CW01663573

A CURSE OF LIGHT

BECOMING LIGHT BOOK 1

SARAH LONG

ALIEN
UNICORN
PRESS

A note to the reader:

Becoming Light contains mentions of mental illness, death (incl. of children), self-harm, and suicide.

For Daniel and Sebastian

ONCE, LONG AGO

A WOMAN in a crimson cape entered the tavern. It was midnight and quiet, save for a small group of men huddled near the fireplace.

She went straight to the plank of oakwood that served as the bar. Behind it stood the tavern's owner. His patrons called him Gus, and though it wasn't his real name, he didn't mind using it. His father had passed the name, along with the tavern, on to him when he was only twenty.

All of the wooden stools lining the bar were empty, but the woman remained standing.

Gus eyed her, all dark hair and piercing black eyes, white skin that seemed like it hadn't been touched by the sun's rays. He wasn't used to seeing someone so young, so deadly beautiful, in this ramshackle old place.

His tavern was a haven for dirty old miners with aching backs and thick beards. It smelled of whiskey, mud, and body odour. Women tended to avoid it.

Seeing this lady here, he knew something was wrong.

"Is a man named Emrys here?" she asked him, her chin raised.

Yes, Gus thought. *Something terrible is about to happen.*

Before he could respond, a grumble came from a man sitting at a corner table. He stood and plodded toward her.

Gus didn't recognise the man. In fact, he didn't remember seeing him come into his tavern this evening to begin with. He was tall and angular, with a peculiar glint in his eyes.

The man called Emrys smiled at the woman. "I didn't think you'd agree."

Gus wrinkled his nose. These two seemed to be in the middle of a conversation that had started ages ago, and he wanted no part of it. Though he rarely drank these days, he suddenly felt the need for a strong whiskey. He turned away from the pair and began pouring.

But still, he lent an ear.

"I haven't," the woman said. "And I won't."

Silence passed. Gus, who had finished pouring his drink, kept hold of the two in his peripheral vision.

Emrys looked like he might explode with rage.

This wouldn't do. Decades of owning this tavern had taught him when to spot trouble, and this pair was bleeding it.

"You two," Gus said, turning to face them. "I think you'd better leave."

Emrys looked over at him as if he hadn't realised anyone else had been in the tavern. His face brightened as he gave an impish smile. "Oh, no need to worry. We're only talking."

Gus took in a deep breath. He'd heard "we're only

talking" from far too many of his patrons over the years, and those altercations almost always ended in violence.

For the thousandth time in his life, Gus fantasised about selling the place and running away to the sea. He'd always wanted to be a sailor.

But then, he'd think of his ill mother and his sister who needed help keeping her children clothed. The tavern was the only thing he knew, and the only way to provide for them.

But perhaps more than that, the tavern and its smelly patrons were an integral part of who Gus had become. He knew how to serve drinks and keep the place going, and those tasks helped him get out of his lonely cot upstairs each morning.

Selling the place was not an option, and never would be.

The woman lowered the hood of her cloak, and in so doing, revealed a pale wrist tattooed with a cross. In the centre of the cross was the form of a white diamond that seemed to glow off of her skin.

More strange than the diamond, however, were the deep red gashes all around the symbol, as if she had been trying to cut it out of her skin.

Gus stared at the woman as Emrys turned toward her.

"This can't go on," Emrys said. "Come back to Camelot and resume your rightful place."

Camelot? Gus broke his gaze from the tattoo. *These two must be lunatics.*

The woman's eyes turned fierce. "You're all murderers. I'll never go back there."

A chill ran down Gus' spine. *Best not to be involved, at least not until they come to blows.* He took a long drink.

"You know we aren't murderers." Emrys lifted his arm, revealing the same symbol tattooed on his wrist, as if this alone was sufficient evidence of his innocence.

"Mordred," she paused and visibly winced, as if the name was an unbearable weight on her shoulders, "would tell you otherwise."

Emrys sighed. "It was necessary. For the greater good –"

"Shut up," she hissed, stepping forward.

Gus' heartbeat quickened.

The woman's hands began glowing. Her eyes shifted from fierce to murderous.

Gus shot a look at the group by the fireplace. They'd been drinking for hours. No chance they'd be able to help him.

He cleared his throat. "You two really should take this – "

The woman lifted one of her glowing hands without breaking her focus on Emrys. A wave of heat suddenly pushed Gus against the cabinet behind him. Bottles rattled on their shelves.

"Leave this world, or you all will suffer." The woman's words were directed at Emrys, but he didn't seem affected by her fury.

"Impossible," he said.

A deep, throaty growl came from her mouth. Her hands began sparking lightning.

The fireside group finally started to notice the growing chaos. They looked, wide-eyed and drunk, at the woman who seemed to command the power of hell itself with her hands.

With one swing, she launched a bolt of lightning at Emrys. He didn't even flinch. Apparently, he didn't need to, because the lightning broke in two and flitted around him without touching his flesh.

One bolt hit a pair of old curtains on the far wall. They burst to flame.

The other hit the window-side table Gus' mother used to sit at when she did her sewing. "Better light here," she'd always say.

The chair burned more quickly than a normal piece of firewood. Gus didn't have time to wonder why that was, because within seconds, the rest of the tavern was in flames.

Gus bolted out the side door for the last time in his life, the fireside group following close behind.

Outside, in the freshly fallen snow, Gus turned around to see his family's tavern burning fast, too fast to save. The thatched roof, which he'd repaired with his father countless times as a boy, was engulfed in smoke.

One of the bedroom shutters on the top floor crashed to the ground. His stomach dropped when he realised it was *the* shutter. The one he'd carved Anna Ingall's initials into after their first kiss. It had been just before she married Jacob Wells and left the county. For months after, he'd traced the engraving with his fingertips every night, wishing for something impossible.

Now, the shutter was lying perilously close to a group of flames near the front doorway. Gus moved to fetch it, to save just one part of his life, but one of the patrons held him back.

Before he could shake the man off, an explosion from inside the tavern burst a wave of heat through his bones. The alcohol had caught flame, and everything was now burning faster, hotter, angrier.

Glasses crashed inside. Crackling heat seemed to singe his skin. The roaring fire burned through his ears. He'd never forget the sound of it.

But there was nothing he could do. His tavern, alongside his childhood, his life, was now burning to ash and smoke, and he was completely helpless.

Everything was now nothing.

Gus stood there, so shocked and empty that he didn't notice a pair of blindingly bright lights hovering over the scene, nor the second pair of lights that shot out of the smoke and into the winter sky.

ONE

HAD I known that wearing Grandmother's necklace on that summer evening would prompt my death, I might have opted for my lace choker instead.

I'd smuggled the necklace out of her jewellery box only hours before, while Grandmother was downstairs gossiping with an acquaintance.

She'd have given me a sound telling-off if she'd seen me wearing it, so I'd hidden it in my wrist purse until I was in the carriage. Now, the necklace glimmered at my collarbone in silent protest of its newest lot in life.

I did receive a warning of sorts upon entering the ballroom that night. It came in the form of an image flashing into my mind – a girl with tiny, pale fingers grabbing at my arms. Her nails dug into my skin as a salty wave hurled itself over our heads. We were spinning together underneath the water, locked in a deadly dance. I was winning.

Was this a memory? No. I wouldn't allow it to be. It was simply a waking nightmare, and such inconvenient ts would not spoil my evening. I pushed the vision away and forced a smile onto my masked face.

The ballroom's gilded mouldings swept across its walls and ceilings, framing deep crimson wallpaper. Silk dresses swished across the floor in time to the melodies of the violins and piano playing at the far end.

The dancers smiled beneath their own masks, too. A tall, red-headed woman hid her laugh behind a lace fan before her dance partner grabbed her hand and twirled her over the marble floor. The crystal chandeliers above their heads seemed to join in, winking and sparkling along with the fast-paced music.

I'd attended dozens of these events in the two seasons since my debut into London society, but they still thrilled me.

"Miss Collins, you've outdone yourself again." Mrs Edwards scuttled through the crowd to greet me. The woman's hoop skirt was vigorously rotund – a fact nobody could ignore when her gown knocked one poor girl into her dance partner's shoulder. This sent Mrs Edwards into a frenzy of apologies.

After we deemed the girl alive and well, Mrs Edwards smiled and turned to me. "Your dress is gorgeous, Emma." She reached her satin-gloved fingers out to admire the tufts of gold lace cascading from my shoulders. "Queen Victoria herself would be envious."

I thanked her and lowered my eyes to appear modest. My dress's green Italian cotton brought out my eyes, which I'd framed with a gold mask. The lace that Mrs Edwards had just admired fell in the perfect spot to reveal my collarbone. I'd spent hours arguing with the seamstress over this crucial detail.

At this moment – which would be one of my last happy moments for an unacceptably long time – I felt like the most splendid creature to breathe air. I walked through a crowd of dancers swaying together in a dizzying wave and breathed in a mix of floral perfumes.

Through the gliding arms and swishing satins, I glimpsed Violet Welch's cobalt dress, spread out over what looked like a horse-length plot of space.

She'd always been proud of her huge crinolines, and this was one to remember. Beside her stood Florence Winston. Mrs Crumbledown once described her as "a brunette with a plain face, but half a dozen royal titles."

I had been furious about such a description of my friend, but Florence didn't seem to mind it. In fact, I think she cared more about her titles than her looks, as the former was admittedly much more valuable.

Both Florence and Violet sometimes drove me mad, but they were my best friends in London. Or, come to think of it, anywhere.

In the ballroom, two men were already fighting for Florence's undivided attention. When she saw me, she pushed through the suitors with the tip of her lace fan and hooked her arm in mine.

"I was wondering when you'd get here." She bopped me on the shoulder with the fan. "There's fashionably late, and then there's just..." her eyes narrowed in what I guessed was an effortful search for an opposing adjective, "... late." Florence had never been one for words.

Violet came to my rescue, placing a warm palm on my

der. "Leave her be." Her aquamarine eyes danced from man to man, her cheekbones highlighted in order to glimmer under the ballroom lights. "You know Emma has already snagged the perfect suitor." She smirked. "The *Light of London* doesn't need to make an effort like we do."

"Speak for yourself," Florence said with a huff. She waved her doting suitors forward and introduced each to me with the musical tone she reserved for men of marriageable status.

Like a moth to a flame, yet another masked man approached Florence from the crowd. Upon closer inspection, however, it became apparent he was staring at *me*. I averted my gaze in the hope he would take the hint and turn away.

Unfortunately, he didn't. "Hello, there." He was an American, judging by his accent. A lock of hair the colour of sawdust fell beside his thick cheekbones. "I don't believe we've met."

Violet sidled in front of me. "And I don't believe you will." She concealed a flirtatious giggle behind her fan before turning to me.

Her eyes said everything: this man was not of status, shouldn't even be here to begin with, and should not, under any circumstances, be talking to us. But, because Violet was such a self-sacrificing friend, she would take the blunt of this good-looking man's attention so that I could have an enjoyable evening. She was a true martyr, so noble and selfless.

The American was not deterred. In fact, he pushed past Violet. "The name's William." He took my hand – without my permission, mind you – and he lowered his face to kiss it obstinately. "Now it's too late. We're already acquainted." His lips curled up at the sides, revealing boyish dimples that almost – *almost* – made up for his blatant American-ness.

Violet's cheeks reddened. She wasn't one to be ignored by a handsome man.

I needed to calculate my options. One: I could nod and make an excuse to leave. That would keep me in Violet's good graces, but it would make this gentleman uncomfortable. Two: I could continue talking to him. That would be terrible on all fronts. Violet would give me a verbal lashing, and I might give this man the impression that I was romantically available. Really, any option I chose would be a social faux pas.

So I bit the inside of my lip, let out a long breath, and chose the wilder option. "Well, sir. Do you have a family name?"

"Do you need it?" He gave a wry smirk that made me want to slap him.

"If I'm to meet you," I said, raising my chin, "albeit against my will, then yes."

"Give me yours, first."

I decided to play his game, mainly because I was terrified of the rageful gaze Violet was firing in my direction. I also hoped my response would be enough to get rid of him. So, I gave him my name without flourish.

His eyes widened so slightly that most wouldn't have noticed. "Miss Emma Collins. Are you Mrs Virginia Collins' granddaughter?"

I nodded and assumed my usual smile – the one that made my eyes crease just enough to convey a pleasant disposition. I wouldn't allow him to know that my mouth was turning dry. Nobody was allowed to know. He would only see congenial Miss Collins. Strong and unaffected by her past, so that nobody needed to be sorry for her.

It must be noted here that anyone with any training in the art of decorum would have quickly moved on after learning my identity, assuming they were aware of my tragic past. Grandmother calls this "the ideal genteel response."

The American just blinked. Many times. And his mouth hung open for so long that I wondered if he could taste the many perfumes undulating in the air. Perhaps Americans enjoyed a good eau de toilette for lunch.

"Well, we must be off," Violet said, grabbing my arm. And off we went, away from that American and his maddening pity.

The music played on, and my stomach was doing a waltz of its own. I wanted to scream. I wanted to tell everyone that I was fine, that I was not to be pitied.

Violet took a deep breath. "You should have let me manage him."

"I can speak for myself." My teeth ground against each other. Hopefully, nobody could see my shoulders shaking.

Violet rolled her eyes. I was the only friend with whom she'd do something so common and vulgar, and she was the only person with whom I could be so rude.

It was an agreeable arrangement, even now, when I was just about ready to pull out a tuft of that American's blonde hair and stuff it into Violet's mouth. He didn't need to feel sorry for me, and she didn't need to speak on my behalf.

I DANCED like a marionette for over an hour until all the people and perfumes began overwhelming me. When the second waltz of the night ended, I escaped to the empty terrace which ran alongside the ballroom. There was a fountain near the end of it, so I sat on its edge and closed my eyes.

A ball was a wonderful thing, of course, but it was also exhausting. Society events could drain the life from a person. There were so many proper behaviours, charming conversational topics, and delicate dance routines to remember. I'd tried once to explain this to Violet and Florence, but they'd only responded with awkward laughter, neither in evident approval or disapproval. I took it to mean the latter.

A buzzing sound came from the pool of the fountain. I opened my eyes to see a poor bee squirming in the water, drowning. Without a second's thought, I tore off my gloves, cupped my hands beneath it, and lifted it out.

The bee sat on my index finger as it wiped its eyes with its front legs and shook out its wings. I couldn't help but smile at the little thing.

"What in heaven's name are you doing?"

I twisted around to see Violet behind me, her hands on the tops of her crinoline and her eyebrows arching toward her curly fringe.

She let out a shriek when she saw the bee. "Emma, get it off you!" She heaved forward and flicked the poor creature with her fan. It tumbled onto the lip of the fountain and jumped around in terror. "You could have been stung. What were you thinking?"

"It was drowning." This seemed sensible enough, at least to me.

Violet didn't agree. She bit her lip and looked at me with stern eyes, like a mother about to scold her child. Instead, she sighed and went back into the ballroom.

I checked on the bee. It was resting on the fountain's edge, still fluttering its wings. One life saved, then. I allowed myself a small smile, then straightened my expression and went to join in with the next dance.

~

LATER THAT NIGHT, after ending a waltz with the bushy-bearded Duke of Sutherland, something in the room shifted. It was nothing physical. But my heart was hitting my ribs like a hammer, warning me of some impending horror from which I couldn't escape.

I turned, more on instinct than anything. And there he was, standing only fifteen feet away. My corset constricted as if Mrs Edwards had put all her weight into pulling its strings back tight. The floor became unsteady. My stomach twisted. It was like being aboard a ship on stormy seas, waves upon waves hurtling beneath my feet.

Richard Jameson was *here*. In this room.

He was wearing his finest Navy uniform. We hadn't seen each other in ten months, and I could see the passage of time on his hardened face. His skin was tan and leathery from ocean suns. He'd grown a moustache and his dark hair was longer, framing his angular jaw.

But even with these changes, his eyes still shone through his crimson mask with the same gentleness they always had.

My legs began working on their own volition to take me closer to him. I was grappling with a flurry of thoughts. He hadn't told me he was coming back. He'd said we wouldn't see each other until this winter. A surge of giddiness and anxiety flooded me, my heart pushing fiery blood into my cheeks. Why hadn't he told me?

It took an eternity to reach him. He still didn't see me, but I knew when he did, those blue eyes would brighten and he'd rush toward me. We'd lock in that familiar, warm embrace. Tonight, I'd forget social niceties and erase all the other names from my dance card.

But Richard was facing a woman I had never seen before. Her golden hair shone beneath the chandeliers, and her eyes were fixed on him. Preposterously long lashes fluttering, she reached up to kiss him on the cheek, revealing a wedding finger adorned with a diamond. Richard moved in to return the embrace.

The ground beneath me rumbled, as if a deadly earthquake was shaking all of England. Only, nobody else seemed to notice. I turned around and limped over to a quiet corner.

Mrs Edwards and her gigantic skirts were soon there with me, swirling and swaying so much it made me feel sick. Her eyebrows lifted to meet her hairline. "Oh, no," she muttered. That tone. That blasted tone. "I'm so sorry, Emma. I didn't know they would be attending."

"They?" My throat was turning to chalk.

Her eyes flitted toward the couple. "You really didn't

know? You poor thing. As if one catastrophe in a lifetime isn't enough, now you must endure—"

"I am fine."

"You don't deserve this," she continued. "Truly. I can't believe Mr Jameson would hurt you like this." Her hand plopped onto my shoulder. "We all love you and your grandmother. Seeing you both hurt, drowning in loss... well, it affected all of us."

Drowning? How dare she choose that word so carelessly?

I jerked my shoulder away. "I didn't realise you were there in the water with me, Mrs Edwards. Watching them die. Certainly, you were most terribly affected."

Her face went white. White as Mama's, under the water. Gasping for air.

I needed to sit down. Black spots blocked my vision, but out of the corner of my eye, I saw Violet rushing toward me, a muffled voice asking what was wrong.

I closed my eyes and focussed on breathing. "Richard."

Violet looked at the dance floor. Her lip curled when she saw the new couple dancing in a nauseating romantic haze.

"What?" she hissed. "He's supposed to be in India. Who is she?"

I couldn't respond. They were dancing in their own little world. I'd known that feeling once.

"Let's go home." Violet's arm wrapped around me.

No. Going home was unacceptable. I closed my eyes, forcing back the tears that were threatening to burst out, the bile rising in my throat. I tightened my lips into a smile and opened my eyes.

"We'll do no such thing. The night's just begun. And he's just one man." I stood up too fast and stumbled.

"Emma." Violet was every inch the stern mother again, but I was already making my way into the crowd.

Mr Bailey stood a few feet away, proud in his uniform, chattering with Miss Hinselton. I snuck my way into the conversation with a twinkling smile. "Mr Bailey, where have you been all these months?" My voice oozed charm as I laid my hand on his shoulder.

Thankfully, he didn't seem to notice I was shaking. He was too busy beaming from the unexpected attention. "I was called away for duty in France," he said, clearly surprised I was talking to him with such affection. "I'm sorry I didn't write to tell you."

"I'll forgive you only if you promise me a dance." I gave him my best flirtatious smirk. It was admittedly rusty with disuse, so I raised a single eyebrow to complement it.

"I'd be honoured." He bowed before taking my hand in his and leading me to the floor. The partner to whom I'd previously promised this dance walked toward me, saw that I was with someone else, and straightened his collar before awkwardly turning away.

I knew this slight wouldn't go unnoticed, but something inside me had grown numb. What did it matter, what did *any* of it matter, now that Richard was no longer mine?

I turned back to Mr Bailey. He was elegant in his officer's uniform and gold mask, which matched mine perfectly. It just so happened that Mr Bailey was Richard's professional rival, and had been awarded an Indian Mutiny Medal five months ago – the very honour Richard had hoped to attain. That medal displayed itself loudly atop Mr

Bailey's breast pocket. Throughout the waltz, I moved my body to make sure the award remained visible to all.

"How have you been, Miss Collins?" Mr Bailey asked as we sidestepped. "We haven't spoken in some time."

"Well, thank you. I sang at the Duke of Wellington's charity ball in April." I nodded to an acquaintance in the crowd. "Everyone still seems to be talking about it."

He took my hand and gave me a modest twirl. "I hear you were spectacular."

"How kind." I crafted my demure smile and lowered my chin just enough to show my humble gratitude.

As we danced, I gazed at Mr Bailey with as much false longing as I could muster. He was admittedly a handsome man, with dark eyes and a chiselled jaw. But he was not Richard.

My smile twitched. Maybe the woman was Richard's cousin, or a family friend. Had I really seen him kiss her? Perhaps I'd been mistaken. And Mrs Edwards was an idiot. How would she know, before *me*, that Richard had begun courting someone else? Much less, heavens forbid, that he was engaged?

I found the courage to steal a glance in Richard's direction, only to see him and his dance partner sharing a passionate kiss on the mouth. The shamelessness of it left me breathless.

"Are you all right?" Mr Bailey sounded worried that he'd done something to upset me.

"Fine." I gasped. "I just need to sit down."

He led me to a chair and fetched some water. "Is there anything else you need? Should I call a carriage to take you home?" He was all but wringing his hands with concern.

"Of course not." My response sounded too forceful, but I had little control over anything anymore. "I was only a little dizzy."

Mr Bailey made a gallant vow to watch over me for the rest of the evening. I didn't want to give him too much hope, though. After all, my heart was now torn to pieces. The poor man didn't have a chance. So I urged him to enjoy the ball, and after some half-hearted argument, he gave up and left me with my little porcelain cup of water.

I sat there for some time, stuffing my new heartache into the deepest crevice of my mind, where my memories of my parents and sister lived. I was Miss Emma Collins. Nobody was permitted to pity me.

As always, though, timing is the devil.

"What's the belle of the ball doing sitting here all alone?" It was that damned American again. William No-Surname. He leaned over me, but I didn't bother looking up. Instead, I stared at his gold cufflinks, each of which boasted bright diamonds that must have cost a fortune. Who was this man, and did he have any sense of modesty?

Regardless of the answer, I pretended not to hear him. The look of pity in his eyes earlier this evening was still burning through my mind.

Still, he sat down beside me. "You know, for a famous socialite, you're not very talkative."

"Famous?" I spun toward him, my arrogant side perking up in interest.

He laughed much too loudly. "Well, all I've heard about since coming to London is some girl named Miss Emma Collins, and how she's the most interesting young lady in all the town. Now I know her personally."

I bit the inside of my lip to hold back a smile. Maybe chatting with an ill-bred man wasn't that bad. My confidence did need a little boosting.

"How long have you been in London?" I glanced at the dance floor in the hope Richard would see me talking to this stranger. What would he think of it? Would he rush to me, pull me away?

Of course not. Richard was busy clutching his new partner much too close for proper company – maybe even for *improper* company. My stomach lurched.

The American seemed pleased by my renewed interest. "Only a month. I've got business prospects here. You English folks are pretty smart about your investments, it seems."

I tried my best to look interested, but it seemed even my supposedly famous social skills were no match for this dull choice of subject.

"Sorry." He shook his head. "I don't mean to talk money with a lady. Anyway, have you ever been to Paris? It's on my list of places to see."

"Paris?" I asked absently. My gaze was stuck on Richard. He was twirling his new love around and around, making me dizzy with it. How was she not getting sick? Did she have the digestive disposition of a farmer?

"Yeah. It's an interesting place." He paused, and out of the corners of my eyes I noticed him straighten his posture. "Would you care for a dance?" Mr No-Surname asked this question in what must have been the most formal tone he'd ever used. It was distinctly unimpressive.

I might have acquiesced if I had been in a better mood.

Instead, I checked my dance card and told him I already had a partner for this song.

As I stood and walked away from the American, I vowed to spend the rest of the evening on my feet. The lustre of the proceedings had faded now. The chandeliers and jewels were dimmer. It seemed I was looking at things through smoked glass.

A memory of Richard suddenly burst through. We were sitting on a park bench in spring. The scent of blooming daffodils filled the air so thickly that I could almost taste the petals on the back of my tongue. He sat so close, clasping my hand, grinning until dimples dotted his cheeks. I thought I might explode into a giant ball of light and blind the world. His smiles always did that to me.

Stop it, I thought. *Not here.* I closed my eyes tight and clenched my fists. *Control yourself, Emma.*

Once my legs had stopped shaking and my hands were steady, I looked around the room for my next dance partner. The night wasn't over, and the Light of London still had time to shine.

TWO

"Mama, help me!" I was screaming, sitting up straight in bed with my heart skipping jigs in my throat.

My bedroom door swung open to reveal our lady's maid, Ms Wright. Her hand went straight to her cheek when she saw me. "Dear heavens, what's wrong?"

Without waiting for my answer, which was wise considering I was gasping too much to speak, she hastened to draw open the curtains. The morning sun warmed my face and I gradually calmed, one last frightened shudder escaping my shoulders as Ms Wright sat down on my bed.

Her forehead was wrinkled with worry as she petted my sweat-dampened hair. Ms Wright was a kind woman, far friendlier than most housemaids I knew. She genuinely seemed to care about Grandmother and me, and wanted to fill the loneliness in our spirits with tenderness and warmth.

I took her hand and smiled. "Sorry. I don't know what came over me."

Ms Wright squeezed my hand, then gave a smile that

didn't reach her eyes. This was a warning that she was about to say something I wouldn't like. "Dr Gibson is back in London, you know. Perhaps —"

I cut in, wincing. "Is Grandmother awake?"

She let go of my hand and sighed. "Yes. She's waiting for you to join her for breakfast."

After a trip to the wash closet, Ms Wright helped me with my morning ablutions. Today she refused me anything but cold water in order to help my circulation. The chill gave me goosebumps, and worse, we couldn't use soap. The stuff wouldn't lather without piping hot water, and though I hated the soap's sharp smell, I'd grown rather dependent on the feeling of purity that came after a sound scrubbing.

I still felt unclean even after Ms Wright gave me a few puffs of rose-scented talcum powder. She helped me into my day dress, a lavender wool number with wide hoops and a coffee-coloured lace trim. It was a few years old, but I refused to give it away just yet. The sight of it always reminded me of Grandmother's beaming face after the seamstress had finished its final alterations. It was as if at that moment, she'd realised I had become a grown woman.

But the happy memory didn't help my aching heart. Ms Wright fixed my hair into a tight bun, and the grim realities of the ball began crashing down on me as I made my way downstairs.

"Emma, I heard you wake from down here." Grandmother stood as quickly as she could from her chair at the dining room table. "Come and sit down, drink some water. Was it a terrible nightmare?" Her blue eyes creased at their edges.

I nodded and did as she asked. Ms Wright handed me a

glass and my usual tincture, meant to stop my monthlies coming. When they'd begun at twelve years old, Grandmother had been adamant I take the medicine each morning. The reason for it was something involving our family suffering from terrible bleeding, but I never really understood it. She'd always had such a strange fear of blood.

Grandmother watched closely as I drank my tincture. She must have seen something of the depths of my misery. "What's wrong?"

Her question did me in. I fell into her arms and began sobbing like a pathetic child. She rocked me back and forth as my tears fell in huge droplets onto her shoulder.

It took some time for me to gather my composure. When I did, I told her about Richard.

Grandmother shook her head. "And we all thought he was such a gentleman." We were silent as the grandfather clock rang in the hour. "Something did feel strange about the way he left, though. One should either propose marriage officially, or wait until one's able before saying anything about it."

I nodded and lowered my gaze. I'd cried myself to sleep the night he'd made that silly promise. Even then, when everything was roses and romance, it had felt too good to be true. But after a few days I'd convinced myself that Richard's promise was a sign that heaven had, in fact, not damned me after all.

Now I knew just how wrong I'd been. The blonde woman's sparkling ring was proof. I deserved the pain, and the shame of knowing I'd been so easily deceived. Soon, half of society would know what Richard had done. The

American had said I was the most loved young lady in town. What would people think of me now?

Probably something like, "Poor Miss Collins, after all she's overcome, now she must suffer a suitor's deception."

Anger boiled inside me. I imagined my hands clasping around each of their necks, one by one, my fingers pressing into their air pipes until there was only wheezing. No voices left to spew pity all over me.

Where did that come from? I pushed away the horrible, violent thought and looked down at my plate. The toast Ms Wright had placed there suddenly looked deeply unappetising.

All I wanted to do was hide in my room and weep like the heroine in a tragic fairy tale. Unfortunately, I had an appointment with my modiste in Marylebone. She was completing the final fittings for my riding dress and was adamant that I be there by mid-morning. So Grandmother and I set off in the barouche, our driver racing his horses through the streets as if we were rushing to the hospital.

Mrs Havendish had been our favourite modiste for years, and she always had a fresh pot of tea ready for us when we arrived. But today, she was in such a hurry that she didn't have anything to give.

"It's my new assistant," she muttered when she rifled through her box of dress receipts. "She's got no sense in her head at all, and now here I am, just about ready to pull my hair out."

When the assistant set to pinning my new dress, I

began to see what Mrs Havendish had meant. She didn't know what she was doing and nicked me at least a half dozen times. The final nick resulted in a bloom of blood from my collarbone. The girl stuttered an apology as she grabbed a handkerchief and blotted my accosted skin. She rushed to the back room in what seemed a bout of nausea at the sight of blood.

Grandmother stood from the chaise longue behind me. "Where's she going with that handkerchief?"

"She's probably just gone woozy." Mrs Havendish sniffed and waved a hand airily, as if to say this was just another in a string of misadventures with the girl. "I'll take over the pinning, Miss Collins."

It should be mentioned here that Grandmother had always had a peculiar habit of immediately either boiling or burning anything soiled with blood. I'd always thought it was some sort of old wives' tale about the dangers of letting blood remain exposed to the air.

Once, before my uncle died, he'd cut his hand while carving a Sunday roast. Grandmother nearly had a panic attack as the blood came, and she didn't stop worrying about it for days after.

So it wasn't too surprising to me that Grandmother seemed nervous about letting the bloodied handkerchief go unwashed. She sat tensely, watching the door.

I placed a hand on her shoulder. "Are you all right?"

She blinked and shook her head. "Ah, yes. If you don't mind, Mrs Havendish, I'm going to check on your assistant." She didn't wait for her reply as she rushed across the shop floor.

The modiste and I exchanged surprised glances. There was some rustling about, and then Grandmother emerged again with the handkerchief clutched tightly in her hands.

"We must go home at once. Emma, change out of your clothes."

"What?" After pulling myself out of bed and forcing my heartbroken body all the way to Marylebone for this appointment, I couldn't believe she was forcing me to leave.

Without answering, she grabbed my arm and pulled me into the dressing room herself. I couldn't get a word in before she stuffed my poor riding dress into a large bag and practically threw it at our driver. Her only words on our journey home were a muttered promise that Ms Wright would finish the sizing adjustments by the end of the week.

She refused to talk about the handkerchief. I saw it one last time that afternoon, when she threw it into the parlour fireplace and stood as still as a statue, watching the flames overtake the bloodied silk.

~

I ALLOWED myself three days of privacy at home to mourn the loss of Richard. But during breakfast on the fourth morning, Grandmother seemed to have had enough.

"You should attend to your charities, or at least take callers." She set her teacup down decisively beside her breakfast, which I still couldn't stomach myself.

I pulled at my sleeve. I'd chosen to wear the lavender dress again today to boost my spirits, but the hem was loosening. This would be the last time I could wear it until

Ms Wright got around to fixing it. The poor woman already had enough work to do, now that she needed to adjust my riding dress.

Grandmother stared at me, waiting for a response. I sighed. "I'll start tomorrow."

She patted her décolletage – a sign she'd like to move on from such unhappy conversation. "Well then, that's settled. And as it happens, I have some additional good news."

I brightened, hoping that this was regarding a new summer hat. Lord knows, I needed one. Last year's hat was... well, last year's, and appearances needed to be maintained if one was to remain the Light of London.

The name had started as a silly joke between Violet, Florence and me. During one of our first dinners after coming out into society, an older man who had partaken in a tad too much wine had loudly decreed that my smile could light up the whole of London. From then on, Violet and Florence would announce my arrival at every soiree with:

"Here she is, ladies and gentlemen. Guaranteed to illuminate any gathering. The Light of London herself, Miss Emma Collins."

Somehow, the nickname spread around our social circle, then around society at large, and stuck fast. I imagined that even the American might have heard the name ahead of our meeting.

I smiled as I asked about the hat. But Grandmother shook her head. "Mr Wentworth doesn't return from Bath until next week." Mr Wentworth was Grandmother's go-to milliner, but he was far from my favourite. His hats were plain. I wanted something bright and daringly French. She ignored my sigh of disappointment and clasped her hands together. "This is something so much better." She looked at the clock. "He'll be here any minute."

He? I straightened up in my chair. A suitor, maybe? No, she couldn't possibly think it appropriate to find me a new gentleman to court, not this soon after Richard's betrayal. My shoulders slumped a little. "What do you mean by 'he'?"

A mysterious smile danced across Grandmother's face. "Mr *Ambrosius*, my dear." She enunciated the name with the splendour reserved for a king. "Do you remember? I used to tell you about our travels when you were small. He's my oldest and most marvellous friend. And it's high time you met one another."

I remembered the stories well. Grandmother had told me of their wild adventures about Europe and the Orient in her youth. Frankly, based on the stories of parties and other hijinks, I'd worried the man had drugged her. Or even that she had made him up. Worse still, her stories hinted that she and Mr Ambrosius had travelled alone together. Scandalous for an unmarried couple.

I didn't know why I needed to meet the man now, of all times.

A knock sounded before I could come up with a decent response. It was probably Mr Ambrosius, and if so, he was already annoying me.

Ms Wright answered. There was a hushed greeting, and then footsteps over creaking wood. She appeared in our breakfast room to announce Mr Ambrosius' arrival.

Grandmother's eyes lit up the whole of London. If

there had only been a way to harness their brightness and heat, we might have avoided another winter of smoggy air. She jumped out of her seat without her cane. She was already being irresponsible, and she and the man hadn't yet breathed the same air. This was going to be a terrible meeting.

I followed her with a defiant thud in my step. Normally, Grandmother would scold me for this. "One should only hear the pleasant rustling of your dress as a signal of your arrival," she'd say. This was years ago, of course, when I'd been more bothersome. At the time of Mr Ambrosius' visit, I hadn't thudded in years.

Grandmother didn't say a word about it, anyway. Instead, she opened her arms wide as she entered the parlour, nearly covering our mysterious visitor from my view. "Oh, Ambrosius. I've missed you." She sounded like a yearning debutante. My nausea immediately returned.

In the doorway stood a man clad in leather breeches, an ill-fitting double-breasted waistcoat and an unfashionably tall buckle hat, reminiscent of the portrait of an American Quaker that Mrs Holstead had daringly hung in her parlour last summer. His aubergine-hued breeches were an inch too short for him – he was abnormally tall – and a pair of canary yellow stockings announced their own arrival so emphatically my eyes ached to look.

Altogether, Mr Ambrosius' flamboyant clothes made him look as if he'd jumped off the pages of some bizarre fairytale.

Even more strangely, I couldn't guess his age for the life of me. He had silver slicked-back hair that reminded me of

Grandmother's prized serving spoons. His forehead was slightly wrinkled, yet his blueish silver eyes had the sharpness of a young man in his prime. His face was completely shaven, a strange sight to see on any grown man. It highlighted his plump, almost childish cheeks and slender, shadowed jawline. He was tall, and stood straight and proud. But despite his seeming youth, there was something ancient in the sparkle of his eyes.

"My Virginia." He kissed Grandmother's hand, and after doing so, examined me. A shiver ran through my body, as if he was reading my soul – and perhaps he was.

"Such a glowing girl. You must be Emma." His voice was disarmingly musical. He released Grandmother's hand, took off his hat and bowed. "I'm Mr Ambrosius, your grandmother's oldest and most audacious friend."

That was impossible. He was far too young to be the famed Mr Ambrosius who had travelled with Grandmother decades ago. Even more harrowing: he had used my *first name* in his introduction. The cheek of it. In what kind of backward place had Grandmother found this ill-mannered creature?

I was about to say something on the matter when Grandmother cleared her throat. "Come, dear Ambrosius. Sit and have some tea." She waved to the chaise longue and two velvet chairs sitting opposite. "Unless," she giggled, a sound that spooked the soul out of my body, "you have some of your miracle wine on hand?"

And there it was. This supposed *miracle wine* was clearly the cover name for a drug – probably opium. My poor grandmother must have had no idea, being such an innocent gentlewoman. I needed to immediately guide her away from such a drink. Later I'd explain the dangers accompanying it.

I opened my mouth to speak.

"Of course." Mr Ambrosius' voice boomed over my own. He reached into his waistcoat and pulled out a full-sized bottle of red wine. How in heaven's name had he stored it there? "I never travel without it, as you well know." He turned to me and winked.

"Ms Wright," Grandmother called. "Bring us three wine glasses, please."

Mr Ambrosius sat at one of the armchairs and put his hat on the coffee table in front of him. Grandmother perched on the chaise longue and waved at me to join her. I sat down, still struggling to think of a way to both politely deny this drink and convince Grandmother to do the same. This situation was far beyond any of my social training and I wanted to remove myself from it.

The glasses arrived and the wine was poured much too quickly. *Think, Emma. Think.* Perhaps I could feign illness. Even better, I could faint. Yes, that always worked. It was one of the greatest tools at a lady's disposal. Grandmother would come to my aid and Mr Ambrosius would have nothing to do but leave.

I began channelling what I hoped would be the most dramatic wheeze of my life when Mr Ambrosius lifted his glass. "Let's toast to a spectacular new adventure, and to becoming light!"

Grandmother shot him a meaningful look and shook her head.

"What's he –"

Grandmother smiled and put her hand on my shoulder. The last time she'd done so, she'd told me I hadn't been invited to the Wentworth Ball. A hand on the shoulder meant terrible news.

"I have an exciting announcement to share with you." She took a deep breath. "Mr Ambrosius and I have been speaking, and we've agreed that he will escort us both on a tour of the Continent. Starting this summer. It's time you saw more of the world beyond London, don't you think?"

The shock sent me reeling. I opened my mouth to ask just why Mr Ambrosius – a total stranger to me – should have any say in such a scheme. Grandmother interrupted before I could utter a word. "You'll surely agree that with Mr Jameson's recent actions, this is perfect timing."

"Oh, how intriguing!" Mr Ambrosius sat forward as his eyes widened. What a terrible man he was, to be so thrilled with my misfortune. "A romantic betrayal, I hope? Those are my favourite."

Grandmother put her hand up to stop Mr Ambrosius from speaking. Some sense was finally returning to the woman's head. She took a long sip of wine. "What Mr Ambrosius means to say is, you could use a good dose of fresh perspective. Travel is wonderful for expanding the mind. For rounding you out."

Mr Ambrosius coughed. "And for making you less tiresomely boring."

Grandmother gave him a look generally reserved for inappropriate conversations and unpleasant smells. With Mr Ambrosius, it could have been both. She turned back to me with a hopeful smile. "What do you say, my dear?"

Before I could respond, Mr Ambrosius laughed in one

of the oddest ways I'd ever heard. It was a literal "Hahaha," spoken in a deep baritone, like a pantomime villain. "She must say yes, Virginia. Why let her believe she has a choice in the matter?"

How could he be so blatantly rude? A pathetic squeak came from somewhere in my throat, drowned out once again by Mr Ambrosius' boorish voice.

"I see you two need time to speak alone. But the trip remains essential, Virginia. You know this as well as I do. I'll arrange everything and contact you with our date of departure." With that, he hopped off his chair, grabbed his half-empty bottle of wine, and marched out of the house.

Grandmother turned to me. Her hand returned to my shoulder. Yes, this was terrible news indeed. "Emma, I –"

For the first time since this foolish, drunken man's arrival, I had a real chance to speak. "Why you would befriend such a nightmarish lushington, I will never know. I'm going to lie down."

Her eyes grew wider than I'd ever seen them, but before she could say a word, I had left the parlour.

~

LYING on my bed with a cold cloth pressed to my brow, I knew that I'd been too harsh to Grandmother. For whatever godforsaken reason, Mr Ambrosius was her oldest and dearest friend, and I'd just compared him to a town drunkard. While I still believed this to be the case, I shouldn't have said it so bluntly.

But of much more concern to me was the sinister secrecy seemingly at play throughout our encounter. I couldn't stop thinking about the way those two looked at each other, the knowing glances they shared, the things Grandmother kept trying to stop Mr Ambrosius from saying. This wasn't simply a trip needed for finishing or refinement. Besides, I was already the Light of London. There was no need to improve.

Also, Grandmother knew full well how much I hated travelling. A jaunt to Scotland by train was just about acceptable, but travelling to the Continent? That was out of the question. I hadn't been on a ship since the doomed *Ocean Monarch*, and I had no plans to return.

So why would Grandmother plan such travels for me? And why would Mr Ambrosius say that I had no choice but to go? None of it made sense.

I closed my eyes and sighed. I felt drained, and sleep came upon me like a blanket before I could fret or theorise any further.

THE GIRL. Her face, so plump and white. Black eyes. She reminded me of a crow. A crow child, her nose turning into a pointed beak. She began pecking at me. I pushed her down, down, into the cold water. Her muscles bulged and contracted as she fought me, but it was no use. Soon, they loosened, and she was dead.

As she should be.

I woke to sweaty sheets. My heart was going so fast, I thought for one harrowing second that I'd faint back into nothingness. Instead, my stomach lurched and I heaved its contents onto the floor beside my bed.

Wiping my mouth, my heart still pounding, I sensed something watching me. My eyes went to the corner of the room. A tall, dark shape flitted in and out of my vision, as if drifting between this reality and another.

It was Mama. She was watching me, waiting for me to join her in the shadows. Of this I was certain. I was going mad, just as mad as she had been. Something shifted beside my bed and I cried out. With a great gasp, I fell back onto my pillow and saw only darkness.

The next thing I remember was the blood. It was smeared on the pillowcase beside my head. I stared at it for some time before becoming fully awake. There were flies on the fabric, buzzing around the stains like crows on carrion. Were flies always so drawn to blood? That didn't seem normal. None of this seemed normal.

I sat up in my bed, still half-delirious. My wrists ached. I looked down to find them wrapped in bloody bandages. Who had done this to me?

"Emma." Grandmother's exhausted voice came from the rocking chair near my bedroom window. She was facing away from me, staring out of the window at the street below. I couldn't see her face, but I was sure she was frowning deeply.

"What happened?" My own voice was weak.

She stayed still. "You don't remember?"

"Only that I had a nightmare." Stupid. I should've kept that to myself.

"What kind of —"

"It was nothing." Better for her not to know about my visions of killing innocent children as Mama stood by, watching. "But I don't remember getting hurt. How did it happen?"

She turned toward me, and in that moment I realised just how grave the situation had become. Her face was pale, her expression lost. "Oh, Emma. You did it to yourself."

THREE

I HAD HEARD stories in hushed whispers about people who took knives to their wrists. Miss Harrison was scandalised and left the resulting child at the Foundling Hospital. She took the public bus to her home in Kensington, filled her bathtub with hot water, got in fully-clothed, then dug a pocket knife into her skin. Mr Wandsworth gambled away his fortune, which put his family on the streets. It was five days before they found his body, mangled on the banks of the Thames, cuts so deep they met the bone of his arm. Those who survived were rushed to the nearest infirmary, never to be seen again.

I would not be one of them.

I was the Light of London.

So that morning I found the dress with the longest sleeves in my wardrobe, put on my day hat, and bid our driver to take me to church. It wasn't proper to go alone, I knew, but considering recent events, I'd have to break the rules. Nobody could know why I was there or what I was praying for.

In fairness, this wasn't the first time I had come to church outside of a Sunday to pray. Grandmother had always joined me on those days, under the half-true assumption I wanted to speak with God about my parents. Today, however, I wanted to be alone.

The pews were all empty as I entered. A twelve-foot high wooden cross stood behind the altar, looming, expectant of something from me. I never knew what it wanted or if I even had anything to give. I stayed in the back row, as far away from it as possible. As much as I wanted to revere it like my good Christian brethren, the cross had always spooked me.

I chided myself. Already I was thinking sacrilegiously, and I'd only been in the church for twenty seconds. That should have been my first warning.

I knelt and interlaced my fingers, bowing my forehead into them and pressing hard. I began reciting.

Dearest Heavenly Father,

in Christ you make all things new:

transform the poverty of our nature by the riches of your grace,

and in the renewal of our lives

make known your heavenly glory;

Through Jesus Christ our Lord.

Faithful and steadfast God,

nourish your people in this wicked world,

and, through prayer and the Scriptures,

give us our daily bread;

through Jesus Christ our —

"Thick bandages you're covering."

My heart leapt so fiercely that it pulled the rest of my

body with it. I jumped to my feet to see the owner of the interrupting voice.

He was tall and broad with red hair, standing square in the centre of the church with his hat on. Wrinkles lined the corners of his eyes, the irises of which were as black as the depths of an ocean. One might say you could drown in those eyes, but it wouldn't be pleasant. You wouldn't survive long enough to write love poems about them.

"Excuse me," I said, trying to steady myself. "But this is a private —"

"What happened when the ship sank?" A smile crept across his face.

The blood drained from my face. "What?"

"You survived. How?"

My throat grew tight. "I don't know who you are or what you want, but please leave me alone." I stepped toward the doorway.

But the man moved forward, blocking my exit. His body, like the cross near us, loomed over me, and my pulse quickened. We were completely alone in this place. He looked strong enough to overtake me, should he decide to do so. I should have brought a chaperone, and not merely for social decency.

"Please let me through." My voice rose in the pathetic hope that someone might be near enough to hear me.

"You should have died." He was coming closer, that wretched smile still widening. "You and your kind are an abomination. It's time to end this."

My kind?

He lurched forward and grabbed me around the waist. I slapped and scratched at him, but he was too strong. Still, I fought, screaming and stamping my foot onto his. He didn't flinch. Nothing I did seemed to matter.

It was as if I was fighting a ghost.

He pushed against me so hard it knocked the breath out of my lungs.

That was it.

The madness deep inside of me burst out, and he was suddenly on the floor. A blinding light bathed the church in white. The man was whimpering, begging me to stop. Begging for mercy.

What was I doing? I didn't know. I didn't understand it. Something was consuming me, and I shook, my skin burning as if fire had engulfed me.

I wasn't strangling the man, I didn't have a knife to his throat. But I knew, somehow, that I was killing him.

And I didn't stop.

He cried out. Then he was silent.

The blinding light faded and the fire on my skin cooled. My head was spinning and I stumbled, catching the edge of the pew before falling to my knees. There was a clanging noise in my ears and everything in my field of vision had turned a mixture of purple and black.

But right when I was sure I'd faint, the chaos died down. I looked to the floor. In front of me, where the man had lain, was a thick pile of ash.

"Oh, please, no," I whispered.

A blue light came from the other side of the room, illuminating the church again. I looked up to see a tall woman in a long, red gown. Her skin was icy white, her eyes the same inky black as the man who now lay in ashes before me. Hair the colour of crow's feathers cascaded in loose, wild ringlets down her torso.

She was not of this world.

When she spoke, it was with a deep sadness, as if all her hope had faded into oblivion. "So, it seems you are the creature we feared."

And then she was gone, nothing more than a mist, drifting up into the eaves of the church.

FOUR

"Emma, my love, no, no, no." I was eight years old, and Mama was crying in her bedroom. I ran to her, my little heart pounding in fear that I had upset her.

She was sitting on her bed, in her nightgown and cap, and tears were streaming down her face. They gave her an angelic sheen under the soft glow of the lamplight beside her. It was morning, but the curtains were drawn so tightly that the room seemed drowned in endless night.

Mama looked up at me. Her face slackened, and her eyes lifted with her smile. "Oh, it was only a dream. Just a dream." She opened her arms toward me in invitation.

I rushed to her and jumped into her lap. She squeezed me so hard the breath left my lungs, but let go just as quickly. "My Emma. Stay alive for me, won't you?"

Of course I would stay alive, I thought. *Why would I do anything else?* I was still too young to comprehend death. But I nodded in agreement anyway, making a solemn promise.

She laughed and shook her head. "I'm so sorry, my love.

Sometimes I have dreams, terrible dreams. They seem so real that I can't tell what's what. I was quite certain that I was awake, and that I was in another realm where," she grimaced, "my little Emma had died."

I didn't know how to respond. I felt only a mixture of confusion and fear. *Was something wrong with Mama, or was something wrong with me? Was I going to die?*

Now, in this church, I knew the truth. I had witnessed my mother's madness building, her reality disintegrating.

Staring at the bare floor where the man's ashes had been only moments before, I knew that my own madness had now taken hold. The man, the woman, and the ashes were all gone. There was no evidence of them in this quiet, empty church.

I must have imagined them.

It was the only sensible explanation. The black-eyed man, the woman in red, and my deadly actions were all a hallucination. And a clear sign that my future aligned with Mama's.

Just as I'd always feared.

FIVE

I STUMBLED out of the church and back to my driver, who didn't seem to notice that anything had gone awry. In fact, the rest of London seemed to bumble along just fine, as though nothing of note had happened that morning, and we travelled home without event.

After Mr Ambrosius's visit and my terrible night of bloodied bedsheets, I'd forgotten all about an excursion to Hyde Park I'd planned with Violet and Florence for that afternoon. The girls rode to my house at one in a two-horse barouche that boasted a wide-open top, gilded in sunlight.

I was unprepared for our outing, and Ms Wright had to rush to fetch me a hat and parasol. Neither matched my long-sleeved dress, which, although it had gone out of style this season, was the best option for covering my bandages. I held my chin high as I emerged through the front door with a starched white parasol, yellow sun hat and sky-blue gown. Perhaps my odd colour combination would become this year's latest fashion, and all the women's magazines would talk about it by the month's end.

The girls, however, were not impressed with my look. Violet knotted her brows together and Florence's mouth dropped open almost a full inch – the widest it had gone since the Great Petticoat Debacle of '58, in which Miss Annabelle Chesterfield found herself in an unfortunate position atop a grey mule.

Violet moved aside as the footman helped me into the carriage. My hands were still shaking from my waking nightmare, and it took some doing to get my legs to move correctly. Thankfully, nobody seemed to notice.

"Your blue dress." Violet's smile twitched at the corners of her lips. "Are we quite sure such a lovely gown is fit for the park today? We wouldn't want it to get damaged."

Meaning: your dress looks awful and you need to burn it – immediately. Violet might have actually said this if Florence wasn't present.

"Leave her be." Florence slapped Violet's shoulder with the edge of her frilly lace fan. "She's just had her heart broken."

Meaning: she's gone bonkers and we must be pitying, righteous women in her time of need. All in our circle will admire us for such selflessness, and it may even secure me a good suitor.

I didn't particularly like Florence sometimes.

"Does my dress really matter?" I sighed, looking out onto the street. An omnibus overflowing with workers ambled forward, and after it passed, our barouche jolted into movement. "It's only a ride in the park."

Florence and Violet exchanged glances, as if they're just confirmed their greatest fear: Miss Emma Collins had, indeed, gone mad.

"Perhaps not. I just never imagined you as the cavalier type," Violet said. "Anyway. Have you heard from Mr Jameson yet?"

I held back a wince. Just like Violet to jump to the subject of Richard without warning. In larger company, she was the perfect gentlewoman, but once we were alone, she tended to let off steam in my direction.

I took a long breath and straightened my skirts. "No. But it's only been a few days since the ball."

"Quite," Florence piped up. "And already, word has spread drastically."

Never mind what I'd said before. I didn't like Florence *most* of the time.

Violet's eyes lit up. "Do tell, Florence. What does this woman have that Emma lacks?" She squeezed my arm and leaned in close to whisper, "Nothing, of course."

Richard's new love was the last thing I wanted to talk about. My throat was already constricting, preparing for a wave of tears that I would have preferred not to show, even to my dearest friends.

"Well, I heard from Mrs Grout that Mr Jameson met the woman in India." Florence leaned forward, her face more animated than I'd seen all year. She seemed more excited about this than even the night they discovered Mrs Price in a state of undress with Mr Hickleman in his downstairs library.

Violet turned to me. "Hadn't Mr Jameson been writing to you, Emma? Did he seem off?"

I swallowed. My friends wouldn't see me weak. I needed to change the subject. With an expert lift of my chin, I spoke with all the bravura I could muster. "It hardly matters now. Grandmother is taking me to Europe to finish my education. I'll be surrounded by handsome Italian nobility in only a few weeks."

Florence gave a delighted gasp and began fanning herself profusely. "Oh, what a delightful revelation. When did you learn?"

"The day of the ball," I lied. "With all the chaos of that evening, I forgot to mention it." Best not to let them know we'd decided upon this trip after Richard's betrayal. The last thing I wanted was word going around town that I was running away.

My friends launched into a barrage of questions about the trip, most of which I continued to answer with lies, considering I had so little information about Grandmother's plans. I also made sure not to mention our travelling partner. They'd demand to make his acquaintance, and Mr Ambrosius was far too odd for that.

Our driver took us into the park and down Rotten Row. It was the best place for those in society to see and be seen. We waved at the Second Duke of Wellington as he drove by in all his finery, his enormous nose protruding like a compass leading its owner through the park.

Soon we were passing through an area where grasses could grow tall and wild amongst the trees. I'd never understood why this portion of Hyde Park existed. Why spend centuries creating vast civilisations and technologies to escape the savagery of the wilderness, only to recreate it in the middle of a perfectly good city? I preferred the controlled dignity of the trimmed green hedges, grand white fountains and lush flower beds found elsewhere.

My driving mates agreed on the matter, and we were

soon enjoying tea perched beside a particularly striking water feature. We looked quite the things there, with the park's beautiful backdrop of trees and trimmed grass. If only Richard could see me, warmed by the sun, twirling my parasol. It didn't matter that I was mismatching. He'd take one look at me and realise his mistake. Wouldn't he?

Violet turned to Florence. "My dear, would you mind terribly if I were to take our Emma on a brief stroll? Just the two of us?"

Florence gave her a knowing look and nodded. I hated when they had these silent, gestural conversations. As if I were too stupid to notice.

But I agreed anyway, and we set off down a paved path that twisted through the trees. Violet let out a long sigh and looped her arm through my own. "Emma, you know I love you dearly."

Might as well get to the point. "What's wrong?"

"I don't think you should go to Europe." She paused to give me a sideways glance. "It'll appear to all that you're running away from the Mr Jameson affair."

"I told you, I'd decided before —"

She shook her head. "It doesn't matter what you say. People will assume the worst. And anyway, there's more to it than that. You're now without a suitor."

I replied through clenched teeth. "Yes, Violet, that has not gone unnoticed."

"Well..." She was choosing her words carefully. "You're nineteen. Florence and I have prospects, but you don't, what with Mr Jameson's false promises. Is it not time to focus your attention on finding a husband?"

My muscles tightened at her harsh words. "I can manage just fine without this talk, thank you."

"Emma, please." The girl was relentless. "We were so glad – relieved, really – that Mr Jameson had taken notice of you, however —"

"Relieved?" What was Violet saying? She made it sound like I had been desperate for a man but ignored by all.

"Well, yes." Her gentle tone only made me feel worse. "You know you've always been a little... off. You've worked so hard to fit in, but the fact is —"

"I'm far from 'off.'" My blood was boiling, inflamed by Violet and her preposterous words. "What happened to being the Light of London? People hold me in high regard. Are you jealous? Is that what this is?"

She laughed, and it wasn't the forced hiccup she gave in polite company. It was hearty and true. I dug my nails into my palms to keep from slapping her.

Violet caught herself, realising how upset I was. "Emma, your uniqueness has always been charming. Please don't misunderstand. People do love you. But we've all thought it odd that, amongst other things, you never leave London, even after the season ends each year. Going now, amid all of this, will only perpetuate talk about you."

"What 'talk' are you referring to?" My voice was growing louder, revealing the raw emotion that I'd fought for so long to hide, even from Violet.

She waved at my outfit, exasperated. "Look at what you've chosen to wear today. It's bordering on a servant's dress, and why? You have plenty of beautiful clothes, all the latest fashions. That's odd, Emma. People will pity you if you insist on presenting yourself in this way."

Pity. The word that had been associated with me since the day I'd found myself orphaned.

"How *dare* you?" The unexpected darkness in my voice took Violet aback.

"Emma, I'm n-not trying to..."

I'd never seen Violet stutter, but I was too furious to care. I swivelled around and began walking away, but she grabbed my arm before I could get very far.

"Listen to me," she whispered. "Please. I only want to help. What with your mother, the way she was... those who gossip say the apple never falls far from the tree. I'm trying to protect you."

Without further ado, because frankly I could feel myself wanting to wring her neck, I yanked my arm from Violet's grasp and rushed off. I was so desperate to get as far away from my so-called friend as I could that I left the path to hurry through brush and unseemly dirt.

I'd worked relentlessly to put aside the shipwreck and blend into society. Spent twelve hours a day with a governess learning good manners and ladylike behaviour, trying my best to ignore the darkness looming within me. I'd hidden the horrible thoughts and visions that I'd inherited beneath frills and lace and a lovely smile, and I thought I'd done well.

Apparently, this was not the case.

The only thing worse than lying to myself for ten years was learning the lie was obvious to everyone around me.

I SOON FOUND myself wandering down a dirt path surrounded by thick trees and brush that blocked the sun. Such a wild place wouldn't normally do for my sensibilities, but my mind wasn't right. In fact, I relished the solitude among the plants, away from the hushed whispers and perfect dresses and grand carriages that were always in my periphery.

Violet was right about one thing: going to the Continent was a disastrous idea. I couldn't do it, not when Richard was showcasing his new love interest around London. I needed to appear strong and unfazed. And, yes, I also needed to find a new suitor as soon as possible. Not an hour ago, I'd assumed this wouldn't be too difficult, but now, after Violet's warning, I wasn't so certain. Besides, no man would win my heart the way Richard had. Maybe potential suitors would see through me and know that I could never love again.

The life I'd carefully crafted was crumbling faster than I could keep track of. Had it only been days ago that I'd dressed for a splendid evening, secreting Grandmother's necklace from her room and knowing I had a wonderful future to look forward to? Now here I was, practically crawling through dirt, snagging my dress on bare branches. The Light of London had become a feral creature with no companions and no means of transport home.

Looking back, I know I had exaggerated my predicament. I was walking through the finest city park in the whole of England, only a few yards from a row of quality taxis, all waiting for me. But at the time, I felt I might as well have been in Africa.

I stomped on a nearby twig and felt a delightful crack

beneath my shoe. Then again, perhaps a *brief* trip out of the city could be good for me, so long as Grandmother didn't continue insisting on leaving Britain or travelling by boat. We could come to a compromise, perhaps.

And maybe, if I was especially fortunate, I'd return home to find that Richard had left his new prospect and had been pining for me during my absence. The thought gave me the first genuine smile I'd had since seeing him the other night.

But the idea of travelling with Mr Ambrosius was unbearable. Couldn't Grandmother and I go without him? Maybe I could raise this with her later in the evening.

As I walked further, the brush thinned enough for me to make out a small clearing to my left.

Leaves rattled, and something moved fast in the corner of my vision. It was a shadow the height of a child, and it danced back and forth a few yards ahead of me and into the brush. I blinked, and then it was gone. A low gust of wind lifted my hat. Perhaps it was simply the wind. Simply my ragged nerves.

And then I heard her laughter. Was that Abigail? Was she playing with me from beyond the grave?

I rushed through the bushes, scanning the area for any hint of her. Nothing. I stood for some time in a pathetic attempt to comprehend what had happened.

All I could ascertain was that this must be another hallucination. As the implications of this became clearer to me, I knew what I needed to do. I walked as fast as I could in my crinolines to the nearest taxi driver and gave him my home address.

I FOUND Grandmother sitting in her usual spot on the chaise longue when I returned home. She nearly jumped out of her seat when she saw my dishevelled state: tufts of hair falling in front of my eyes, a feather on my hat bent at an awkward angle, and a stain near the bottom of my dress. Then there was my expression – that of anxiety mixed with something like determination.

"Were you run over by an omnibus?" Grandmother's voice raised an octave for the occasion.

I took off my hat and shook my head. *Time to be strong, Emma.* "I'm not going with you and Mr Ambrosius."

Her eyes narrowed into a squint. I couldn't guess whether her expression conveyed confusion or a sudden bout of pure contempt.

"And why is that?" she asked.

Another octave higher? Oh God, it was the latter.

I opened my mouth to mention Richard and my lack of potential suitors, but the truth came out instead. "You'll have me travel by ship."

Grandmother let out an exasperated sigh. "Emma, the wreck was over ten years ago. You were a child then, and you're a woman now."

"You know I still struggle –"

"Of course I do." Her eyes bore into mine like ice picks. "You're frightened, and you have good reason to be. It horrifies me that you watched them drown."

My nails dug so hard into my palms I could almost feel blood soaking my gloves.

"However, you're also smart enough to know that not

every ship burns. It was a terrible accident, but that's all it was. An accident, and it won't happen to you again."

She really didn't know. It *hadn't* been an accident.

Now the room was spinning. I leant against the doorframe. *Stop talking*, I wanted to say. I wanted to scream it, in fact, but my body wouldn't allow for more than a pathetic moan. And then I was there, dropped into the ocean, flailing for air as waves crashed over me. My mouth, my lungs, all filled with water, swishing in my stomach.

And Mama's face, bubbles escaping her lips as her eyes flickered back and forth, searching for air. And fire everywhere. The fire she had started. Waves upon waves upon waves.

Somehow, back in our London home, I'd ended up sprawled indelicately on the floor.

"Emma." Grandmother was leaning over me. Her eyes were soft again, and filled with worry. She patted my forehead with her handkerchief, despite the fact that my skin was bone dry. Everything was dry, no seawater in sight, thank God.

I sat up as Ms Wright rushed in with a cup of tea, which was the obvious remedy for any ailment, including fainting.

Thanking her, I turned to Grandmother. "See? I can't go, not when I'm so unwell."

But she would not be swayed.

"You'll be all right, my dear. You need to face your fears, and the rest will be easy. Mr Ambrosius and I believe in you."

Had Mr Ambrosius so influenced her that she no

longer knew her own mind? I shakily got to my feet and leaned against the wall.

Grandmother took my hand in hers. "I love you dearly, Emma. And it's because of this that I am insisting we go."

I tore my hand away. "So you will disregard my feelings completely, then. This Mr Ambrosius has taken you for a fool."

Grandmother opened her mouth to speak, but I'd have no more of it. I was still dizzy, but I managed to climb the stairs and make my way to my bedroom, away from the increasing madness of the world around me.

It seemed everything was falling to pieces. First my life with Richard, then my friendship with Violet, and now my relationship with Grandmother. I knew I shouldn't have spoken so sharply to the woman who'd raised me, but it wasn't right of her to do this. She was forcing me back into that terrifying place. What kind of grandmother would do such a thing? She'd grown so heartless in only a night, right after Mr Ambrosius' arrival. It was clear that this was all his fault.

I collapsed on my bed and stared through the chiffon canopy at the ceiling. I would leave town, it seemed, as I had no other option. But if I must go, I wouldn't be boarding any ship.

I would choose to do things my own way.

SIX

THAT EVENING, Grandmother announced we would leave London the first week of August. This gave me only one week to plan my own secret departure, one that would take me far away from Grandmother, Mr Ambrosius, and all their talk of seafaring.

The races at Royal Ascot sat in the middle of this final week. I'd be out of the city– and away from Grandmother – for a few days. It was the perfect opportunity to make preparations. Considering recent events, it would also be a necessary break from Grandmother.

Violet's carriage picked me up early the following Friday morning. The fog was so thick I could hardly see my hands stretched out before me, let alone the horse and buggy waiting outside our house. Violet was nestled inside, covered with a wool blanket and huddled beside her mother, who herself sported a sleepy grimace. Mr Welch sat on the opposite side, looking tired but dashing in his riding suit and silver mutton-chop sideburns, which peeked out from under his top hat. Thanks to Ms Wright's swiftness with a needle, I was wearing my new riding outfit for our day. Now Violet had nothing to say about me wearing outdated clothing.

We bid good morning to one another and rode out of London. When Mr and Mrs Welch were both asleep, Violet nudged my side. "I'm sorry," she whispered. "We both said things the other day... things I believe neither of us meant."

I'd meant every word I'd said, but I nodded anyway. After all these years, neither of us wanted to end our friendship over a single fight, no matter how hurtful it had been.

Still, I was now second-guessing myself. Was I really regarded as *odd*? I was crushed that Violet thought such things of me, but I could not afford to show this. Together we were two of the most well-known ladies in society. Should our friendship wither, so too would our own statuses.

In fact, it was with Violet's help that I'd met Richard. We had both just turned eighteen and completed our formal presentations to the Queen – our official coming out into society. That evening we attended a grand ball.

I entered the room wide-eyed and innocent, holding Violet's arm for support. We made our way through the crowds, and there he was, wearing a fine suit and fashionable hat. But I barely noticed his clothes, his blue eyes blinded me so. We locked gazes and moved toward each other whilst I pulled poor Violet alongside me, hoping someone could properly introduce us.

For this, I will forever thank Violet – or perhaps, now, blame her. She'd already met Richard through a relative and could make the introductions.

Richard and I were inseparable from then on. We spent months courting, but as Richard was the youngest son in his family and unable to receive much inheritance, he was forced into joining the Navy. It all happened so fast. One moment we were laughing together in Hyde Park, the next he was bidding me a tearful goodbye as he left for India.

That had been the moment. Standing in front of my house on that painful, rainy afternoon, he'd made his promise: as soon as he came home with money to his name, he would ask Grandmother for my hand. It wasn't quite an engagement, but a vow nonetheless.

And he'd broken it. I turned my head away from Violet and looked out of the window at the sun peeking through the dissolving fog, praying it would dry the tears blocking my vision.

He'd be at the races, and likely with *her*. I needed to find my strength before we arrived. With any luck, the gossip and pity would die down if I showed off my usual, carefree smile. *Nobody could hurt Miss Collins,* they'd all surmise. *She's far too plucky for that.*

"I heard that preparations for your trip are underway," Violet said in a careful tone. "Are you sure you should go? I must admit, I still think it's an ill-advised idea."

I let out a long, tired sigh. "Tell that to my grandmother."

She turned to me with wide eyes. "Is she forcing you into this?"

I nodded.

"How dastardly." She looked horrified about my predicament. "She always seemed so reasonable. What happened?"

It was time to take a chance and mention Grandmother's partner in crime. As humiliating as it was to admit that such an eccentric was to be our touring escort, I needed information about him. And if anyone in society would have it, it would be Violet. "Have you heard of a person named Mr Ambrosius?" My voice cracked a little at his wretched name.

Violet looked at me blankly. "Well... Um, no. I don't think so." We both sat in silent shock. This had never happened to Violet Welch. She knew every society man in the book, including his age, marital status, and the number of positions away he was from the throne. Such knowledge was crucial, as her goal was to marry one of the first fifty names in line for the crown.

This could only mean one thing: Mr Ambrosius was not a proper society man. Which perhaps wasn't too surprising. But still.

Violet patted her forehead with her handkerchief, seemingly to calm her nerves. "He must be quite unknown. What does he have to do with your trip?"

I'd been hoping that she wouldn't ask, but there was no escaping it. I explained everything – the stories Grandmother used to tell, his outdated clothing and their strange obsession with his *miracle wine*.

Violet gasped at each turn. "He sounds like a deviant. No wonder I didn't recognise the name." This revelation seemed to comfort her, and she relaxed her shoulders.

"Indeed. And I've no choice but to join them." I picked a piece of lint off my lace glove and sighed. "Unless, of course, I were to disappear..."

I hadn't mentioned my plan to anyone yet. Violet seemed as wary as I about the trip, but I couldn't know for sure what her reaction to my scheme might be. Running away was scandalous, something a lower-class girl would do. But going to the Continent now of all times might also destroy my reputation.

Violet blinked a few times. Then she smiled.

"Perhaps you could stay with my cousin Madge." She leaned in and whispered so that her parents wouldn't wake and uncover our plan. "I'd invite you to our estate, but I'm sure your grandmother would find you there. Madge lives in Cheshire now. She married Mr Frankmore and moved to the country. And she still thinks the world of you."

For the life of me, I couldn't remember who Madge was.

"You met her last year at the Hammersmith Ball." Violet, thankfully, knew my facial expressions well. "She wore that revolting pink petticoat and matching hair bows, remember?"

"Oh, yes. Madge was quite sweet." And timid. The girl had looked like she might be sick with nerves at any moment. Which made it less likely that she would blab to anyone about my movements. "And you think she'd let me stay for a few weeks until Grandmother gives up on the idea of our trip?"

"Of course."

My original plan had been to stay alone in a hotel somewhere up north. But if anyone had caught me doing so, I would have been ruined. Now, thanks to Violet, I had a respectable place to stay.

She put her hand on my shoulder. "It seems your entire world is shattering, but things will blow over. They always do. There is one further piece of bad news I have to give you, though."

"What?"

"Richard will be in our picnic group at the races today. I'm sorry, Emma, but I couldn't do anything about it."

I mumbled something about it being fine, though of course it wasn't. Outside the carriage window, the pastures rolled by like waves on a stormy sea. My stomach flipped and I looked away, preferring instead to amuse myself by watching Mr Welch's shuddering shoulders as he snored.

~

VIOLET and I joined our picnic party after unpacking our things at the Hammersmith Estate. We were both wearing riding dresses, although neither of us intended on getting anywhere near a horse. My own was a new demure crimson number with a gold striped underskirt. Violet eyed me up and down, silently judging my choice, but I was rather pleased with the look.

It seemed the others in our group were as well. Mrs Hammersmith nearly jumped out of her shoes at the sight of me, so happy was she to see such a fine quality dress. Miss Ainsley commented on how nicely the colour brought out the flush in my cheeks, and many of the gentlemen nodded in approval.

We found a choice spot just next to the race track, only a few hundred yards from the finish line. From our place, we could make out the royal seating area in the stands, which was still empty save for an overeager duke or two.

The rest of the stands, however, were overflowing with people, all in fine hats that fluttered their feathers in the afternoon breeze. I smiled. The races were one of my favourite events of the year, one of the few in which it was acceptable to be outside all day.

Before long, though, I found myself scanning the crowds, searching for Richard's beard and uniform. A quarter of the men present were similarly attired, which meant my heart was constantly skipping about like a fearful rabbit.

A hand tapped my shoulder. I swivelled around, terrified of the face I might find before me.

But it wasn't Richard. In fact, it was the person I was least expecting to see – that incorrigible blonde American from that masked ball. Mr William No-Surname smiled. "Nice to see you again, Miss Collins."

"And you." I forced my own dainty smile and turned to speak with Miss Montgomery.

The American, as seemed to be his habit, didn't take the hint. He leaned forward on one leg to keep his face in my line of sight. "I didn't peg you as a race enthusiast."

"How amusing." I turned to him, still smiling politely. "I didn't, what's the word, 'peg' you as someone who would receive an invitation to this event."

"One of the Navy men invited me." He seemed unfazed by my insult and gave an amiable shrug. "Can't remember his first name. We only just met the other night. Last name's Jameson. Real friendly guy."

The flush Miss Ainsley had admired quickly drained from my cheeks. "Oh, y-yes. So I've heard."

Violet noted my stuttering and came to my aid. "The handsome American has arrived." She beamed and took him by the arm.

I felt the deepest sense of gratitude as I watched her lead him toward the track, animatedly waving her arms at the horses.

Of course the American would befriend Richard. Everyone befriended him. He was one of the most beloved men I knew – a perfect match for the Light of London.

Until he'd ruined everything. Beneath the shattering heartbreak, I wondered how the rest of society would treat him after such a debacle. Unfortunately, I was to find out sooner than I'd liked.

Richard arrived, handsome as ever, with the blonde woman hanging on his arm. She wore – to my horror – a crimson riding habit that nearly matched mine, and her blush seemed to entrance the entire racecourse.

She was perfect. Men paused mid-conversation to take a second glance at her, women whispered behind fans. Everyone and everything stopped for her.

The treacles I'd devoured only half an hour ago threatened a return up my throat. This wouldn't do. I patted my skirt, raised my chin and, deciding to be bold, waved a cheery hello to Richard and the woman.

He stopped in his tracks and looked at me like he'd seen a phantom. His arm dropped, and he gave a jolting nod.

To hide my heartbreak further, I made my way over to poor Mr Bailey. As guilty as I felt abusing his kindness so, I knew it was the only way I'd keep my head about me.

We engaged in some banter regarding which horse would win, though all the while I kept one eye on Richard. He was canoodling with his new love. I did my best to ignore them, despite their attention-seeking behaviour.

It seemed Violet, however, had other plans. She and the American returned to our group and made a beeline for Richard. She dipped into the lowest, most formal curtsy I'd seen her perform since our introductions to the Queen, and asked to be introduced to his fiancee.

Mr Bailey was still droning on about horse facts and statistics, so it was easy for me to lend an ear to this more pressing conversation.

Richard's face grew unsurprisingly pale. He knew Violet well enough to guess what she might say next. "Uh, yes, of course... Miss Welch, this is Miss Klepakhov."

"A *Russian*." Violet's eyes lit up. A smile – her most devious one – crept across her face. "Well, Mr Jameson, no wonder you left our dear Miss Collins in the dust." She leaned in, as if to whisper, but her voice only grew louder. "We all know how well they powder their hair, which I'm sure leads to a great deal of fun. Far more than we English ladies can provide."

Miss Klepakhov turned to Richard. "Powder their hair?"

Richard looked furious. "It means to drink excessively." He turned to Violet and raised his perfect nose. "And it's completely untrue. I'd appreciate, Miss Welch, if you'd pay

Miss Klepakhov the same respect you would to any English lady."

"A lady, is she?" Violet let out a giggle that stopped even Mr Bailey's horse-related monologue. He turned to observe the scene with more than a hint of fear on his face.

Violet leaned toward Miss Klepakhov this time. "Ladies don't go around stealing betrothed men." She straightened and shrugged. "But I suppose cultures are so different around the world, aren't they, Mrs Hammersmith?"

Mrs Hammersmith was white as a sheet. "Ah, well... we are all different, are we not?"

"Hmm." Violet nodded and returned her attention to her prey. "Well, let's hope we don't see another Crimean War anytime soon. You may be forced to do away with her brothers."

Richard grabbed Miss Klepakhov's arm and began moving away. "I believe we have another picnic to attend. Good afternoon, all."

Everyone silently waved as they left. I was in shock – Violet had defended me like a champion, putting her own reputation at risk in order to give Richard the telling off he so deserved. She was incandescent in her fury, and I had never loved her more for it. I only hoped that the rest of our circle would similarly admire her voracity.

Before the group could round its attention on me, I took the nearest arm – which happened to unfortunately be the American's – and whisked him away, toward the racecourse's stands.

"What a terrible thing to do," he muttered as we walked.

"She was only trying to stand up for me," I replied. "Though her approach was perhaps a little heavy-handed."

He looked down at me and furrowed his brow. "No, I wasn't talking about Miss Welch. Mr Jameson's a cad. And a ninny, at that."

To both of our surprise, I let out a long, hooting laugh. Never had I heard Richard Jameson referred to as a ninny, but now it seemed fitting. "Oh, I apologise," I said through hitched breaths, my cheeks flushed. "I think I'm losing my mind."

"Not something I'd blame you for. I'm sorry I mentioned him earlier. I didn't know you two –"

"It's fine. How were you to know?" We stopped beside one of the stands and I pressed my back against it for support. It was louder here, which forced me to speak up. Still, it was a small price to pay to be away from our gossip-hungry picnic group.

The American extended an arm to block the lowering sun from my eyes. He was closer than necessary, but his breath smelled like a mixture of honey and mint, so I had little to complain about.

He sighed and shook his head. "I just, well... for a man to have a fine lady like you and then drop her like that... It's a terrible thing. The worst."

Without warning, a sob escaped my throat. I thought I'd built a thick wall between my heartache and the outside world, but somehow, the American had made it crumble to nothing.

Before I knew what I was doing, I found my face buried in his chest, drenching his fine waistcoat with my tears. I heaved indecorous sobs into his ascot until, with his arms wrapped around me, I let out a long, shaking sigh.

The American looked concerned as I gathered myself, apologised and dotted my face with Grandmother's handkerchief. I rushed back to the picnic before he could say a word. Hopefully, nobody had seen us.

SEVEN

I WAS glad to return home to London. The drama at the races had quieted down after the first disaster, but the air was still charged for the rest of the event. I'd avoided the American, Richard, and Miss Klepakhov as best I could. The latter two had been much easier, as Richard had ensured that they kept their distance.

The following week slid by. Grandmother and I didn't speak much. I was still fuming at her for forcing this trip upon me at such a delicate time, and she still seemed unable to care about my feelings in the slightest.

Worse, she and Mr Ambrosius had agreed we should pack lightly. This meant no crinolines with hoops. Such a prospect was beyond unthinkable, yet here I was, standing in my bedroom and making final decisions about which of my oldest dresses should join me on my travels.

Ms Wright had laid out my choices: an apple-red riding habit I wore when I was fourteen, before crinolines or my hips had emerged; a yellow tea dress that I'd stained with pink cake icing when I was fifteen; my sky-blue dress, which still boasted the marks of my Hyde Park misadventure; or the eggshell gown I'd worn only twice before the crinoline came to England.

Had I known that one day a man in an ill-fitting Quaker costume would come barrelling into our lives and force me to wear outdated clothes, I might have kept more. But my choices were limited, and I only had a day to make my decisions before Ms Wright set to refitting them.

At least Madge had confirmed my place at her estate in Cheshire. Even better news was that Mr Ambrosius and Grandmother agreed Bristol would be the first stop on our voyage.

This meant I could leave London with them, rather than sneaking off before their departure, which had seemed wrought with potential complications. I would stay in Bristol until they chose their next destination. Then, I'd make my secret diversion to Cheshire.

Despite knowing I had social wounds to heal here, the prospect of leaving London was growing more appealing by the day. The season was still going strong, and Richard and Miss Klepakhov were frequenting events.

Worse, everyone had lumped me in with Violet after her outburst at the races, and now both of us were paying for her social sins. Upon our return to London we had both been dropped from the invitee list to the Hammersmith Ball and the Hyde Park Picnic.

I was growing tired of trying to keep my status as the Light of London. It was exhausting, and what was it for, anyway? To secure a husband? I no longer had Richard and couldn't imagine anybody else filling his shoes, so why bother with it all?

Mama. That was why. As long as I could cover memories of that day with lace and laughter, I could distract myself from the darkness inside. Without society life, I'd lose my mind, perhaps quite literally.

Whatever road I took would be horrible, and regardless of what I did, the Emma Collins I'd so carefully crafted over the years was dying. A new question now lurked: Who would stand in her place?

~

In more pressing news, I decided upon the eggshell gown and sky-blue frock, despite its new stain. With any luck, Ms Wright could get rid of it. I'd add my crimson riding suit to the luggage, since a couple of extra petticoats would be enough to support it, and heaven knows I wouldn't survive without at least one fashionable piece in my travelling wardrobe.

I picked out a few current pieces. Violet would come fetch them after our departure and send them straight to Madge's so that I would have appropriate clothing during my stay.

I called Ms Wright to my room when I had finished choosing my outfits that evening. She arrived in a fit of anxiety, wringing her hands and muttering something about the devil's work.

"What's wrong?" I asked.

She looked up at me and shook her head. "I was certain I'd turned off the lamp in the arbour earlier, but I must have forgotten. You know how I hate going out there at night."

I knew it well. She was terrified of the dark, even when

confined within our own walls. I sighed and began making my way downstairs. "The blue dress has a stain. Please see to it and I'll turn off the blasted lamp."

Ms Wright struggled to hide a gasp at my foul language, but otherwise seemed comforted knowing she wouldn't need to venture outside. She thanked me a half-dozen times and picked up my dresses with gusto.

Our back garden wasn't expansive – this was London, after all – but it was larger than average. On a misty night such as this, it was big enough to look like it had no end. The fog kissed the stony ground and whirled around in the air, dimly reflecting nearby streetlights that someone would soon put out. I held my lantern as I walked down the path, past waist-high hedges and two stout cherub statues framing the arbour's entry.

The oil lamp hung in the middle of the space. It was nestled behind our wisteria, lending the flowers a ghostly, grey hue. I was starting to see why Ms Wright was terrified of nighttime walks here.

As I reached up to the lamp, my own lantern's flame whiffed out. *Nothing to fear,* I reasoned. *Just the breeze.* I knew the garden well enough to feel my way back to the house, so I snuffed out the arbour lamp and turned back, our kitchen illuminated in the distance to guide me.

An odd tingling crept around the back of my neck, and a soft glow appeared in the corner of my vision.

I turned my head to find the arbour lamp blinking on again.

Hadn't I completely snuffed it out? Maybe I hadn't been paying attention. I let out a silent breath and returned to the lamp, ensuring that I extinguished it this time.

I made my way toward the kitchen.

Again came the tingling on my neck.

Again, the soft glow.

I turned to see the wisteria moving with the breeze. The lit lamp began jolting around, sparking and playing tricks of light all around the arbour. The cherubs' shadows moved back and forth, elongating and shrinking. Someone was giggling, somewhere just out of sight. A girl's shout. Someone was here.

I summoned the courage to speak. "Who's there?"

Silence.

The lamp stopped moving. The breeze dropped, leaving stale air behind it. Fog thickened around the arbour until I could hardly see a thing.

And then a rush of breath inside my ear. "*Go.*"

I fell back into a hedge and cried out. That voice. Crawling indecorously among the plants, I scrambled for the safety of the house. Had the back door grown more distant? It seemed miles away.

"*Go.*"

More giggling, more voices with bodies I could not see. I screamed for Grandmother, for Ms Wright, even for Richard.

"*Go. Go. Go.*"

I hurtled forwards and clawed my way through branches and fog, my hair soaking wet, dress dripping, throat full of salt. The kitchen's light only grew farther away. The ghosts would keep me here forever, buried where I belonged.

I made it to the patio, only a few feet from the back door. Grandmother stood there huffing, asking a million questions I couldn't decipher. The taste of salt water was still overwhelming in my mouth. I stuttered something about the arbour and the voices.

Grandmother paused her questions and peered at me, concerned. She took my arm. "It's all right. Come and sit down."

We entered the kitchen, safe and bathed in light. I slumped on the table reserved for household staff and rested my forehead on the cool wood. My stomach began lurching and I was quite certain I'd lose my dinner, but Ms Wright was already on hand with a cup of tea.

"It's that garden. There's something wrong with it. You mark my words," she muttered as she set the cup down in front of me.

I took a careful sip and glanced up at Grandmother. Her eyes darted to the window, but she was shaking her head. "There's nothing out there, Ms Wright," she said. "Merely the darkness playing tricks."

Her expression, however, betrayed her words. She looked just as frightened as Ms Wright. There *had* been something outside, and it wanted me gone.

EIGHT

As one might suspect, I wasn't able to close my eyes that night. I stayed in Grandmother's bed, curled up next to her, something I'd done often in the months after the shipwreck.

But even the comforting rhythm of her breath couldn't lull me to sleep. I sensed shadows moving all about, watching me, waiting for a moment of weakness. That voice – "*Go!*" – still echoed like a haunting tune that wouldn't go away.

So it shouldn't have been any surprise to anyone that I was feeling unwell the next morning, least of all Grandmother. But when I muttered a tired "Yes" to her remark about the nice weather at breakfast, she set down her knife and sighed.

"Must you be so downhearted? Plenty of girls would love to be in your shoes, Emma – travelling, seeing wonders—"

I dropped my half-eaten slice of toast onto my plate. "May I leave the table?"

I hadn't asked her for permission since I was fifteen. This would send Grandmother the message I wanted: she had succeeded in controlling my entire life, including my movements and my emotions. I was as broken as a horse.

But Grandmother didn't seem to catch my meaning and merely waved me off. I pushed back my chair and left the breakfast room, my blood pumping fast.

Where was the woman who used to dote on me? This startling change was Mr Ambrosius' fault. That much was obvious. Everything had changed after that first visit.

I walked into our parlour, which Ms Wright had half-covered with white sheets to prepare for our absence. There was only Grandmother's chaise longue and an armchair in the corner. I opted for isolation.

Just then, Ms Wright entered in a panic, carrying a pile of Grandmother's folded petticoats, asking questions about how many extra stays I might want, and if I would mind giving up one of my hair combs, as they weren't all fitting into my toiletry bag.

It was too much. My head was pounding, and a looming nausea crept into my stomach. As if on cue, a knock sounded at the door.

Ms Wright nearly dropped the petticoats. "This isn't calling time." She threw everything down on the hall table to answer the door.

If I'd had time to guess, I would have assumed that it could only be Mr Ambrosius committing such a faux pas. And I would have been entirely wrong.

"Oh, Mr Jameson. I apologise, but we aren't taking visitors at the moment."

My breathing turned shallow. *Richard? Here?* I patted

my hair, which, to my dismay, Ms Wright hadn't yet fixed up. It hung in long ringlets down the back of my dress. *Dear God, why was he here?*

"I'll just be a moment. Please." His voice, like velvet, drifted through the hall. "I need to speak with Miss Collins before she leaves."

He couldn't see me like this. The only escape route was through the side door to the breakfast room.

I jumped from my chair, which was quite the mistake considering I was wearing my largest crinoline. A hundred inches of wire toppled the chair over with an unwholesome crash, which drew both Richard and Ms Wright to the parlour before I could flee.

I stood above the upturned chair, my arms flapping toward the breakfast room door and hair flailing wildly around my body. It was not my most graceful moment.

But there Richard was, in my doorway. He gave me a formal bow. "Miss Collins."

"Mr Jameson." I raised my chin and patted my skirts. "You've arrived at an inopportune moment."

His eyes flickered to the fallen chair. "My apologies, but I heard you were leaving town."

"Yes. Tomorrow, in fact."

"May I sit?" He gestured toward the furniture. "There are things I need to say to you. Before you go."

Oh, there certainly are. I perched on the chaise longue. He chose the chair. The last time Richard was here, we'd sat so close to each other that I could feel the warmth of his legs radiating through mine. Now he wanted to be nowhere near me.

"You didn't tell me you were coming home. How long

has it been since your return?" My voice cracked and I prayed he wouldn't notice my face flushing red.

He stared at his shoes, polished to the highest shine. "About a month now."

A month? He'd been here a month and not a word to me? My throat was so constricted that all I could muster was a strangled noise in response. I stared at my blurry form in his shoes.

"And... how's your grandmother?" he asked, clasping his hands together as he sat forward.

My throat managed to loosen enough to respond with something about her being well.

He looked up and caught my gaze. His eyes were filled with guilt, but not sadness. It was worse. Pity, for the pathetic creature he'd thrown away.

"Why did you deceive me?" I blurted it out. Tears of frustration welled at my lashes. *No, not now. Don't cry, silly girl.*

Richard's eyes grew as wide as two moons. He coughed. "W-well, I— I never deceived you. Not intentionally."

My anger and confusion spilled out with the force of a hundred volcanoes. "You promised me we would be engaged as soon as you returned." I was surprised at my newfound fury, the heat bursting from me. How could he be so brazen?

"I thought we would." His voice had turned into a meek whine that stung my ears. He wouldn't meet my eyes. Instead, he fidgeted with the sleeve of his blazer. "I truly did, but things changed."

"You mean to say that you found someone new." I

fought to keep my body from shaking by digging my fingers into my palms.

Richard shook his head. "No, not that. My feelings for you...faded. We were apart for so long."

He shrugged, as if our relationship had been dust on his shoulders, easily brushed away.

I closed my eyes and breathed as deeply as I could. Only when my anger cooled did I open them. "And this had nothing to do with your new Russian friend?"

Richard gulped, his Adam's apple skipping beneath his tan skin. "Miss Collins, I-I came here to make amends. Let's not part on these terrible terms. I don't want you leaving England with hatred in your heart for me."

A mirthless smile flickered across my face. "So, you admit that you've replaced me, yet you still care about what I think of you?"

Richard dropped his shoulders. Had he responded with anything resembling a "Yes," I would have presented him with a barrage of choice words, including: coward, hornswoggler, ninny, skilamalink, liar, gongoozler, muck snipe, and – worst of all – cheat.

"I hoped you might be more forgiving than this." He looked down. "It's been so long since we—"

"You promised you'd *marry* me." My nails remained stuck in my palms. My voice was growing louder. "Do you understand what that word means, or do you use it freely and with everyone?"

He looked up and rubbed his jaw. Then he let out a sigh, as if he had suffered too much for one day. I bit back a dark laugh at the idea. "If I tell you what happened, can we part as friends?"

"Oh, of course," I replied, sarcasm dripping from my words. "Why, I'm so grateful that you would grant me the honour of the truth."

He groaned and dropped his head into his hands. "This isn't easy for me."

"For *you?*"

"I'm sorry." He ran his fingers through his hair and sat back. After a moment's pause, he continued, head turned toward the china cabinet to his left. "We met on the way from India. She was a nurse. I was visiting a wounded friend."

My nails burned deep red crescents into my palms. "And she gave you what I clearly couldn't." I lowered my chin and looked at him through wet lashes. "Did she win prizes for her stitchery? Was she invited to sing at the Duke of Wellington's charity ball last year? What made her so su*perior* to me?"

"Come off it, Emma." He snapped his head around to me. "Do you think all those things matter? My God. You only care about what's on the outside." His eyes returned to mine, glossy, full of guilt and something else I couldn't comprehend. "You never loved me. You know it. I know it—"

"How dare you. I loved you more—"

"You loved the life I'd give you," he muttered, his shoulders slumped in defeat.

I wanted to leap up and strangle him. "I see. That's your excuse, then."

Richard buried his face in his hands. A silent minute passed. I breathed in and closed my eyes in order to summon the courage for my final question. "So. She's already wearing a ring. Will you marry her?"

His gaze remained aimed at the Persian rug beneath his feet.

"Yes."

The rest of the day was a daze after that. My response to his answer was admittedly less than ladylike. Objects were thrown, curses were yelled, and Richard was gone soon after. I remember fighting against Ms Wright as she dragged me to my bed, and Grandmother asking if they should call Dr Gibson. I answered the question with a banshee scream, and Grandmother brought me a cup of tea instead.

They must have laced the drink with a sedative, because I soon found myself in a glorious stupor. Everyone around me seemed more affectionate than usual, and my bedroom took on a gentle haze.

Grandmother smiled and patted my head. I couldn't stop revelling in her deep blue eyes. They were so lovely, so pure. I beamed up at her and let out a giggle. My laughter grew stronger, until I was so exhausted I felt like I'd walked across the world twice.

Ms Wright's outline drifted toward the oil lamp next to my bed, hand outstretched. Just then, my eyes flitted to the corner of the room.

Behind Grandmother stood a girl. Nobody else seemed to notice her.

There was something familiar about this girl, though her features were hazy.

Abigail?

She was motionless as she stared at me. Her face was battered with purple bruises.

Before I could warn everyone of her presence, Ms Wright switched off the lamp and blanketed us in darkness. I tried to speak, but no words came out. My body would not obey my commands.

Through the inky black came a familiar voice. It was not Abigail's childish lilt. It sounded far older, smoother, and calmer.

"Hello again, Emma."

It was the woman from the church, the day I dreamt I'd turned a man to ash. I'd all but forgotten about her after I'd convinced myself that her red gown and black eyes were a delusion.

Grandmother and Ms Wright apparently couldn't hear her, because they had already left me without a word, closing my bedroom door behind them.

We were alone.

My drugged haze prevented me from giving a vocal response, so I simply blinked. My eyes adjusted enough to make out Abigail's slight frame and, beside her, the woman.

"You have done some terrible things, Miss Collins," the woman continued. She moved closer to my bed. "Including killing one of my own."

The man who had turned to ash. No, I hadn't killed him. How could I have?

"I don't normally do this," she continued, stepping toward me. "But after seeing what you did in that church, you leave me no choice."

I tried to ask what she meant, but it came out as a low groan.

She seemed to understand anyway. "My name is Morgana, and I'm here to right the wrongs of your family."

My family?

"And it seems," she motioned toward the girl who looked like Abigail, "that you already understand much of what is at stake."

I understood nothing, but had no ability to say as much.

"Your time is ending. You will be free of this soon." She was standing over me now, a hand reaching out to caress my cheek. Her fingers left what felt like a trail of ice in their wake. My eyes closed again, and the darkness took me.

~

AND THEN IT WAS MORNING. I hadn't slept, hadn't felt the passage of time, yet somehow it had shifted. A golden glow shone through my linen curtains.

Something was prickling on the back of my neck. I rubbed my hand over the spot and felt warm liquid. Blood.

I stumbled out of bed and over to my vanity mirror. Long, angry marks made a path down the back of my neck, and under my night shift, which was already stained red. I pulled it off to find scratches careening down my torso and around my hips.

There were only two explanations:

Last night had all been a terrible nightmare and I had clawed at myself in my sleep.

Or, that vision had been real. And a woman named Morgana had given me these scratches after announcing my imminent death.

NINE

Ms Wright came into the room just as I was inspecting my newest injuries. She looked mortified. It was clear now that she thought I was losing my mind.

By midday, Grandmother knew about them, too. She demanded we call the dreaded Dr Gibson. That godforsaken man was the last person I wanted to see. His beady eyes would scan me up and down, judging me from behind spectacles as big as tea plates. Then he'd proclaim me mad and send me to the nearest woman's institution.

I'd avoided this sentence as a child, but now, with these marks, I knew there was no hope of escaping.

For the first time in a long time, however, I found myself lucky. Dr Gibson would not be in town until weeks after we'd left on our travels.

That was my only bit of fortune that day. Over the next few hours, the rest of London began hearing of my encounter with Richard. Violet and Florence called later that evening with information regarding the story, which was apparently no longer my own.

"Poor Miss Collins. Her mind has grown so fragile, she is soon to be admitted to an institution," Mrs Edwards had confided in Miss Evans over tea.

"You do realise why Miss Collins was so distraught over Richard's denial?" Miss Evans had whispered loudly to a curious Ms Smith afterwards. "I hear she had disreputable relations with him a few months ago, and is now in a most delicate position. That's why, of course, Mrs Collins is sending her away for the next few months."

"A trustworthy source tells me Miss Collins is not only with child, but attempted to murder poor Mr Jameson with a kitchen knife she had hidden in her dress pocket!" Ms Smith told this to all, and the rumour travelled from mouth to mouth until it met Florence's eager ears. "He barely made it out of the house alive, and only did so by feigning his undying love for her."

The gossip had almost become worse than the heartache itself. I wished more than anything that I'd never allowed Richard to enter my parlour in the first place. Or I should have pretended he had meant nothing to me.

But it was too late. Society was turning its back on me, and I had no choice but to leave London with a mad Quaker and his hypnotised comrade. And while travelling, I would only have my own thoughts to occupy my time. I shuddered as an image of Morgana and a sea-soaked Abigail flashed into my mind's eye. Such idleness would only bring me closer to the demons lurking within.

MORGANA'S FACE continued filling my mind on the morning of our departure. I was queasy with fear by the time Ms Wright and the driver finished loading the luggage into the carriage.

Grandmother was standing beside me on the walkway, staring up at our house with a look of sadness in her eyes. For one shining moment, I thought she might change her mind and tell us we'd stay home.

That hope was immediately dashed when she turned away and said, "What a lovely day to see the countryside."

My shoulders slumped, but I picked them back up when I saw Violet and Florence approaching. The former was already dabbing her eyes dramatically with her lavender handkerchief.

"I-I just can't believe you're leaving us." She sniffled into the fabric as they arrived at our carriage.

My current disposition allowed no patience for such silliness. "Oh, Florence, do stop it," I snapped. "The season is ending in a few weeks anyway, and then everyone will leave the city, including you. You're making it sound like I'm about to perish."

Violet let out a shocked gasp. "Don't say such things!"

I turned to her with narrowed eyes. "The dying may say what they like."

Violet was raising her fan to bash me on the shoulder just as a taxi came to a stop behind our carriage. Mr Ambrosius peeked out from the window with a huge smile.

Both Violet and Florence stopped everything they were doing to stare at the man.

"What a spectacular travel day." He jumped out of the taxi.

My knees threatened to turn to jelly beneath me.

Violet frowned, put her fan away, and grasped her parasol rigidly with her other hand. "If you don't write every day, I'll send detectives out to find you." Her orders were loud enough for Mr Ambrosius to hear.

My eyes filled with tears at her words. For all her judgement and bluster, Violet was still the best friend I'd ever had.

"I promise."

We hugged and Florence followed suit. What would life be like without them? There was no guarantee when I would return. What if I was years older, and it was too late for me to marry? Spinster life was not something to which I aspired.

The driver finished loading Mr Ambrosius' belongings into our carriage.

"Come along now, Miss Collins," Mr Ambrosius said. "We have a long way to go and not much time."

Violet let me go. "Wire me when you're ready for Madge," she whispered. "And don't worry. We'll mend everything by next season."

I swallowed hard and dotted my cheeks with my handkerchief, turning toward the carriage. Mr Ambrosius held out his hand to help me get in.

I stared at the hand. It was slender and pale, the skin devoid of flaws or freckles or wrinkles. A perfect specimen, as unnerving as its owner.

Thinking of Madge and her Cheshire home, I took a deep, shaky breath and gave my hand to Mr Ambrosius. I sat down next to Grandmother. As the carriage started moving, I looked out the back to see my closest friends waving their goodbyes.

Their figures grew smaller and smaller. The carriage turned a corner, and they were gone.

WE ARRIVED AT VICTORIA STATION, the fear I'd suffered earlier now replaced by a warm enthrallment. It had been years since I'd been on a train, and I remembered how much I'd loved the swiftness of wheels on tracks.

Travellers crowded the station, most carting enormous pieces of luggage. Some spoke in languages I'd never heard. Many of them were immigrants from India, searching for a new home amongst the smoke and havoc of London. An older man with a hunchback tried to sell me flowers, his two-toothed smile beaming at me amongst the chaos.

Mr Ambrosius moved gracefully through the crowds, twirling around a woman carrying baskets of fruit, tiptoeing past a group of street children smoking pipes, ducking under a megalithic trunk being carried by two muscular men. He moved more like a breeze than a man walking. Despite his quick pace, he never once stumbled or crashed into anyone. It seemed this entire station was filled with dancers choreographed to Mr Ambrosius' design.

Grandmother and I stayed a few feet behind, her arm in mine as we made the journey across the station to Platform Four. Our train was already preparing to leave, and the porters rushed to get all of our luggage on board.

We had only just entered our cabin when the car lurched forward, and I careened indelicately into the wooden siding. I looked up at Mr Ambrosius, incorrectly assuming that he would come to my aid.

Instead, he regarded me with an accusatory raised eyebrow. "Not much of a natural traveller, are you?"

I decided not to grace him with a response and sat beside the window to watch the passing city.

Factories pushed smoke into the grey sky. We spied a gaggle of children playing cricket in a park, then the last of London's buildings swept by, replaced by vast fields of grass and sheep.

Grandmother pointed out various pieces of land belonging to old friends long gone, her eyes shining at memories I'd never be able to inhabit.

Now that we were actually on our voyage, a new question arose that began nagging at me. I turned to Grandmother. "What's in Bristol?"

She smiled. "What do you mean?"

"Why are we going?"

Her eyes drifted out the window. "I wanted to see an old friend. Mr Ambrosius will take you to one of his favourite villages nearby."

I bit the inside of my lip. Spending time alone with Mr Ambrosius sounded about as palatable as eating a block of rotting cheese. "And can I not join you on this visit instead?"

She shook her head. "This is your opportunity to get to know our lovely escort. You'll have a splendid time."

Her words weren't so much a promise as they were a command.

We arrived in Bristol that afternoon. It was quieter than London, and its cobblestone streets were less grimy than those in the capital city. Our hotel was more of an inn, with rough-hewn walls that looked like piles of stones.

The driver transported our luggage to our rooms, while Mr Ambrosius craned his neck, looking up at the clear sky. To my horror, Grandmother excused herself for a nap, which meant I was left alone with the man. The atmosphere between us was awkward, especially when he licked his index finger and pointed it up to the heavens.

After five minutes of this pose – not without a few odd looks from passersby on the street – he hopped once and smiled widely.

"Tomorrow shall be a perfect day for St Michael's Tower."

Before I could ask him what the blazes St Michael's Tower was, he grabbed my arm and dragged me – to my acute horror – into a neighbouring public house.

"I don't believe this is an appropriate location for dinner," I protested.

"It serves food. How is it not appropriate?" His reply wasn't a question.

We were already inside as it was, so I sighed and stood behind him, in hopes I could avoid being seen by anyone.

This, of course, was impossible. Gruff, pipe-smoking men filled most of the pub, and they all turned to look at me. A flush came to my cheeks. Whistles and much-too-encouraging smiles weren't the types of attention I enjoyed.

"'Ello there, lovey,"crooned a large man sitting at the bar.

His friend, who was peeling an apple with a worn knife, smiled wide at me, revealing a broken, rotting front tooth. "You look thirsty," he said. A sheen of saliva laced the edges of his mouth.

I ignored both of them and thought about the Mansfield's Annual August Roast, which was happening in London today. Soup might have been served already. Mr Mansfield was probably cutting into the beef, a task he only performed for a minute before he had a footman take over the rest of it.

The guests, including many fine London gentlemen, were probably commenting on Mrs Mansfield's choice of china for the event– for nobody of good upbringing made remarks regarding a lady's need for hydration.

"She's *hungry*." Mr Ambrosius was unaware of the lewd tone in the man's voice. "Good woman, what does your cook have for us tonight?"

A red-faced barmaid scowled as she replenished the tooth-man's cup. "'Erring soup." She gave me a suspicious glare. Apparently, we would not be forging any kind of womanly bond against the male indecencies lurking here.

Mr Ambrosius was unfazed. "That sounds spectacular. We'll take a bowl each and a pitcher of ale." He handed the woman some coins and traipsed off to an unoccupied table. As I followed, I gave the pub's patrons my gentlest smile in the hope it would improve the atmosphere. This, of course, was an idiotic idea. All the men who saw me perked up much too animatedly. I lowered my head, sat down, and focused all my attention on a wayward splinter poking out of our dining table.

Thankfully, a bowl of soup swiftly replaced it. Not thankfully, an herring head floated up from its murky depths to lock eyes with me. The accusatory glare from my meal made my hunger disappear, and I pushed the bowl away.

At this point, I should not have been surprised that Mr Ambrosius had a most unusual approach to eating a meal.

As for the specifics of his strange behaviour, I shall illustrate it with a poem my governess had me memorise as a child:

> A lady who is at all polite,
> Finds table manners a delight.
> Her mouth with food she must not crowd,
> Nor while she's eating, speak aloud.
> The table cloth she must not spoil,
> Nor with her food, her fingers soil.

It seemed my grand escort may have learnt the same poem, because he was endeavouring to do exactly the opposite of what the rhyme suggested.

Food flew across the room from his hands and lips, travelling further than I imagined possible. Had the accusatory herring head not put me off my dinner, Mr Ambrosius would have done the job himself.

"So, what has your grandmother told you about me?" Mr Ambrosius asked, mid-chew.

I lifted my chin and worked hard not to grimace at the spittle running from the corner of his mouth. "She's told me about your travels, which were quite interesting."

In proper society, *quite interesting* was a nicer way of saying *appalling*. Once again, however, Mr Ambrosius made it clear he knew nothing of proper society.

"'Interesting' is such a boring word. I prefer

'invigorating.' Or 'enlightening.'" He waited for some kind of reaction from me. When he didn't receive it, he continued. "Anyway, what else did she say?"

I shrugged. "Not much. I must ask, though... when you travelled, did you do so alone?"

He raised an eyebrow. "That's it? That's the only question you have? Gods, you really are a disappointment."

"E-excuse me?" I had never been so insulted.

"Did she not tell you *why* she travelled with me? Did you not ask?"

I was silent, because I actually hadn't asked. From Grandmother's stories, it seemed clear that they were travelling only for hijinks and pleasure. It wasn't as if Grandmother, a wealthy woman with a title, was doing business all over the globe. Such an idea was laughable.

Mr Ambrosius shook his head in disappointment. "I hope you aren't as hopeless as you seem. Because if you are, I fear the entire world is doomed."

The herring head in my bowl stared at me with one glassy eye, as if waiting for my response. I tried to stay calm. I needed to know what Ambrosius was getting at, and if I lost my temper, he might close the conversation down altogether. "Why don't you tell me the entire story now, then?"

He shook his head again. "I'd very much like to, but your grandmother forbids it. She thinks that when the time comes for the truth, it should be from her, and no one else. She's worried, I suppose, that you might suffer your mother's fate."

Mama.

He was peering at me over his soup, as if measuring my

reaction. Did he know what had happened in her last weeks? There was only one way to find out.

I straightened my spine and raised the edges of my lips into a forced smile. "And what fate was that, Mr Ambrosius?"

"A fate worse than madness. Worse than eternal damnation. A fate of nothingness."

My bones turned to ice. He knew about Mama's madness. Worse than that, he seemed to know even more about what had happened to her than I did.

~

SLEEPING on an empty stomach wasn't something I enjoyed. Neither was waking up to the memory of Mr Ambrosius' words playing over and over in my mind throughout that wretched night. *A fate of nothingness.* What did that even mean?

I thought of my visions of Abigail, with her long hair and sweet brown eyes, begging for life, crying. My hands around her neck, my fingernails digging into her soft skin, leaving marks. The dark part of me wanted to squeeze harder.

And now there was someone new stalking across my nightmares. Morgana. She had said that my time would end soon.

As one might imagine, I was thankful when morning came. That was, of course, until Mr Ambrosius began slamming his fists on my door. "Up and at 'em, Miss Collins. We're running late."

I muttered some half-blasphemous response and began

my morning ablutions. Never in my life had I done them without help from someone else. The inn had provided a basin of fresh water the evening before, so I set to dabbing my face with a wet towel.

After a long, arduous struggle with my corset and its lacing, and a tiring swim through the yards of taffeta in my dress, I turned to the mirror.

My long hair flowed wildly over my shoulders. I groaned and grabbed a brush. It usually took at least twenty minutes for Ms Wright to put it up.

Mr Ambrosius began banging on the door again, just as I'd wrestled my hair into a simple bun. I glanced at the mirror with not a small hint of pride at my accomplishment before hastening to the door.

An infuriated Mr Ambrosius stood on the other side, his eyes wide and glinting. He dangled his cracked pocket watch an inch from my face. "We're late."

"I needed to get dressed." I leaned back from the watch and brushed past him. "It takes some time to do."

"Pff. Takes me two minutes. You won't be needing those frills anyway, not where we're going." He flicked a tuft of lace on my shoulder before pushing past me down the hall.

I was about to scold him for his rudeness, but then I noticed who was missing. "Where's Grandmother?"

"This is a side trip," he called without bothering to look back. "Just for us two. She'll be staying in Bristol today."

So this was the day Grandmother would be seeing her supposed friend. Something about that conversation on the train yesterday had seemed off, but with a loose corset and a night of little sleep, I didn't have the energy to think much more about it. My temples were already pounding.

We stepped into our carriage outside of the hotel and were soon driving into the countryside. It was a lovely August afternoon, warm and bright. The rolling green hills were dotted with trees that reflected the sun, lending them a gold hue at their peaks.

Long-buried memories of picnics with Father and walks with Mama began stirring in my mind. But remembering my parents was never a good idea, so I dismissed the thoughts as quickly as they came.

"I remember the morning you were born," Mr Ambrosius mused as we passed a flock of sheep spread out over a wide green pasture. "It was much like this morning, except warmer. Strange day, though."

My head swivelled from the sheep to him. "What? Why on Earth were *you* present at my birth?" The idea was absurd. Aside from Grandmother, he was a stranger to our family, as far as I was aware.

I imagined my poor, exhausted mother dealing with Mr Ambrosius' antics while trying to settle a crying newborn.

"Are you listening? That's not the part of the story that matters," he replied with a raised eyebrow. "The day was strange."

My brow furrowed as I turned his words over in my mind. "In what way was it strange?"

"Your birth itself was abnormal. It was very peaceful, too much so. You didn't cry when you were born. The midwife thought you were dead."

My mouth dropped open. "Grandmother never told me this."

"When the doctor established that you were indeed alive and well," he continued, "we came in to see you. Your grandmother cried, of course. And Maxwell seemed like the usual proud father. Nothing else was amiss, at least that anyone else noticed." He stopped and licked his lips like he was gearing up for some grand revelation. "But I saw an oddity."

I waited again for him to continue, but he stayed silent.

"...Go on?"

"Ah, yes." He laughed and pointed a finger upwards, to the sky beyond the roof of our carriage. "Well, it was your energy field. It wasn't changing colours at all."

I blinked. "My what?"

"The energy surrounding you." He lowered his chin. "Everybody has an energy field. It changes colours depending on disposition." He waited for me to respond, as if monitoring how I would digest this information.

I stared at him.

"Your grandmother never told you about this, either?"

I shook my head.

"Gods, she wanted to keep *everything* from you."

It was difficult, to put it mildly, imagining my reasonable grandmother telling me about colourful fields of energy that nobody else could see.

"Well." Mr Ambrosius let out a long sigh. Had he not been so rude, I'd almost feel sorry for him being forced to travel with somebody as mundane as myself. "Energy fields change colour. Yours, however, always remains white."

I waited for him to explain further, but apparently he felt he'd been clear enough. "And that means...?"

"Humans don't have purely white energy fields." His silver eyes were intense. "Ever."

I laughed. "Are you suggesting I'm not a human being?"

Mr Ambrosius was silent. Only the sound of wheels bumping on rocky ground disturbed the carriage's thick atmosphere. I stopped smiling.

It was bad enough that I'd had to leave London. Bad enough that I couldn't live a normal life free of Mama's madness, free from violent visions of my drowning sister and red-robed strangers, free from inexplicable scratches all over my body – but now this man was insinuating I wasn't human?

A moment passed as I contemplated the social ramifications of such a revelation. What would my stitchery circle say about it?

"No. Of course you are," Mr Ambrosius stated with a heavy finality. "Your mother and father were, so you must be. But that doesn't mean you're normal, not by any means."

"Thank you," I replied dryly.

"You're welcome." He smiled and looked out of the carriage's window. "Oh, good. There's the tower."

I followed his gaze toward a tall, oddly-shaped hill jutting out from the others around it. Just off-centre from its summit sat an old tower built from grey stone that reflected the reddish hues of the afternoon sun.

This must have been the St Michael's Tower that Mr Ambrosius mentioned. The thing cast a long, dark shadow over part of the hill. Mr Ambrosius closed his eyes and began humming.

Thankfully, the carriage ride only lasted another half

hour. It was late afternoon and I was famished, so we went straight to a small inn in the village and ate a delicious spread.

The sun had set by the time we finished, which seemed to agitate Mr Ambrosius to a near-manic excitement. It wasn't until we emerged outside that I understood why.

The sky was filled with the most dazzling green, red and blue lights I'd ever seen. They waved across the heavens, granting colour and brilliance to the moonless night. One of Father's astronomical books mentioned this phenomenon: the *aurora borealis.* But if I remembered the text correctly, they rarely appeared so far south.

"Did you know they were coming?" My gaze was affixed on the spectacle above us.

He snorted. "It was obvious. The sun emitted a solar flare a couple of days ago. The aurora arrived faster than usual, but that's to be expected, what with the current placement of the Earth's rotation and its magnetic field."

"Right."

He sighed. "Come with me." We walked across an extensive field, the colourful sky illuminating it in quasi-daylight.

There was an owl flitting back and forth ahead of us, its white feathers bluish under the painted sky. It hooted at our approach and flew off to the top of the hill before us, toward St Michael's Tower.

Mr Ambrosius led us up the incline and I leaned forward, huffing cool air as my heels poked into the muddy grass beneath me.

"Stop." Mr Ambrosius stood still. He took a stick from his belt and whipped it through the air in front of us, so that it extended telescopically into a walking cane. I blinked at this latest bizarre affectation, and he began humming again.

I put my hands on my hips and sighed. "What are you doing? And where are we going? You've so far held my interest today, Mr Ambrosius, but my patience is reaching its limits."

Mr Ambrosius didn't answer. He put his cane out horizontally before him, as if he were fishing, and began walking. It seemed that the cane was leading him as he drifted to the right. "Follow."

I could have walked away and returned to the lovely inn with its tasty food. I could have stayed the night in a warm bed and taken the morning carriage back to Bristol and Grandmother.

And in doing so, I wouldn't get any answers. As silly and ambiguous as Mr Ambrosius was, at least he was giving me information at all. It was evidently more than Grandmother had done all these years.

So I let out a breath and followed behind him.

We walked around the hill, only slightly ascending each time we made a full circle around it.

"Why are we going around and around?"

"Have patience." His deep concentration had deadened the musical tone I'd grown accustomed to.

I closed my eyes, counted to five, and continued walking. Best not to get into a fight with a madman on a lonely hill in the dead of night. I quietly followed him until we made it to the top.

Once there, I steadied myself against the ancient grey tower and took a few deep breaths, dotting my forehead with the handkerchief I'd borrowed from Grandmother. "Will you please explain now?"

Mr Ambrosius began flailing his arms above him in some kind of dance. "We were following the Old Way. The path the ancients took to ascend the hill. It follows the ley line they called St. Michael."

"What in heavens is a ley line?"

Mr Ambrosius smiled. "A ley line is a line of energy. One of the Earth's veins, if you like."

"And you found it based on your humming and your cane?"

"Yes, of course."

I crossed my arms and stared at him in disbelief.

"I see you still doubt me," he noted. "Stop that."

The wind picked up, sending a chill through the exposed skin of my neck. I looked back up to the painted sky, wishing Grandmother was here to see it.

He sighed. "I cannot explain everything to you, Miss Collins. Right now, I can only assure you that you need to trust me. Indeed, your life may depend on it."

Mr Ambrosius began humming again and plodded around the tower, waving his cane. Then, as I was pondering the madness of all of this, a long-forgotten memory crashed into my mind.

"Mr Ambrosius," I called out. "I think I've been here before."

"You have?" His voice was laced with false surprise as he appeared from around the other side of the tower. "When? With whom?"

Their faces – smiling, laughing, bright – filled my mind. "I was young, maybe... five?"

Mr Ambrosius dropped his arms and gave me a serious look. "Who were you with, Miss Collins?"

My parents. And Abigail.

In my memory, Father was walking around the tower, much like Mr Ambrosius had been doing. I was chasing him, laughing and tripping on tufts of grass. Everything around me sparkled, bathed in sunlight.

Mama was dancing, drinking in the noon warmth. She didn't have a parasol or hat to cover her skin. Instead, she let the sun hit her face. Her eyes were closed and there were tiny lines trailing from their corners.

I was too young then to be confused by how little she cared about getting freckles. But now, remembering it, I wondered if she'd been going mad for some time before the shipwreck. No sane woman of her standing would have done such a reckless thing as exposing her skin to the sun.

"Emma?" Mr Ambrosius yanked me out of my reverie. I only then realised that tears were streaming down my face.

"I was here with my parents and my sister. It was a picnic." I wrapped my arms around my chest. "Just us."

"And how did you feel? When you were here last time?"

I took a deep breath. "Happy. I was innocent then." If only I could bring that innocence back. Wipe away all of my evil thoughts and be who I was before I watched Mama set that ship on fire. Before I watched hundreds of people screaming, drowning. Before Abigail and I found ourselves together in the waves...

The Tower began glowing red.

Mr Ambrosius approached me. "And you're not innocent now?"

Did he know the truth? That gentle Miss Emma Collins, the Light of London, suffered from dark fantasies – visions of killing a poor little girl. Visions which could also be memories. There were still parts of the fire and the wreck that I couldn't recall.

For a moment, I could have become as mad as my mother. I could have killed someone. Just as she had.

Mr Ambrosius chuckled. "Your silence is an interesting answer."

"I... I've done nothing wrong."

The aurora was reflected in his bulbous forehead as he smirked. "Then why say such a thing? He began walking toward me. "You don't remember doing anything... dark?"

The Tower was now bathed in bloody light. Mr Ambrosius looked up and shook his head. "It's stronger than I feared."

"What is?"

Mr Ambrosius turned to me. "Have you been having terrible visions of violence? Dark shadows that wake you in the night? Has a phantom visited you, warned you of your impending doom?"

My stomach dropped.

"How about hearing things, like children laughing? Or seeing lamps snuffing out? Scars that appear from nowhere?" He took in my frozen expression and nodded. "Yes, you are in danger, Miss Collins. Mortal danger. Powerful beings want you dead. But do not despair. I am here to help."

One might imagine a long, dramatic silence might then

ensue between us. Perhaps I would faint at his words and Mr Ambrosius would catch me to keep me from falling in the mud. Or maybe I might devolve into fits of crying and denial, pushing my fists against him, telling him what a cad he was for feeding me such a story.

But the reality was much more unexpected. Much to Mr Ambrosius's confusion – and my own – I burst into laughter.

"What's so funny?"

I took a breath to gather my senses. "The irony. Of all the saviours one might imagine, all the dashing princes in storybooks, and you are the hero I am sent to deliver me from evil." I shook my head, tears of laughter (or perhaps despair) running down my cheeks. "If I *was* being tormented by some kind of ghost... well, forgive me, but you would not be the first person I'd expect to save me."

Mr Ambrosius looked only a little affronted. "It's not a *ghost*, my dear. But I suppose that's the most similar creature someone like you could comprehend."

There was a clear insult in that statement, but I chose to ignore it, deciding that we were now even. "So what am I to do about this... thing?"

It was Mr Ambrosius' turn to laugh. "Quite the question. These creatures don't have life to lose, so you cannot simply kill them." He paused. "No, I'm afraid we have an arduous task on our hands now, Miss Collins. In fact, there's a probability that you are about to experience a most horrific death."

TEN

Mr Ambrosius and I didn't speak much for the rest of the night. I'd half-run, half-rolled down the blasted hill after he'd made his deadly assertion.

However, my racing thoughts calmed after a good night's sleep and a morning bath. I needed to see Grandmother and tell her everything I was experiencing. More importantly, I needed to ask her what she knew about my past and my parents. There was no more time to dance around it.

Grandmother was in her room when we arrived back at the hotel in Bristol the next morning.

I paused for a moment as I looked at her. She was sitting on a sofa with the sunlight streaming over her face. Everything I needed to know was there, in the wariness of her eyes, the creases of her down-turned lips. There was a sadness that I had never noticed until now.

Why had I been so blind?

She noticed my entry and turned to me with her usual smile. Of course. I knew that smile well. It was just like my own. We Collins girls were apparently perfect at showing false happiness.

"Can we talk?" I asked her. There was no time for pleasantries.

She cocked her head to the side in surprise. "Of course, my dear. What's wrong?"

I had been rehearsing this conversation in my head during our ride back to Bristol, but now the words escaped me.

Instead, I joined her on the sofa. We sat in silence for some time.

"How was St Michael's Tower?"

"Mr Ambrosius told me I'm in danger. He asked if I've been suffering from dark visions." My breath hitched. "And the truth is, I have."

Grandmother's face was unreadable.

Then, to my surprise, she waved her hand in a way that suggested this was all tomfoolery. "Oh, do not listen to Mr Ambrosius. He has such a colourful personality, doesn't he?"

My eyes widened. "You're saying he was simply playing with me?"

"Oh, absolutely. But he doesn't mean to be cruel." She shook her head. "It's simply his way of having fun. It means he likes you."

I decided then that being liked by Mr Ambrosius was not a prudent aspiration. That being said, however, I also knew that Grandmother was lying to me.

It seemed I needed to uncover our family secrets myself.

AT DINNERTIME, Grandmother came to my room in good spirits. She was wearing her finest evening gown – a deep crimson velvet and silk number with dark crystals cascading from her shoulders.

Glimmering from her collarbone was the necklace I had purloined the night of the masked ball. The crystal sparkled mockingly next to my own plain clothing. Why had she brought fine evening wear along on this trip, when I had packed so frugally?

I inwardly fumed as she led me downstairs to the hotel's restaurant. Mr Ambrosius was already eating everything in sight, and the two of them spent the better part of an hour lost in laughter and memories which I'd played no part in.

After dessert, I excused myself to the restaurant balcony. The fresh night air rejuvenated me. As my eyes adjusted to the darkness, I noticed a small cemetery just past the hotel grounds.

Then there was movement.

Behind the gravestones, standing beneath an oak tree, was a short statue. A statue that then stretched its arm up and began waving at me.

So it was a child, clearly lost and in need of comforting. But then it was moving toward me much too fast, without the usual jolt of feet hitting the ground. Within seconds, it was past the cemetery and nearly halfway to the balcony.

It was a girl. Her eyes, black beneath the grey moon, locked onto me like a cat stalking its prey.

This wasn't just a girl. At least, not a normal one. It was Abigail.

Her mouth opened wide, gaping as she continued toward me. Her bruised arms stretched forward, white hands spread wide.

A screech came from somewhere in her throat. The sound of it was far more animal than human.

I fell back into the restaurant and ran into the hallway. I couldn't discern up from down, couldn't find my footing.

All I could do was try to move forward. The dreadful screech echoed in my ears so loudly I wasn't sure if it was a memory or another cry. Was she following me?

The hallway lights snuffed out. Darkness covered me, my screams smothered. Someone was breathing heavily beside me and I reached out blindly, seeking with my hands the person who must have been there. But they found only cold stone.

The breathing rasped again.

I crawled forward, crying for Grandmother, even for Mr Ambrosius. Anyone. Whispers came out of the walls, fast and hushed. Giggles. Someone ran down the hall beside me, bare feet slapping against the wood floor, the edges of a skirt brushing past my cheek.

Another cry, but this sounded different. Arms wrapped around me. Grandmother's. She held me so tight it seemed I'd become a part of her.

Mr Ambrosius stood behind her, holding a lantern that brought light back into the hallway. "Heavens above. What was all that about?"

I tried to spit a smart retort, but couldn't. I merely slumped onto Grandmother's shoulder and let out another whimper. As per my weak request, they led me to Grandmother's room. I slept for a few hours huddled beside her, a peaceful respite from the racing terror and flashes of frightening images.

One scene that stuck in my mind was an old memory. Months after the wreck, Dr Gibson had spent a tireless afternoon trying to convince me to speak. As if just telling me to do it was enough to bring the words out. I didn't have the ability to say anything. My mind had made it impossible, so afraid was I of accidentally telling everyone what I'd seen Mama do.

Dr Gibson had just left our house when Grandmother sat me in the front parlour. This room was only meant for guests, and I felt instantly ill at ease. Grandmother perched opposite me and clasped her hands in her lap.

"I know you won't answer my questions, Emma," she began. Her voice had grown lower, the tone she used for adults. It frightened me. "So I will simply tell you what's on my mind."

I waited as she took a long sip of Earl Grey.

"You survived a nightmare I can't imagine, and I won't pretend to comprehend what you're suffering. However," she paused and furrowed her brow deeply, "I will not stand by and allow you to destroy your future. Many people are aware of your current affliction, and it's already affecting your standing."

I bit my lip hard to keep from crying.

"Right now, you may feel it's impossible to imagine a happy life. But I promise, if you fight for it, you'll have it. We must look to your future. And you must learn to look outward now, my dear. Your pain won't go away until you find comfort in the company and love of others. You can't do that if you don't speak. Do you understand?"

I nodded.

She let out a long breath and patted her skirts. "I've sent for a governess. She'll be here by the month's end. I expect you to greet her with a smile befitting a good, diligent young lady. Dr Gibson will not return to help. This is your fight now."

She excused me and I plodded up the stairs with tears streaming down my face. Grandmother was right. I couldn't hide away forever.

So I set my favourite doll on my bed in front of me. She was a fine porcelain thing with dark curls and pink cheeks that Father had brought me from a trip to Germany. Her glass eyes looked at me expectantly, waiting for my words. I waited, too.

It took me days of practice with my little doll, but I was determined. I crafted a new persona – a new way to speak, to act, to be. Miss Emma Collins, the unshakable socialite and most beloved girl about town.

The same Miss Emma Collins who was now curled up in her grandmother's bed, praying that the monsters would go away and leave her be.

Perhaps I would not have survived socially had I allowed the silence to remain. But I couldn't shake the suspicion that I'd made a mistake. Perhaps I should have focused my efforts not on speaking, but on something deeper. Something like healing.

THE NEXT MORNING, I caught Grandmother and Mr Ambrosius enthralled in a heated discussion over the hotel restaurant's breakfast tarts. I'd just entered the lobby and was about to join them when I saw Grandmother's deep frown.

They hadn't seen me yet. I leaned casually against a nearby wall, out of sight, fanning myself so that witnesses could assume I was merely feeling faint. From here, I could hear pieces of their conversation.

"... can't tell her those things... ready." Grandmother's voice was urgent, with dark undertones preserved only for sound chastising. I rather enjoyed knowing Mr Ambrosius was on the other end of it.

"I'll not censor myself, Virginia," Mr Ambrosius wasn't bothering to whisper, and for once I was thankful.

"... not saying... but Emma needs..."

"She needs to know what's happening to her." Mr Ambrosius' voice was rising. "It's stronger than her mother's. It's moving faster. We need to go to France immediately."

Someone tapped me on the shoulder. I let out an indecorous chirp and swivelled around to find a young porter. "Sorry, Miss. Are you feeling all right?"

"Just fine." My words came out as more of a hiss than a kind reply. The poor boy straightened and scurried away. I turned back to the restaurant, but all I could hear now was the quiet tapping of forks and knives.

I DIDN'T EAT breakfast that morning. Grandmother asked me repeatedly what was wrong, but I didn't have it in me to craft a false smile and tell her I was fine. She'd know the truth, anyway. Grandmother had always seen through what she called my "society face."

However, I also couldn't tell her what I'd heard. She'd only deny everything and admonish me for trying to eavesdrop.

I needed to go to Mr Ambrosius. It seemed he wanted to tell me things, despite Grandmother's command not to.

My plan was to wait until we were alone and he was in a good mood. Unfortunately, the entire day passed without such an opportunity.

In the afternoon, Grandmother and I took a stroll through some open fields nearby. Clouds were obscuring the sun, so I left my parasol closed and carried it beside me as I breathed in the wet air. The countryside did suit me, much to my surprise and modest dismay.

Richard had once expressed a yearning to escape to Wales and live in the mountains with only a small estate and a dozen servants. He would become a wild mountain man, he'd said with a grin.

Neither I nor my satin heels had been intrigued by the idea, but I'd returned his beaming smile and said something about what good the air would do for one's lungs.

He would love this walk. A patch of trees was obscuring the town, so from here, it seemed the world was only fields and forests.

Perhaps if I'd brought him here, he'd have seen the good in me. I sorely wanted my corset tightened to vanquish the emptiness in my chest, but with no Ms Wright at hand, I could only wrap my arms around myself and stifle a whimper.

He was with someone else now. Almost as painful was knowing she was quickly replacing me, going to all my favourite charity balls and picnics.

She'd soon be the new Light of London. And here I was, in damp fields with a loose corset and no friends.

How quickly the great can fall.

Grandmother broke through my miserable thoughts. "At least it looks like your fever has broken. Your cheeks have their flush back."

I couldn't believe she was still insisting I'd suffered a fever. Clearly I hadn't. My visions of Abigail had simply become stronger than ever.

A wave of guilt washed over me. If I told Grandmother about my dark visions and Morgana and what had happened to Mama, there was every chance she would think me a monster. Nothing would ever be the same.

But I had to start somewhere. These secrets were getting too heavy to carry for much longer.

"I can't stay here." My voice was steady and clear.

Grandmother tilted her head back and sighed. "I understand that you're not used to being outside of London, but —"

"No, it's not that." I paused. It was suddenly impossible to put into words in a way that made sense: Abigail screaming, chasing me. So, I changed tack. "I just don't feel comfortable here. There's something wrong with this place."

Grandmother sighed. "There's nothing wrong. You had a fever. You saw things that weren't there."

"I didn't tell you anything about seeing things." My throat was going dry. Grandmother knew something. My thoughts went back to the hushed conversation she'd had with Mr Ambrosius at breakfast.

"You did." She spoke earnestly, but didn't sound convinced of her own words. "During the fever. You told me."

I'd had no fever. I knew that with certainty, and I also knew that I hadn't said a word about visions last night. Grandmother was lying to me, something completely out of character. She had always claimed to abhor keeping secrets, and was never afraid of being blunt with me. In fact, she'd told me more than once that lying indicated severe moral weakness.

So why would she lie about this? I had so many questions, and none of them were being answered.

Grandmother stopped walking and turned her gaze to the far-off fields. "Are you sure you want to leave?"

"Quite sure."

She nodded. "We'll leave tomorrow. On one condition."

My heart flooded with such gratitude for her I was willing to do anything she asked. I nodded profusely.

"We must go straight to France."

I blanched so white I might have matched Ms Wright's jars of clotted cream.

"Why?" As far as Grandmother knew, I'd heard nothing about Mr Ambrosius' mention of France during their breakfast chat. Now she had the chance to tell the truth.

But of course, she didn't.

"I haven't been in ages, and the food is divine," she said with a false smile.

We walked in silence for some time. I considered my options, which were few. Stay here, next to a cemetery apparently haunted by my sister, embark on a terrifying journey to France aboard a ship for some mysterious cause, or go through with my plan to run away to Cheshire.

The last was clearly still the most palatable, but I couldn't help feeling awful about lying to Grandmother.

I turned around, back toward the house. "All right. We should tell Mr Ambrosius of our plans, then."

Grandmother looked at me softly. "We'll have such a lovely time. You'll see. I promise."

I nodded and began walking back along the path toward Bristol.

ELEVEN

THAT AFTERNOON, I went to the village post office and wired both Madge and Violet. Our train to Southampton would stop in Reading, which provided connections into London and then on to Cheshire.

At Reading, I would excuse myself for a breath of fresh air on the platform before our train left the station again.

With any luck, Grandmother would be too tired to join me, and Mr Ambrosius wouldn't care enough to serve as an escort. I would simply disembark and then lose myself in the crowd.

I didn't need any belongings, save my purse, as Violet had already sent my dresses to Cheshire. I would simply buy a train ticket and be on my way.

As can be imagined, I spent most of our train journey anxiously awaiting Reading as I fought bouts of nausea.

The heavy jolting of the train meant I was staring into a bucket for a good portion of our jaunt across the English countryside.

Grandmother slept most of the way and Mr Ambrosius

seemed always deep in meditation, occasionally humming some strange melody.

When Reading was finally announced as our next stop, both were thus preoccupied. My stomach lurched. Mr Ambrosius stopped humming and straightened in his seat. He checked that Grandmother was still sleeping and leaned toward me. "I know your plan, Miss Collins. Looking forward to arriving at Reading, aren't you? It's rather obvious."

Something caught in my throat, and for a moment, I thought I would choke.

"You're free to go." He sat back and crossed one leg over the other. "It's your choice. But I can promise you one thing." He stopped, waiting for my reply.

I swallowed. "And what is that?"

"You will not survive alone."

"Why do you keep saying these dreadful things? And never explaining what you mean?"

"I told you. Your grandmother forbids it," he continued, as he set his hands on his lap. "But believe it or not, I am trying to help. I want you kept alive."

His words sent a shiver up my spine.

"Cheshire will hold a far worse fate for you than any silly ship," he said. "And if you stay planted firmly in your seat until we pass Reading, you'll find out why."

I didn't say a word.

My body tensed when the call sounded for Reading Station and the train slowed. It was time to jump up and run. This was my last chance. So why wasn't I moving?

I looked at Mr Ambrosius, whose eyes were now closed in meditation. It seemed he was pretending not to care about my decision. Grandmother let out a snore that, had she learned about it later, would have made her blush. She'd be so unhappy with me if I abandoned them here. I was, however, also quite unhappy with her. I hadn't wanted to go on this trip in the first place, and worse, she'd still not explained its true purpose.

Once, I'd imagined a comfortable, quiet life in London, even with the dark memories and fears that sometimes overwhelmed me. I would have a husband and children. There would be dances and charities and stitchery circles. A beautiful home.

But instead, here I was. Lost and lonely Miss Collins. And the train was moving again, away from Reading.

TWELVE

My reasoning for staying on the train was twofold.

One: it seemed that Mr Ambrosius knew far more about my family than I'd previously imagined. I needed to know who this man really was, and how he had acquired his information.

Two: My encounters with Abigail were only getting worse, and I feared what would happen to me if I simply let them continue.

Mr Ambrosius had said the only way I would survive would be if I continued on this journey. Perhaps there was a chance, however small, that if I successfully set foot on that ship, travelled across the Channel and made it to France in one piece, Morgana and my terrifying visions would be banished.

I wrote letters to Violet and Florence as our train sped on toward Southampton. They'd want to know of my new travel plans and where to send communications. I directed them to the postal office in Paris, hoping we'd spend a considerable amount of time in the city.

If I'm to be truthful, there was another reason for my change of heart about travelling to France: fashion. If I was to be forced to journey far from home, then at least Paris would allow me to fill my cases with all the latest styles, buy dozens of pattern books, and ensure I was the best-dressed socialite next season.

Next season. Would I even be able to return to Society, after the scandal I'd left behind? Perhaps, no matter how hard I might try, things would never be the same. I let out a sigh and sealed my envelopes. No use in worrying about that yet. A greater challenge lay right before me, and it would take all my energy to overcome it.

~

My heart was dancing jigs in my chest when we arrived at Southampton's docks. Salty air accosted my nose, throat and lungs. I stared up at our ship, a looming steamer with two masts ready to stand against the wind. It was smaller than the *Ocean Monarch* by a considerable amount and decorated differently, but my body still shuddered violently at the sight of it.

Father's face flooded my memory. His expression was a mixture of terror and rage as flames engulfed the ship. He'd seemed more furious than frightened that night, barking at me to listen, to follow him. At the time, I thought he was angry with me.

My feet felt heavy as they took their last steps on the dock. What if I never felt dry land again? What if I only had an hour or two before salt water filled my mouth, forced the air from my lungs?

Visions returned of Abigail, water filling her mouth. Looking at the all-too-fragile vessel floating in front of me, I couldn't imagine any version of this voyage in which I wouldn't swiftly perish.

The ship was already listing back and forth, despite being securely docked. I fell against a wall as we entered the passenger lobby. Mr Ambrosius looked at me with more than a hint of judgement. "Really? We aren't even at sea yet."

"That tells you something about the stability of this ship," I muttered, pressing my hands hard against the wall. A dockhand passing by gave me a rather unfriendly frown. God forbid I insult his precious conglomeration of splinters and metal.

I graced him with a pointed glare right back.

"I'd say it tells you something about *your* stability," Mr Ambrosius smirked. "Mental stability, that is." He skipped down the hall toward our day cabin before I could whack him around the head with my handbag.

Grandmother merely sighed and put a comforting hand on my shoulder. At least she understood me and my fears a little.

The day cabin was tiny. There was only room for our bags and one resting cot. A small porthole let in a circle of light. I looked through it and my breathing grew shallow. That view of an endless horizon was too familiar. My lungs turned to iron.

"I can't breathe."

Mr Ambrosius set down his top hat and groaned. "Oh, no. You're not going all silly on us already, are you?"

I felt too panicked and sickly to even glare at him.

Grandmother asked if I needed fresh air. Before I could protest, Mr Ambrosius had taken my arm and led me into the hallway, up some stairs I could only vaguely see and out onto the deck.

There, a gust of salty wind smashed against my face and filled my lungs. I immediately rushed to the rails with a violent stroke of nausea.

"Really?" He turned to me with a raised eyebrow.. "We haven't even left the harbour."

I ignored Mr Ambrosius and focused on my breathing, praying the world would stop spinning. But then the ship began to move. A wailing sound came from its horn, signalling our departure.

"Oh, God," I whimpered. Tears came to my eyes as I grasped the railing harder. All I could think about was the deep, dangerous water beneath us.

I had only been eight years old. That was too young to witness such horror. I buried my face in my hands and a muffled cry escaped my lips. Hollow shouts filled my ears, life slipping from bodies all around me. Corpses floated past on the waves, pale and foggy-eyed.

Hands grasped my shoulders. "Emma. Emma! Snap out of it." Mr Ambrosius commanded.

"They're drowning..." I whimpered.

"Everyone is safe. No one is drowning. There's no shipwreck here."

No, it wasn't happening right at this moment. But in some ways, that day had never ended. It had stretched out into my past, present, and future, and would forever replay in my mind. I found my voice just as the wind picked up.

"Grandmother told you I was in the wreck?"

At first I thought Mr Ambrosius had not heard me. But then, in the gentlest voice I'd ever heard escape his mouth, he spoke. "Yes."

"So why are you doing this to me? Tormenting me with a journey by boat." A sob jolted my torso, but I was too distraught to be embarrassed.

He didn't answer, but instead responded with his own question. "What do you remember?"

I breathed in deeply and looked up. The sun was too bright, the air too sharp. "This isn't the time to talk about it."

"Why not?"

It took everything in me not to scream my next words. "Why do you think? I'm on a *ship*. Leaving the safety of land, for the first time since I watched my parents and sister drown."

If he was shocked by my outburst, he didn't show it. "A truly terrible thing for a child to see, no doubt." He paused, but only briefly, before carrying on. "And you were in the water with them?"

Another wave of nausea sent me reeling. I saw Mama, suspended under the water like a marionette. She was fighting, her wild eyes black and wide, struggling until her lungs finally heaved in too much of the sea.

I remembered how I had felt then, in the water. How numb I was. "Yes. I thought I would die, too."

"But you didn't."

"Oh, really?" I managed a sarcastic tone, despite my miserable state. "I thought I had been dead this entire time. Thank you for informing me otherwise."

Mr Ambrosius chuckled softly. "Sometimes one does need to be reminded."

He raised his index finger and held it up to the wind, just as he had back in Bristol. "You know what, Miss Collins? I do believe it's wine time."

I dabbed at my face with a handkerchief, but paused to glare at him. "Have you not noticed how distressed I am? How nauseated?"

"Of course, and that's why I'm suggesting it. Miracle wine cures all." With that, he grabbed my arm and led me back down to our cabin.

When Mr Ambrosius flung open our cabin door and declared to Grandmother it was time for wine, she clapped her hands together in delight.

I stood in the doorway, quite dumbfounded. Had she not noticed my red eyes, damp hair, or the pastiness of my cheeks? Before I could protest, Mr Ambrosius pushed a glass into my hand and began pouring.

I clutched my side and mumbled something about seasickness, but Grandmother and Mr Ambrosius were having none of it. Without a pause and in terrifying unison, both cried, "Drink! It will help."

They looked at each other and laughed. And despite both my turning stomach and growing fears that this wine was poisoned with hallucinatory medication, I drank. Better judgement be damned.

My theory was that if it made me sick, at least I'd have something to keep me busy for the next few hours. And if it did make me hallucinate, with any luck I'd see something jollier than the visions I'd been having of Abigail and

Morgana. Even if not, my mind would sooner be anywhere else but on this ship.

My travelling companions chatted amiably with one another as I sipped. Time passed. Strangely, the wine soon started giving me something entirely unexpected: *courage.* I wanted answers. I was tired of waiting, of being restrained and obedient. I looked straight at Grandmother, and spoke without fear.

"Grandmother," I said, interrupting their chat. "Mr Ambrosius has been telling me some interesting things."

Grandmother's eyes flashed, and she turned to Mr Ambrosius. He merely grinned and shrugged.

I continued. "Apparently I am about to die a most horrible death. And only by continuing on this journey will I be saved. I'd be ever so grateful if one of you could elucidate?"

"You told her *what*?" Grandmother stood up so fast, her legs wobbled.

But Mr Ambrosius was not unsettled. It seemed the miracle wine had given him a kick of confidence, too. "Virginia, please. She needs to be told the truth."

"The truth is," Grandmother said, her voice raising an octave, "you are overstepping your role."

Mr Ambrosius snorted. "Overstepping? Really?" His eyes were bright and sparkling, as if he'd been yearning for a good argument for some time. "I'm here to protect the two of you, and this is the thanks I get?"

"That's right," Grandmother hissed. "Protect us. Simply that, and nothing more." Her face had grown ashen, and she turned to me. "Emma, please leave us at once."

I shook my head.

She blinked. I was expecting a verbal lashing for my blatant disrespect, but instead, her shoulders slumped forward. She looked at Mr Ambrosius, sighed, then sat down and closed her eyes. "Very well. Since you are both insistent on defying me, we will do this now.

"I had hoped – oh, I don't know." Her eyelids lifted slowly open, as if they were heaving anchors with them. "I'd hoped to keep your life as normal as possible, for as long as possible. Sometimes I even thought you might never need to know."

"Pure silliness!"

We both gave Mr Ambrosius a pointed glare.

Grandmother let out a long breath. "Here it is, then. Our family is... cursed, for want of a better word."

"Cursed with silliness," Mr Ambrosius added.

"Can he leave us?" I asked, making a point to speak as if he weren't in the cabin to begin with.

"I certainly can," he replied with a snort. "But I won't."

I decided to ignore him. "What do you mean,'cursed'?"

Grandmother turned to Mr Ambrosius. Unfortunately, she clearly wanted him involved in this maddening conversation. "You do it, Ambrosius. You're better at explaining than me."

"With pleasure," he nodded, his face suddenly serious. "There are a race of beings that want you dead, Emma. Inhuman, insidious beings. They wanted your mother to die, your aunts and uncles, your grandparents, and all of the people who share your bloodline."

"Demons," Grandmother added. "That's how my mother described them. Demons from hell itself."

A wave rocked our cabin. I tried to process what I was

being told while clutching on to the nearest piece of furniture.

Grandmother continued, unperturbed. "Mr Ambrosius is our protector. He has stood by our family's side for many, many years."

This time, I didn't fight back a snort. "Then it's no wonder we've all had such bad luck."

But Grandmother was looking at Mr Ambrosius with undisguised warmth. Adoration, even. A thought struck me then. Was Grandmother... in love? Surely not. It hadn't occurred to me that theirs could be a romantic relationship, as well as a practical one. But had she ever gazed at Grandfather the way she gazed at this madman now?

"Be kind, Emma. Please," Grandmother said, raising her chin. "Vicious talk is a sign of demonic possession. Do you remember when your mother started speaking to people so cruelly, in a way she never had before? That was when the demon took her."

An icy jolt ran down my back. "Mama was possessed?"

Her eyes filled with tears. Grandmother rarely spoke about Mama, and never talked about what I'd previously thought had been a descent into madness.

It was Mr Ambrosius' turn to speak, and it seemed as if he knew my thoughts. "It wasn't insanity that took her – not as humans usually define it, anyway. It was the so-called demons. The Annunaki."

The cabin swayed, though this time I wasn't sure it had anything to do with the sea. I needed to keep my head, so I swallowed hard and steadied myself.

"All right. So these... Annunaki. They want our family dead. I understand that. What I don't understand is why?"

Grandmother raised her eyebrows. "A very good question. Mr Ambrosius?" The exaggerated pleasantry in her voice told me that she had been asking him the same thing for some time.

He blinked, then looked away. "I... No. We don't know why."

Even I, who had known Mr Ambrosius for only a few weeks, saw that this was a blatant lie. Grandmother shook her head and adjusted her skirt. Clearly, this had been a heated topic of conversation between them for many years.

"Well, the mystery continues. I imagine we will learn nothing more from Mr Ambrosius today." She glanced at him rather sadly and gestured toward the door. "Emma and I need to have a private conversation now, if you don't mind leaving us alone."

Mr Ambrosius looked forlorn, but nodded. "I'll get some fresh air." With that, he left the cabin as lightly as a butterfly.

As soon as the door shut solidly behind him, I turned to Grandmother. "Who is that man?"

"Our protector." She stared at the door through which he'd left. "An angel, maybe."

"Is he... human?" The question tasted strange in my mouth.

"I don't know. He's always just been Mr Ambrosius to me." Grandmother paused and turned to me. "I know that sounds strange, but... he saved my life. And my mother's. I couldn't keep pressing him for information he did not want to give."

I understood. But I needed to know more. "How old is he? Has he always looked the same?"

Grandmother nodded and stared past me. "Ageless. Always the same. Always Mr Ambrosius."

"And these demons," I said. "How does one know..." I trailed off, unable to say the words.

"When they're possessed?" Grandmother said, her eyes distant. "For me, it started with visions. The Annunaki presented itself as a man with black eyes, but only I could see him."

A man with black eyes. That horrid memory of the man I'd apparently turned to ash flitted through my mind. And now, apparently replacing him, was Morgana.

I swallowed. "And how long does one have, when the demon takes hold? Before... the end?"

Her lips twitched. "It takes time for the Annunaki to fully possess us. Years, sometimes. If Mr Ambrosius can work his magic fast enough, they won't succeed. But once the more severe symptoms start..."

"How long?"

"Days."

"But you and your mother were never fully possessed?"

She nodded. "Mr Ambrosius caught it early and saved us."

"But he couldn't save Mama."

Grandmother's body went rigid. "No."

That single word had a weight to it. Once again, there was more she wasn't telling me. Her lips were pressing hard against her teeth in an attempt to keep from revealing the depth of her pain. I wasn't sure I had ever seen her struggle so much with an emotion.

She so rarely talked about Mama, probably because she was so focused on my own welfare. But shamefully, for the first time in our years living together, I only now understood the extent of the loss that Grandmother had suffered – the loss of her only daughter. What kind of waking nightmare must that be? And there was I, worrying about suitors and dresses and dances, thinking the only grief of import in our house was my own.

She had more secrets, yes, but that did not matter just now.

I wordlessly stood, walked over to Grandmother as she sobbed, and wrapped my arms around her as tightly as I could.

THIRTEEN

WE ARRIVED in France after sunset, guided in by the glimmering lights of the shore, which cut off the water's inky blackness. Upon boarding the ship in Southampton, I'd imagined myself gleefully stepping onto land again and breathing in deep relief.

However, after learning about our family's curse and seeing Grandmother in such a state, I was not in as much of a celebratory mood as I'd expected. A weight, one that was even heavier than my fear of the sea, had planted itself upon my chest.

If everything I'd been told was true, and demonic creatures were following my family... Well, the odds of surviving to old age were not in my favour.

Mr Ambrosius didn't seem as concerned as I was, perhaps because he was not familiar with feeling a fear of death. As we set foot on the dock, he grabbed my hand and began twirling me about. "A little dancing will cheer you up!" he chirped, pulling me into a second, more forceful twirl that might have sent me over the edge of the dock, had I not collided with a helpful stack of shipping crates.

I found my footing and turned to give him a piece of my mind, but he was laughing so hard I knew there'd be no hope of him hearing.

"How funny would it have been," he giggled to Grandmother, "if she'd survived the ship, but then drowned by twirling?"

Grandmother and I both gave Mr Ambrosius the same deadly glare, and finally, I felt I had an ally with me on this journey.

We left the port on the first train to Paris the next morning. My mood had improved at the prospect of being surrounded by French fashions.

It was the perfect distraction from my troubles. In London, we'd heard so much about the flamboyant and chic styles that were sported here. Most of my friends deemed their low-cut silk necklines and frilly bonnets to be too ostentatious. But I'd secretly admired these pieces and wondered just how lavish they would feel on my skin.

I planned to visit the city's finest dress shops and get fitted for the grandest gowns. If the Annunaki killed me here in France, at least I'd go out in style.

When the train slowed on its way into the Gare du Nord, I rushed to the window to see everything I could.

Paris was much dirtier than I'd expected. Some streets looked even worse than sooty, rubbish-filled Whitechapel in London's East End. Parisians filled the streets everywhere I looked. Many wore fine designs, but most were disappointingly clad in the same dreary clothing I'd grown accustomed to in England.

My eyes darted from sight to sight. Each multicoloured building boasted delicate curlicue iron balconies that jutted out from shutter-style doors. Streets overflowed with donkey-drawn carts filled with grape vines, driven by men in frayed flat caps.

A teenage boy stood on one of the busiest street corners. He wore a withering tuxedo, its formerly white collar now stained a smoky brown.

The boy didn't seem to care that his fine clothes were all a mess. He was much too busy playing a lively jig on his violin for the passersby. A tall woman with a blue hat dropped some coins into his bucket.

Soon, we had made our way to the hotel and were resting in its marble-floored lounge to escape the city's summer heat. Grandmother took to her room for a nap, and Mr Ambrosius began humming his meditations in the lobby. This inspired me to sit a distance away from him, pretending we were strangers and burying myself in a book.

We spent the afternoon this way, as I didn't want to go outside in such uncomfortable weather.

However, one lingering question continued to nag at me. I set my book down and approached Mr Ambrosius.

"Ahem, Mr Ambrosius?"

Silence. Not even a twitch to suggest he'd heard me.

"Mr Ambrosius," I continued, raising my voice. "I have a question for you."

He kept his eyes closed. "Can it wait?"

Best to be assertive. "Not if you want me to continue on this trip."

He lifted his head and looked at me with a sigh. "Fine. What is it?"

"Why are we in Paris? What is all this travel meant to do?"

"This is only a stopover. The main event is at the Carnac Stones, in western France." He closed his eyes again.

"And how will these stones help me?"

"They will purge the Annunaki within you, with any luck."

"And you're sure I have this... Annunaki... possessing me? How do you know?" It was a silly question. I already knew Morgana was lurking within.

He nodded. "St Michael's Tower illuminated that thing for me, as bright as those auroras. It's a strong one. Usually, the tower can also purge the Annunaki, but this creature stayed put. The Carnac Stones are stronger. Hopefully, they'll get rid of it once and for all. But we need to act fast."

The bellman approached us to light the crystal chandeliers above our heads. I sat down beside Mr Ambrosius and let his words sink in.

Some time later, Grandmother joined us downstairs, and a waiter led us to the hotel's dining room. Mr Ambrosius ordered the two largest ducks they had, plus a tureen of onion soup, a whole baguette, a platter of vegetables, and a log of foie gras.

I winced in embarrassment as an ashen-faced waiter delivered the hefty order to our table, though I had to admit, it did all look delicious.

When we had cleared our plates, Mr Ambrosius sat back, rubbed his belly, and sighed. "I believe it's time for some after-dinner absinthe. Don't you agree, Virginia? I know a café near L'arc de Triomphe."

I frowned. "Isn't absinthe a rather strong drink?"

"Yes, remarkably so." He grinned at Grandmother. "And Virginia loves it."

Grandmother responded with a sheepish smile and flushing cheeks. I was stunned. She would never partake in such a beverage. After all, she was a proud member of the London Temperance Chapter, and the most that she and her comrades ever drank was half a glass of wine during dinner.

It had been odd enough to see her drinking miracle wine outside of supper, but to see her entering some degenerate French cafe in the middle of the night to imbibe even stronger substances? What was my world coming to?

I lifted my chin. "What would Mrs Bromeley think of absinthe, Grandmother?" I gave her a pointed stare before turning to Mr Ambrosius. "Mrs Bromeley is the president of the London Temperance Chapter, of which Grandmother serves as an elected chairperson."

He snorted and looked at Grandmother. "Is she telling fibs now?"

Grandmother rolled her eyes – another concerning development. "I've been campaigning for stronger restrictions on alcohol usage, yes, but that doesn't mean I'm against the idea of enjoying it myself now and then."

"That sounds more like the Virginia I know and love!" Mr Ambrosius grinned and stood up from the table triumphantly.

Grandmother giggled. I simply sat there in dismay.

As they were going to partake regardless of my concerns, I agreed to join as a chaperone. We walked down uneven cobblestone streets that smelled of all sorts of unpleasantness.

Upon arriving at the cafe – which was quite lovely, with blinking lights strung up about its entrance – the barkeep greeted Mr Ambrosius with a hearty hello. Within moments, we were sitting at the bar, each with glasses of green liquid in front of us.

Mr Ambrosius lifted his cup into the air with a flourish. "Ah, the green fairy of my dreams. We meet again." He turned to us. "A toast to our perilous voyage!"

Thinking of the Annunaki dwelling within me, I decided just one drink might be suitable for my nerves. I picked up my glass, clinked it against those of Mr Ambrosius and Grandmother, and drank.

Absinthe was even stronger than I'd expected. The world around me turned hazy after only one drink. I vaguely realised that for the first time in my life, I was drunk.

From what I could discern, Mr Ambrosius still seemed his normal self. Of course, *normal* was not a word that suited the man. I began giggling uncontrollably at the thought.

"What's so hilarious?" Mr Ambrosius asked.

I sputtered and set my empty glass down hard on the counter. "You."

"Why?" He opened his mouth and grimaced. "Do I have food in my teeth?"

"Everything about you is so silly. I can hardly believe you are real! I mean, take your hat – it's *purple*!" I pointed a wobbly finger at the thing, which I'd tried my best to ignore for some days, and burst into peals of laughter again.

Grandmother sighed, seemingly also unaffected by the drink. Was I the only one incapable of holding my liquor? She gave Mr Ambrosius a knowing look. "We should retire to our hotel before she's tempted to have another."

So we left the bar and joined the locals filling the streets. Each Parisian seemed more amusing to me than the last. In fact, I found everything around me hilarious. I decided I could get used to being drunk on absinthe. Blast the Temperance Chapter. They were all nosy old busybodies, anyway.

My merriment subsided, however, when I saw the most magnificent sight. Pearls of brilliant light were floating down the street, all around us, like glowing flakes of snow that never reached the ground. I stopped still to wonder at them.

"Are they not beautiful?" I said with a sigh.

Mr Ambrosius swivelled around to look at me. "Are what not beautiful?"

"The lights."

He blinked.

"These little white things," I giggled and gestured all around me.

"You see them?" Mr Ambrosius sounded confused, and Grandmother stared at me like I had grown a second head. The thought made me laugh even more.

"Of course I do, you *silly* man."

Ambrosius rubbed his chin. "Huh."

I didn't understand what all the fuss was about. "Don't you see them?"

"I do, yes," he said, smiling. "All the time."

I HAD the most dreadful headache I'd ever experienced in all my life when I awoke the next morning. It seemed a thousand hammers were smashing at my temples over and over.

Worse was that Grandmother's knees were still aching from the sea voyage, so she couldn't join me in our explorations of Paris. That left only Mr Ambrosius as my escort.

And so there I was, in a city I'd only ever dreamt of visiting, with a madman and a nightmarish migraine.

As we left the hotel, Mr Ambrosius turned to me with a wrinkled brow. "You look miserable."

"How adept you are at reading emotion," I said. My sarcasm went unnoticed.

"How about a romp to a dress shop? Virginia tells me you're quite the fashion fiend."

"I — Yes! I mean, yes, please." My mind was buzzing with pleasant surprise at his offer. "I would like that very much."

Mr Ambrosius took my arm and twisted us down a side street. We arrived at a small storefront with dark windows and an entrance framed by an archway of stone.

Above the door in gold lettering was the name *Worth and Bobergh*. We walked inside to find a rather scant room with black-and-white floor tiling and a woman idling at a table.

She looked up and rushed over to us, giving an enthusiastic welcome in French and showing us to two chairs.

She disappeared into the back room and emerged with a tall man wearing a fine tweed suit. He seemed excited to see a customer, which made me uneasy.

"Welcome," he said in an English accent. "My name is Charles Frederick Worth and I've just opened this shop."

A male dressmaker? I turned to Mr Ambrosius, who seemed completely comfortable with the oddity of the situation.

"Delightful," he cooed. "This is Miss Emma Collins, and I do believe she'll love your dresses. How about we make her something for next year's season?"

I'd been hoping for a new dress, despite the fact that my actual presence in London society next year was in serious question. I decided to overlook the fact that a man was to be designing it and nodded energetically.

Mr Worth studied me for some time. "Your eyes are a haunting hazel. I will design everything to match." He began feverishly drawing.

Within minutes, an intricate dress had appeared on the page, his pencil delicately shading each aspect and bringing forth a most interesting sartorial vision.

And then came the fabrics – cream silks and, strangely, spangled green tulle. It all came together like a dance, with Mr Worth rushing about, fabric flailing, his assistant whisking her measuring tape all over me. But even in the frenzy, there was organisation.

After some hours, we left his store with a fitting appointment and a copy of Mr Worth's design. It was a dress that would be quite daring in London, with a slim front crinoline and a puffier back. I was giddy to wear it to a ball.

Assuming, of course, that I'd ever be invited to a ball again. Or that I would be alive to accept the invitation.

I eyed Mr Ambrosius suspiciously as we walked. "Why are you being nice to me?"

Mr Ambrosius shrugged. "Your grandmother thought I should get to know you better. Bond with you, if you will. Considering your interest in fashion, I thought I'd take you to Mr Worth. He's a delightful man and an artistic genius."

"You must really care for Grandmother, to do as she asked. You've spent all day doing just the things I like."

He smiled. "This is about so much more than simply caring for someone."

There it was again. Did he mean *love*? The question came quite unbidden from my lips. "Mr Ambrosius, are you keen on my grandmother?"

He looked uncertain. "Keen?"

"Are you in love with her?" My voice was raised high enough to turn the head of a young woman passing by with a pram.

Mr Ambrosius paused, then scoffed. "Love! You don't know what you're going on about."

He was clearly avoiding the subject. Had I been dealing with anyone else, I might not have dared to ask such a direct, impertinent question. Better to get answers with honey than fire, Grandmother always said. But Mr Ambrosius brought out an unseemly side of me.

He cocked his head to the side, his expression as innocent as the newborn baby who had just passed us. "Did you love Mr Jameson?"

I wanted to pummel the man. Instead, I took a deep

breath and prayed the air coming out of my lungs would poison him. "Yes, I did."

He squinted. "Really?"

"You think I'm lying?"

"No. Of course you *think* you loved him. But did you?" His eyes were not mocking, merely curious. There was no judgement behind them. "Did you find yourself crying in bed at night, staring at the stars through your window, thinking of just how much you needed him? Shedding tears that were ecstatic and agonised all at once, because you had found the greatest love of your life, but you could not share infinity with him? Because even if the love didn't break apart, then mortality would one day separate you?"

I was stunned, but Mr Ambrosius was in full flow and did not notice.

"And when he did leave you, what did you do? Go into a fit of enraged tears and complain to your friends? Or did you transcend time and space itself, escaping to a dark dimension with no light or sound or smell or material to touch, in a desperate attempt to find a moment of numbness, just for a second of relief from the pain?"

Until now, I'd seen Mr Ambrosius as merely an oddity. He was a man to be tolerated and kept away from delicate social situations. But there was more to him than that. He had loved Grandmother deeply, that much was now obvious. He seemed to love her still, and she thought the world of him. So what had broken them apart?

Even as I asked myself the question, I already knew the answer. He was an unacceptable marriage prospect. Grandmother must have known this, and forced herself to let him go.

But still. Their love had blossomed in the face of shallow social constraints and expectations. And it had endured in their hearts, even though there was nothing to be gained from its presence. Could I say the same for Richard and myself?

Mr Ambrosius let out a long, tired sigh. "You wouldn't understand." His voice was so low, I could barely hear it. "You're a society girl, just like all the rest. To you, love is a business proposition."

I opened my mouth to protest but found no words. To some degree, he was right. My heart was most often filled with fine dresses and charity balls and gossip from my friends.

I searched for genuine feeling and found only whispers of sadness and fear stirring within. Perhaps there was something wrong with me. Perhaps I had no soul at all.

Before I could say anything further, we arrived at the large square that housed Paris' international post office. Enough time had passed for Florence and Violet to have received my letters and to have sent their own to me. My heart lifted a little as I took Mr Ambrosius' arm and led him inside.

Sure enough, Violet had written to me. I opened the letter as soon as we returned to our hotel.

Dearest Emma,

I know you explained your reasoning for the change of plan in your letter, but I remain quite concerned. Did your Grandmother learn of our scheme and force you to continue on?

Should I send out someone to save you? I still worry

for your future, especially now, with the latest gossip going around.

Everyone is convinced you are in a delicate condition, which is why you rushed out of town in such a hurry. Mrs Goodworth even claimed she had seen you in a ladies' home in Scotland! I try my best to snuff out the rumours, but they seem only to multiply.

Mr Jameson has also done little to help matters. He is so enthralled with his Russian woman that it seems he has forgotten our social circle. Apparently they are to marry next month. I, of course, will only attend the wedding as a spy. I'll observe and tell you all the details of her awful dress and disgraceful countenance (as I am sure both will be in clear view during proceedings).

I hope things are going better for you on the Continent. Perhaps you could take an afternoon to call at the Rushley's Paris residence? She is there now and respected on both sides of the Channel. She could serve as a witness to your arrival in Paris, to prove that you are not waiting on a child.

Dear me, what maddening times we live in! To think that my sweet Emma could be accused of such unsavoury actions. I only hope the rumours dissipate along with the summer heat and all will be forgotten come Christmas time.

I also hope, of course, that you'll be returning to us before then. I miss you so.

Yours with eternal love and concern,

Miss Violet Welch

Everyone thought I was *with child*? I fought back a gag. How dare they say such a thing? The moment Richard had arrived in town with Miss Klephakov on his arm, it seemed I had been dropped from society's favour like a burning coal.

As I sat on my bed ashen-faced, I remembered, for the first time in much too long, poor Miss Stevenson. Only last year, she had been a favourite on the London scene. She and I were rather good friends, but then she'd been caught alone with a married Lord. Despite both of their assertions that nothing untoward had happened, rumours spread, and within days society had shunned her.

I, along with all the others, had stopped calling at her family home, stopped inviting her to soirees, stopped being her friend altogether. Perhaps I had never really been her friend to begin with.

Now that I was on the unfortunate end of the same treatment, I realised how badly I had behaved. I'd been unfair to Miss Stevenson, and to so many others whom I couldn't even name now. Bright, interesting women who made one perceived mistake and found themselves cast out. Was I to be next?

No. I wouldn't have it. Demonically possessed or not, I'd be home by Christmas to take my rightful spot as the Light of London. I had to. I had nothing else.

~

A FEW HOURS LATER, Grandmother's knees had recovered enough to accompany me to a cafe across the street from our hotel. Mr Ambrosius was busy meditating, and I was glad to have some time away from him.

We chatted about the dress I'd ordered earlier that day as I waited for a croissant and a tea. Grandmother, as seemed to be her newfound Continental habit, opted for a glass of wine.

When our drinks arrived, she took a long sip and lifted her gaze to the air above me. "Do you remember Abigail's tenth birthday?"

The cafe swirled around me at the mention of her name. I gave a nod and took a long sip of tea.

"Your father gave her a book about ancient Egypt." Grandmother's eyes were hazy with tears.

We so rarely spoke of my sister. I gripped the edge of my chair for stability.

"She read the entire thing in a few days. Such a smart girl. You were too, of course, but she had the most natural fascination with history. I'd planned on taking her to Cairo for her sixteenth birthday."

We were both silent for some time. Abigail never turned sixteen, never got to see Egypt. I remembered the book. It was a thick tome with a cover gilded in gold at the edges. I'd traced it with my stubby fingers when no one was looking. I'd hoped to read it too, one day – then I'd be just like Abigail. Of course, that never came to be. I was nothing like her.

Grandmother sighed. "If there is one thing I've learned, it is that only two things matter in this life. Love and family."

Love and family. I'd likely have neither now, and perhaps I didn't deserve it. After so many years of forcing away my guilt by doing good deeds, I was realising that nothing could take my past away. No matter what I did, I would be forever marked.

I thought of Violet's words in Hyde Park – that I was odd, and everyone knew it. I thought of Richard and how lucky I had been to court him. He was with Miss Klephakov now, but he had come to my home to ask for my forgiveness. To beg me not to hold hatred in my heart for him. And I'd refused.

I stared at my reflection in my teacup. Should the Annunaki win its battle for my life, I had little time to absolve myself of my own sins. But I could at least put another person's mind at ease.

And so, when Grandmother and I returned to our hotel, I began writing the longest, most difficult letter of my life.

FOURTEEN

LATE THE NEXT AFTERNOON, as Grandmother and I rested in her room, I handed her Violet's letter.

"We need to call at the Rushley's."

She blinked in confusion and read. "Oh, my poor girl." She stopped reading and folded the letter several times, as if trying to further conceal its message. "These rumours are terrible, but you must keep a stiff upper lip. Miss Welch is correct. By Christmas, all of this business with Mr Jameson will be forgotten."

My jaw tightened. "I don't want to end up like Miss Stevenson."

"Who?"

"Exactly my point. Let's call on Mrs Rushley's first thing tomorrow. Without her, I have no chance of keeping my reputation."

Grandmother said nothing. She turned the letter over in her hands. "Please." I was getting desperate. "I'm begging you. Come with me. I can't call on her alone. We haven't been introduced and —"

"Emma," her voice was gentle. "I believe that now isn't the time to worry about your social situation."

The world spun. Forget everything else she had revealed: Mr Ambrosius and their escapades, her love for miracle wine, and our familial demonic curse. "*Now isn't the time to worry about your social situation*" was the most shocking string of words I'd ever heard.

All I could manage was a look of sheer confusion.

"We're on our way to Carnac first thing in the morning," she continued. "Perhaps on our return – "

"No. It will be far too late. Grandmother, please. You have to –"

"I'm sorry, Emma. We have already set the plans in motion." Her lips sucked in, my cue that the subject was to be dropped.

Plans? There was a grimness in her tone. She was referring to more than just travel arrangements. A shiver ran down my spine.

Before I could think much of it, though, she clasped her hands together. "Now, the bellman told me of a lovely park around the corner. How about a stroll before supper?"

Half an hour later, with barely a word between us, we were walking down a leafy Parisian street. I was lost in thoughts that pulled me in a thousand directions. Society thought I was a ruined woman. A demonic being was threatening my life. Both issues needed to be addressed. So what was one more day in Paris to redeem my social standing?

But they had set plans in motion. What did that even mean? And why was Grandmother being so quiet on our stroll?

If the rumours continued, I'd lose any chance of finding a decent husband. Grandmother knew this. Yet she wanted us to leave Paris at once, without taking one afternoon to snuff out these accusations. Perhaps the Annunaki was overtaking me faster than they were letting on, and I wasn't even aware of it.

The sun had set by the time we arrived at the park. It was a shadowy place, thick with evergreens. The dark outline of windswept branches sent a chill through the air, one that bit at the exposed skin on the back of my neck.

There was something wrong with this place. Perhaps it was the lack of people. Grandmother and I were the only souls in sight, which was strange, because there was still enough sunlight to enjoy the fresh breeze.

I turned to Grandmother, who walked solemnly beside me. Her own eyes were haunted with something untold, a deep memory that she would never share. I'd always loathed those moments, when her gaze turned hazy and there seemed to be a million miles between us.

It was especially terrible now, in this strange park at twilight, when I needed her comfort.

"What's on your mind?" I asked.

She turned to me, and a sob choked her throat. "Oh, Emma."

I stopped walking and clasped her hand. "What's wrong?"

"I'm so afraid. For you, and for our family. For myself." She looked at the path beneath us. "I have been so selfish."

"How could you say such a thing?" I squeezed her hand tighter. "After you brought me into your home and raised me? You saved my life."

A sob escaped her, and she shook her head. "I didn't, my dear. It's my fault she's gone."

"What do –"

Before I could finish, a wail sounded from somewhere behind me. Grandmother didn't seem to react, but I turned around to look. Nothing.

"Did you hear that?"

Grandmother looked up at me. "Hear what?"

We were both silent for a moment. Neither of us wanted to admit that something dark was in our midst.

"Should we turn back?" I couldn't find the right words to voice my unease.

She looked at me, her gaze soft and distant. "Are you frightened?"

My expression must have given away my nerves. Confirming my fears seemed dangerous, as if it might breathe life into them. But my senses were sounding alarms. There was something here. An unseen predator watching me.

Silence overcame the park, muting the sounds of carriages and horses and people on the surrounding streets. Shadows played off the gravel pathway before us.

Someone had already lit the park lamps. They were flickering now, blinking in and out. My eyes followed them, taking me deeper into a reverie I wasn't sure I'd escape from.

Further down the path, beside a tree, flitted the form of a girl. Abigail. Covered in bruises, dress ragged. There was a breath in my ear. *"You watch me all the time. But you never see who I am."*

It was her voice. Inescapable, undeniable. A shout

escaped me, or I think one did, because Grandmother looked back as I wrapped my arms around my chest and bent double.

I needed to get away. I turned around and ran out of that blasted park with its all-seeing shadows and into the street.

The last thing I saw were the shins of a horse as they crashed into my chest. Then there was no air. I was in the sea, reaching out, grasping for breath, and failing.

ONE MIGHT PRESUME, due to the grand proportions of most horses, that my unfortunate meeting with such a beast would only result in my death. Or at least a gruesome injury.

This thought was all I could grasp as I lay half-conscious on that muddy, manured road. That, and the horror of knowing I was sprawled in the muck. There were also screams, and the screeching of wheels as drivers halted, but these were considerably less disagreeable.

I slipped into a gentle slumber, one so deep I felt lost to reality. It was daylight when I awoke again. I was lying in bed in my hotel room, and there was a nurse sitting sentry beside me. She saw my open eyes and rushed out of the room to fetch someone. At least, that was what I hoped she was doing. A terrible pain was crackling through my ribs.

My eyes must have closed again, because I heard the familiar voice before I saw him.

"Miss Collins, have you woken?"

There was only one man I knew who spoke in that

whining tone, like a young boy who hadn't yet grown into his voice. Had I not despised him so much, I might have pitied him for it. I sighed and forced my eyes open.

Dr Gibson's long, angular face peered over me. His beady eyes scanned me from behind ridiculous jam-jar spectacles, with the lack of emotion only a self-centred man could muster. "You're a very lucky woman," he continued. "Only a bruised rib and a few scrapes. It's a miracle, really."

There were many reasons I despised the man, but the main one was his heartlessness, his cold careerism. He was Grandmother's only doctor and had been treating our family since before I could remember.

Dr Gibson wasn't an ordinary physician. He had practised for many years at an asylum in Brighton, and acted like he knew everything about the human mind, as well as the body. He seemed to find our family just fascinating – like specimens in a lab, or animals in a zoo.

After the wreck, Grandmother had pushed Dr Gibson upon me for months. He'd tried to draw out my story.

And what a tale it would have been for his medical career: a child aristocrat, forced to watch her parents and sister die in a horrendous fashion. Even worse was that he had been the closest of anyone to figuring out the fire's true origin, and who caused our ship to sink.

I silently cursed as he checked my heartbeat and administered mild sedatives. Why the blazes was he in Paris? I had nowhere to go, no way of escaping him. Despite having only bruised a rib, my body felt like it had been broken in two. I was like a limp doll.

Hours passed in a haze until dinnertime. I found myself famished, and after a hearty meal of duck and vegetables, Dr Gibson returned with a dose of pain medicine.

Now that I was more conscious, he grabbed at the opportunity for an impromptu therapy session. "So I hear you're having problems in London."

I shook my head and lifted my chin. "Just a temporary social setback. I'm sure I'll be singing at the Duke of Wellington's Charity Ball next year and everything shall be forgotten. You heard about my last performance, I imagine?"

Dr Gibson's smile stretched above his pointy chin. "I believe the whole of England has heard about it. You must be very honoured. But it's not your social standing I'm worried about."

I shifted my eyes to the window next to my bed as Dr Gibson leaned forward in a sinister bid for attention. "Your grandmother tells me you've been seeing things. Disturbing phantoms. Visions of violence."

I said nothing in response to this. Dr Gibson squinted his eyes and changed tack. "You know, I'm not surprised that you're feeling down, after your recent encounter with Mr Jameson. Miss Welch and Miss Winston have been campaigning throughout London with stories that you're doing well, but outward appearances can sometimes deceive."

I lifted my head. "I thought you weren't interested in my social standing?"

Dr Gibson blinked a few times, seemingly surprised that I could hold my own in an argument. "Not in itself, no. But I am interested in your wellbeing, and a person's wellbeing is connected to their world, their relationships."

He paused. "Emma, as my patient, you have full confidentiality. I will keep your secrets. You know that, don't you?"

I gave him a blank stare. Did he actually think I'd bare my soul to him? Had I ever done so before?

Still, he persisted. "If not me, then you can tell your troubles to a confidant. Do you have such a friend?"

"I speak to Grandmother. Really, Dr Gibson. We don't require your services."

Dr Gibson sat back, a look of discomfort burgeoning on his face. "Of course. But do you talk to your grandmother about your parents, or your sister? About the shipwreck?"

My polite smile disappeared. I lowered my chin and glared at him with naked contempt, my jaw set firm. Poor Dr Gibson squirmed in his seat. He knew he had crossed a line.

"I'm exhausted, Dr Gibson. Would you please leave?"

Dr Gibson sat forward in a pathetic attempt to appear powerful and convincing. "Miss Collins, you need to talk about them. It's the only way to process what happened. If you don't talk, you will never heal."

"Then so be it!" I shouted, and he jumped at my outburst. I contained myself with a deep breath. "There's nothing more to say. I apologise, Dr Gibson, but I must sleep."

With that, I laid my head back and closed my eyes. There was a loud sigh, a chair squeaking, then light footsteps leaving the room. The door closed, and I was free.

Grandmother didn't come to see me at all that day, or in the evening. I asked for her on multiple occasions, but the nurse tending to me shook her head and apologised in French.

I thought Grandmother would at least visit me once before bedtime, but that hope was dashed when the night nurse bid me a good evening and snuffed out the lamp beside me. Bathed in darkness, I let myself cry just a little.

Here I was, in an unfamiliar country, alone. No Grandmother, no Violet, no Florence. And no Richard. This was the first time since the wreck that I'd experienced such a deep sense of loss.

I felt like I was ten years old again, curled up with my knees to my chest, crying for Mama. Thinking about my last sight of her, floating like an angel, suspended forever in the water. Wishing I could pick her up and bring her home, wrap a blanket around her, serve her tea all by myself. Make her better.

My aching rib brought me back to the present moment. Another pain had emerged too. The skin around both of my wrists was itching so much that it burned. I had to press my fingers hard into the mattress to keep myself from scratching it to shreds.

Minutes later, I felt warm liquid wetting my wrists. I didn't need a lamp to know that it was blood. It was drenching my mattress, but I couldn't move, so great was the pain.

So I stayed still, hoping someone would hear my sobs and come to my aid before I lost too much blood. I pressed my wrists into the sheets beneath me, trying to stem the flow.

There was movement in the darkness, a shadow within a shadow. Someone, or something, was in this room with me. My eyes focused, though I regretted this the moment it happened.

The shadow creature was tall and thin, stretching its dark form from one corner of the room to another. It inched toward my bed slowly and methodically, like a cat about to pounce on a mouse.

I came to realise that I was, unfortunately, the mouse.

My body began shaking, telling me to run from this blasted room, but I couldn't. This thing was coming closer, and I knew it was here to kill me. It would suffocate me, slice at me, drown me in my own blood. And I could do nothing to stop it.

I was under the water again, watching Mama and Father and Abigail die. This time, I would go with them.

FIFTEEN

"You JUST HAD to go and get yourself possessed, didn't you? Honestly." Mr Ambrosius' voice came to me in the darkness.

My first sight upon waking were the two glistening, silvery orbs of his eyes. It was an unnerving experience so early in the morning.

"What?" My voice was gravelly, and my entire body hurt. I was about to ask about the shadowy form that I'd seen last night, when I noticed Mr Ambrosius' gaze move from my face to the bed.

I followed his eyes to see my sheets stained red, every inch soaked in blood. Oh, good God. How on Earth was I still alive?

Mr Ambrosius provided a swift distraction, pressing his palm against my mouth to stop me from speaking. "Listen to me," he whispered. "You must remain calm. The Annunaki has grown even stronger, and we have little time to destroy it." He waited a moment before lifting his palm.

"I'm going to die, then." My voice hit a high pitch that made me sound like a whining child.

He shook his head. "We still have options. But you need to stay calm. It is easier for the Annunaki to influence you if you let your fears take hold."

"Influence me how?"

Mr Ambrosius looked away as he spoke. "We should have explained all of this to you sooner. I told Virginia you needed to know for your own safety." He sighed. "Their mode of killing is through psychoses. They can alter certain chemicals in your brain. These cause visions, make you hear voices that aren't there, and cause such despair as to make you want to end your own life. Eventually, you'll do just that."

His voice had taken on such a sombre tone that all its usual musicality was gone. He sounded like a level-headed doctor, and this terrified me even more than his gruesome words.

"Could I not simply... choose otherwise? Surely I can refuse to take my own life?"

Mr Ambrosius laughed. "Do you want to know how many times I've heard your ancestors ask that exact question? It's not a choice, Emma. By the end, the Annunaki will have convinced you that death is the only way."

Once again, Mr Ambrosius was revealing his age. I took a deep breath and asked him what we would do.

Mr Ambrosius shut his eyes tight. "Virginia has a plan. She wants you to know she is taking care of it. For now, we need you to rest and stay calm."

"What is she doing?"

He said nothing and refused to meet my gaze.

Something was wrong. Mama's face illuminated in my mind. The memory was foggy and confused. I was trying to work out what it was when Mr Ambrosius cleared his throat.

"I trust Virginia to save your life. You'll be fine as long as you stay calm – and you'll be stronger now that you're aware of what the Annunaki are attempting. Just try to keep yourself separate from your thoughts. Whenever you see a shadow, or hear a voice that doesn't seem natural, remind yourself that it could be the chemicals in your brain. They've been tampered with and they're jumbling things up."

I nodded and chanced another question, now that Mr Ambrosius was being so forthcoming.

"You're not an angel, are you?" I asked, in the most matter-of-fact tone I could muster in the current circumstances.

He laughed and shook his head. "No. And you're the first person in your line to deduce that for yourself. I'm glad you're not a complete dullard."

I ignored his insult and continued my line of questioning. "But you're not human either."

"Correct. And neither is your pal, Dr Gibson."

I bit back a dark laugh. That explained a lot. "I see. So both of you are ageless beings? Immortals?"

He shrugged. "Time is relative."

More riddles. It was time to get to the point. "If you're not human, then you must be something else. So what are you?"

Mr Ambrosius grinned, and I knew he would not

answer the question. "Why, I'm the Great Mr Ambrosius. What else is there to know?"

This was an invitation. He wanted me to figure it out on my own.

"Get some rest," he continued. "I'm in the room at the end of the hallway. Just knock if you need me. However, I won't be available this evening, as your grandmother and I plan to dine at a lovely little restaurant on the Seine. You should be fine, though. The nurses are here to assist you."

Yes. Definitely an invitation.

I WAITED until the only light coming through my window was from the dim, golden street lamp outside. By now, Mr Ambrosius would be out at dinner with Grandmother. She still hadn't visited me since my run-in with the horse. Under normal circumstances, I would have been upset by this. Strangely, though, all of the longing and loneliness I'd felt the night before was gone.

Were my feelings already being jumbled up by the Annunaki? I could almost sense the thing, a cloud of smoke billowing ever larger in the back of my mind. It was like an invisible curtain, making me feel separated from the world around me.

My dinner – roast duck with cranberry sauce and heaps of warm bread – sat uneaten on the side table. With all the fear and anticipation, my stomach couldn't take it.

I was about to break into Mr Ambrosius' room and uncover all of his secrets. My heart was pattering in my chest; I stepped – or more accurately, sort of leaned and rolled – out of bed, onto the floor. My rib screamed at me and sent my pulse racing. How could a mere bruise cause so much pain?

There wasn't time to dwell on it. I needed to get to Mr Ambrosius' room as fast as possible. At this rate, he'd be back before I'd even reached my bedroom door. I clenched my teeth, forced myself to stand, and shuffled to the door.

Before me was the long, dimly lit hotel hallway. It reminded me of our garden back in London, with the lamp that kept snuffing itself out. I felt as if I was there again. There was even a hint of wisteria in my nose.

No, this was all in my mind. I was far from home and about to sneak into a maniac's bedroom.

I stumbled down the hallway. The pain was much worse than I'd imagined it would be, but I soon found myself at his door.

Breathless, I twisted the knob.

And then I was inside.

His room was...ordinary. No bright clothing draped over the furniture, no smells of frankincense or incomprehensible gadgets. Nothing that seemed like Mr Ambrosius. I didn't like it one bit.

The only personal item was a travelling chest by the opposite wall. At least this made my sleuthing easy. I went straight over to it, expecting to find it locked, but it opened easily. Too easily. Was this a trap? I ploughed on regardless.

So far, all I could see were his clothes: white puffy shirts that my great-grandfather might have worn, and a pair of hideous, bright purple breeches. I dug my hand down to the bottom of the chest to find something hard and smooth. It was small enough to pull out through the folded clothes without making a mess.

In my hand was a cloudy, white crystal, a flat oval about the size of my palm. In its centre was a faint blue light, flickering like a candle. *How in heaven's name was that possible?*

I'd heard of inventors using wires and carbon to produce a spark of electricity, but I knew there was no scientific explanation for a light trapped inside a crystal – especially one secreted away inside Mr Ambrosius' clothes chest.

It was beautiful, but also terrifying. I found myself mesmerised by it for some time.

At least, until the crystal started vibrating. I threw the thing across the room. It fell with a clank against the floor, a shaft of blue light escaping its confines and beaming upwards.

I ducked behind a chair, only peeking out again once I'd caught my breath. And then I nearly passed out from shock.

Standing before me was the American. But it was *not* the American. It was an image of him, made of light, as if the blue beam was a clay that had moulded itself into his form.

He stood there with that bothersome smirk on his face. He was staring at me like he had a secret he wanted to divulge, because he was American and couldn't keep anything quiet.

Then his shape changed. It was no longer the American who was standing in the room.

It was Morgana.

SIXTEEN

"So, you've discovered Ambrosius' messenger." Morgana's voice was just as I'd remembered it from our encounter in the church, which now felt like a century ago. Only this time, she sounded amused. "I thought you'd have learned by now to not mess around with technology you don't understand."

She was speaking to me. *How?* I had only just grasped the idea that someone's image could emerge from a crystal, but now, somehow, a live person was speaking directly to me.

Person, of course, being a broad term.

Morgana's brows knitted together. "You look like a frightened little lamb."

Her eyes softened then, and her expression turned almost motherly. She opened her mouth as if to say something more, then closed it again. The hard line of her jaw reappeared. "You will die soon, Miss Collins. You have to. Do you understand?"

"Are you trying to convince me of this, or yourself?"

My words came out like a river, wild and untamed. My sudden brazenness shocked me.

She blinked in surprise at my response. There was silence for a moment, and I could see her mind working, as if she was fighting an inner battle. "I don't *want* to do it, you know."

"Then... don't?"

Morgana smiled and shook her head. "It's the only way. By killing you, I preserve the rest of humanity."

She was trying to *save* people?

I was sure that Morgana could see the confusion all over my face. "The security protocols in this messenger will cut off our communication soon. I don't have time to explain everything, but as I'm sure you've already surmised, there is more to Mr Ambrosius than meets the eye. And you are a small but integral pawn in one battle of an infinitely larger war."

She paused, and her eyes softened once more. "I'm sorry, Emma, for what they've done to you. I'm sorry for what we must do next, but it's unavoidable. You will die. We can make it fast and painless, but you mustn't fight. Simply let me in."

My head was spinning. She wanted me to let her kill me? Who in their right mind would agree to such a thing?

Someone who wanted to save humanity, I suppose. But in what way was I a threat to begin with? Morgana was making no sense to me, and I would not continue playing her game.

"You're mad. And no, I will not, 'let you in.'"

Morgana's lip curled. "Then, unfortunately, we remain enemies."

The blue light casting her image flickered, and then she was gone.

About five minutes later, the screaming began.

~

I HAD RETURNED to my room, my mind racing with everything Morgana had said. The Annunaki, however, did not have the decency to give a lady time to regain her wits before commencing another attack.

The screaming emerged from the walls, as if banshees were crawling behind the brocade paper.

Seasoned Londoners are used to screeching foxes rampaging through the streets at night. I'd heard stories about visitors to the city, who, upon hearing the foxes, called the authorities to report what they could only assume was the sound of a gruesome murder.

But fox cries were nothing compared to these noises. I clasped my hands over my ears. The sound was still screeching, and I realised it was coming from inside my head.

My body began shaking. Ice was rising in the veins of my legs, into my torso, curling around my aching ribs.

Morgana was taking control of my body. Soon, she would find her way to my heart and my mind, infecting them with lies, misery and despair, until I broke.

And then, there were screams coming from Grandmother's room. Muted, concerned voices which sounded like Mr Ambrosius and Dr Gibson.

I found some feeling in my legs and rushed to the door, ignoring the pain coursing through me. The hall was dim and filled with flickering shadows. Figures moved up and down the hall.

I scrambled to Grandmother's door and pushed it open.

The scene before me was unreal. Grandmother was stretched out across the bed. Her wrists and ankles were tied to the bed posts with thick rope, and her body was convulsing against her constraints.

Dr Gibson was beside her, tapping on an instrument I didn't recognise. Mr Ambrosius stood close by, holding a candelabra over Grandmother's flailing body as he hummed a gentle meditation.

Then, Dr Gibson's instrument emitted a blue beam, the same as the light I'd seen inside the crystal. He angled the beam until it shone straight at Grandmother's forehead.

This time, it was my turn to screech like a street fox.

Mr Ambrosius whipped around. His eyes were filled with sorrow, all the life in them gone. I felt ice course through my body again, but this time, I knew it wasn't Morgana's doing.

"Get *out*," he said, in a low hiss.

I stood in place. "What are you doing to her? Leave her alone."

"She's not well, Emma." Dr Gibson's voice was gentle as he continued tapping at his wretched device. "We're helping her."

I knew there was little chance I could apprehend both men at once, but that didn't stop me from trying. I catapulted myself forward and attempted to wrench the device from Dr Gibson's hands.

Mr Ambrosius grabbed me in an instant. "Stupid girl," he whispered, as I writhed and fought against him.

"Emma." Grandmother's voice sounded weak. "Please, let them help. Trust –"

She broke off with a guttural scream.

I stomped on Mr Ambrosius' foot. He let out a howl and I was free from his grasp.

"They're hurting you!"

Grandmother heaved in a deep breath. "No, Emma. They're saving me. You must leave us."

I didn't believe a word of it, but I didn't know what to do. These men would continue with their ritual, whatever its purpose was. I was totally powerless.

I didn't know if it was this revelation, Morgana's presence, or my bruised and broken body, but I was suddenly too exhausted to stand. Mr Ambrosius watched me as I sank to the floor, sobbing. I could feel the weight of a sinking ship on my shoulders. All I wanted to do was sleep.

THE NEXT THING I remember was waking up in my bed, Mr Ambrosius looming over me.

"You've slept much too late," he said, his tone clipped. "We need to leave, now."

My memories of the previous night resurfaced, and I felt a wave of nausea course through me.

"Grandmother – what did you do to her?"

Mr Ambrosius' face gave nothing away. "She's alive, but we need to get out of the city."

"Why?"

His face remained unreadable. "Things that are about

to happen to her... things which shouldn't take place in a populated area. It'll be safer for everyone if we get your grandmother to the country."

My head was still ringing with screaming echoes, my body aching from Morgana's assault. My only choice was to trust Mr Ambrosius and pray that he really did love Grandmother as much as I did.

We were soon on the road and out of the suburbs, travelling west in a clanky buggy with an irate Parisian driver. Dr Gibson and Mr Ambrosius sat facing Grandmother and me. We had spoken little in the hours since leaving our hotel, and Grandmother was still weak, her eyes foggy and distant. I told myself that the traumatic night had simply exhausted her.

But I couldn't comfort myself with that fib for very long. Grandmother had begun humming off-key and tapping her fingers against the edge of the buggy's window. I knew those tics all too well. They were the same as Mama's.

Dr Gibson noticed them too. He watched her twitching fingers, his lips set in a straight line.

Mr Ambrosius, as always, seemed not to notice – or to have a care in the world, for that matter. He was staring out over the golden, empty grassland surrounding us. At one point, I thought I spied a single tear rolling down his pale cheek, but I couldn't be sure. It might have been a trick of the light.

No one was going to explain Grandmother's current predicament to me, so I spent the rest of the ride leaning my head against the window and watching the landscape wobble by.

Our carriage soon began passing fields of grapes and wheat – an intermingling of striking greens, purples, and golds. It was late afternoon when we stopped at a small house, alone in the middle of an acres-wide farm. Stalks of wheat shimmered beneath the reddening sky, and low hills rolled across the horizon like a sea of sunlight.

"May I ask where we are?"

Mr Ambrosius brushed off his hat and secured it to his head. "My nephew secured this home for us. Quite the spiffy character, if I do say so myself." He turned to me and squinted. "So be nice."

Was he telling me to mind my social cues? I was furious. Grandmother and I stepped out of the carriage and followed Mr Ambrosius up to the farmhouse, while Dr Gibson paid the driver and helped unload our trunks.

I didn't much like the house, upon closer inspection. Its wooden clapboards were painted a queasy salmon pink in a failed attempt at cheeriness that only made the old house spookier. There was one lonely tree in the garden. Its dark, barren branches seemed barely able to hold up an old rope swing, which swayed beside it in the wind.

For the first time all day, Grandmother perked up. "What a lovely little home." She clasped her hands together in delight.

Was she seeing the same house? I scanned the countryside for another house – perhaps I'd missed one – but this was the only building for miles. She really must be unwell to think this sinister place was lovely.

Mr Ambrosius knocked on the door, and we waited. Moments passed, then it creaked open to reveal half a face.

To my dismay, I recognised it.

A smile curled the ends of his mouth, followed by a hearty American laugh. He opened the door wide, and his arms wider. "Miss Emma Collins." The American turned to Mr Ambrosius and gave him a tight hug. "And Uncle, how nice it is to see you."

"And you, Nephew." Mr Ambrosius patted the American on the back, dropped his arms and introduced Grandmother in as formal a manner as he could manage.

The American led us into a cosy front parlour, which smelled of pipe smoke. Thick navy curtains covered the windows and a single oil lamp sat lit beside an old chair, its cushion flattened with use.

He turned to me and smiled. "The shock on your face is very becoming, Miss Collins."

"I – I just didn't expect to find you here." Had I just stuttered? What a strange thing.

Even stranger, it didn't seem that Mr Ambrosius was at all surprised that we knew one another. He merely sat in the old chair and took out a bottle of miracle wine.

Grandmother, on the other hand, was flush with delight at our existing acquaintance. For the first time since our fateful walk in the park, she seemed her old self again. The tension in my shoulders eased with relief.

She began asking the American all about how and where we'd met, through whom, and how London had behaved for him.

He answered her questions with a grace and dignity befitting our brothers to the West. "Well, I met her at a ball and she threw me off like a sack of burning potatoes. Didn't help much that Richard Jameson had just broken her heart." He turned to me. "You feeling any better?"

I stammered my pathetic assent and found myself looking at Mr Ambrosius, wishing he'd pour his miracle wine faster.

"And what of your relation to our dear Mr Ambrosius?" Grandmother continued.

Mr Ambrosius handed me a glass. "He's my sister Gwendolyn's son. You see his striking eyes? Stole them from her."

I bit the inside of my lip. This familial revelation still didn't tell me what the American's surname was. It couldn't be 'Ambrosius', as his mother would have dropped the family name upon marrying her husband. Unless they were unmarried, and the American was born out of wedlock.

What trying times these were.

The wine relaxed me, though, and soon my worries dulled into a simple desire to wander alone, one which I appeased by finding my bedroom upstairs and going out onto its balcony.

I leaned against the rails, enjoying the view of the garden beneath me and a small village in the distance.

Another view, one which I wasn't as happy about, was of Mr Ambrosius pacing about with his cane next to the garden's lone tree. He seemed to be muttering inane, angry comments to nobody in particular. That was, until I saw an orange tabby cat perched on the fence beside him, mewing.

To my dismay, Mr Ambrosius swivelled on his heels to look at the cat and began raising his voice. I couldn't hear all of his words, but I thought I heard him say "Morgana"– and that alone was terrifying enough to send me back into the safety of my bedroom.

Knowing of Grandmother's undying devotion to the

man, I decided against reporting his antics. She'd probably only laugh and say something about his brilliant imagination, and frankly, I wasn't in the mood to entertain it.

So I went downstairs to dinner, which was a spread of baked potatoes, green beans and roasted chicken. I avoided sitting next to Grandmother.

The American took the seat beside me instead, which only led to more stuttering awkwardness on my part. What a terrible affliction this stutter was becoming, and for no discernable reason. I retired early simply to avoid dealing with it.

Despite the enduring pain of my bruises, I slept well. But in the middle of the night, a knock sounded at my door.

It was a startling noise, and I sat up straight in bed, clutching my chest. There was another knock, so I stood up and called Grandmother's name. Nobody answered. I walked toward the door, which was haloed by a soft light coming from the hallway.

I opened the door, but nobody was there. Odd. I looked down the hall to the stairway.

An inky, blurry shadow – or was it smoke? – suddenly came into view, moving toward me. It ambled its way over the top step, reaching into the hallway.

I slammed the door shut and locked it. There was a screeching of ragged fingernails down the other side of the wood. Stifling a scream, I jumped back into the middle of the room.

The noise stopped. Everything was silent. I grabbed the vanity chair and propped it beneath the doorknob, listening for any movement. Was it gone?

As if on cue, a little voice spoke.

"Let me in."

This time, it came from the window, and the garden beyond. I looked outside and shrieked.

It was just as I feared. Abigail. A yellow nightgown hung from her body in tatters as she stood alone, looking up at me.

I shut the curtains fast. Taken by some childish instinct, I jumped into my bed and hid under the covers. My panicked heart thudded in my ears – I steadied my breath, shaky gasps bursting from my lungs.

Something hit the balcony door. I jumped and whimpered. Was Abigail throwing rocks at my windows now? No, of course she wasn't. I was only hallucinating. This vision was all in my mind.

Then there were footsteps lightly pattering along the balcony. Against my better judgement, I got out of bed and crept to the balcony window. I knelt down on the floor and peeked through the curtain. Nothing. But then the footsteps sounded again, and Abigail's yellow nightgown and dirty purple fingernails flashed past the lace curtain. We were only inches apart.

I stifled another scream as I fell to the floor and scrambled back to the centre of the room. This couldn't be. She was just a little girl. She wasn't even real. Why did I keep forgetting this?

I looked around, unsure of where to hide. No place was safe. So I stayed where I was, shutting my eyes tight and pressing my hands over my ears, legs curled up to my chest. I whimpered the Lord's Prayer over and over until everything went dark and silent.

SUNLIGHT HIT my face the next morning as I lay on the rug in front of the bed. My back and chest hurt from the rough sleep, so I lifted myself up and crawled to the window. The curtains were open, just as I'd left them the night before. I pushed them aside and looked outside.

A cheerful bird chirped as it soared by. Still nervous, I forced myself to look down at the garden. It was empty. There was only wet grass and the lone tree, made darker by last night's rain. But then, something on the balcony caught my eye.

A bare, muddy footprint. The size of a little girl.

There were more footprints, too, all over the wood. All of them the same. Was I still hallucinating, even now?

Abigail had come closer last night than ever before. One evening, not long before the shipwreck, I remember Mama grabbing my arm and whispering in my ear. *"The nightmares are coming closer."*

Is this what she had meant?

A knock sounded at my door. "Who's there?" I called.

"Your dearest Mr Ambrosius," came a familiar and sarcastic voice. I opened the door to Mr Ambrosius' unwrinkled face looking back at me. He was grinning, but there was something else in his eyes. I couldn't quite pinpoint it until he pushed past me and into my room.

"You shouldn't be in here. It's improper," I said, edging toward the hall.

He shook his head. "It'll only be a moment. I need to have a private word with you."

My bones grew cold. Did he know about my most

recent nightmare? I glanced at the balcony, where the footprints were still visible.

"You and Will," he said. "It can't happen. I'm sorry."

I blinked. "What?"

"Don't pretend innocence," he said with a snort. "I see the way you act around him." He tapped his cane decidedly on the floor. "It won't work." Tap. "It's impossible." Tap.

"I don't understand what you're talking about." It wasn't a complete lie. Mr Ambrosius was being as vague as ever. Though he seemed to insinuate I had a romantic interest in the American, he might have equally been warning me against slapping him.

His eyes narrowed. "You may not, under any circumstances, start a romantic relationship with my nephew."

Well, that clarified things.

I scoffed. "Of course I won't. He's almost as insufferable as you are."

Mr Ambrosius' face was unreadable. I wasn't sure if he was about to laugh or launch into a tirade scolding me for my indecency.

He let out a sigh. "Well, good. That's sorted, then. Let's have some breakfast."

He pushed past me and back into the hallway.

Grandmother seemed alert and well that morning. She was the only one who noticed my lack of appetite at the table. When breakfast ended, she took my arm and led me back to my room. As she closed the door behind us, a small, tired sigh escaped my lips. "I didn't sleep last night."

Grandmother stepped forward and placed her hand gently on my shoulder. "What's afflicting you?"

My eyes drifted to the balcony and the lace curtains, letting in the gentle morning light. It was difficult to find the words.

"I've been seeing strange things. For a while now. A little girl." I wouldn't tell her who. I couldn't, and besides, did it even matter? It couldn't be the real Abigail. She was in heaven. She had to be.

Grandmother's lips turned down at the edges. "Nightmares, perhaps?"

"More like visions," I said. "Like Mama had, before she died."

Grandmother looked away. "That makes no sense. We..." Her voice was shaking. She closed her eyes. "We need to get you to the Carnac Stones."

I touched her arm. "Are you all right?"

She turned to me, tears filling her eyes. "Oh, Emma. There are so many things I hid from you. I told myself I was doing it for your benefit but really, it was for me. I am so selfish."

"You keep saying that, and it's not true. You're wonderful and –"

"I let my daughter die." Her words came out like a gunshot.

It took me a moment to compose myself. "You know it couldn't be helped. Mr Ambrosius –"

"There's more than one way to remove an Annunaki." Her voice was raspy. "But it requires courage. Selflessness. I had neither, and to this day, I hate myself for it. You lost your mother because of me. I am so sorry, Emma."

"I'm sure that's not the case," I reasoned. Even with Grandmother's harrowing revelation, my mind went to Abigail, to my own guilt.

She was silent for some time. Finally, she let in a long breath. "I'm doing everything I can to put things right, and I pray it will work. But I need you to trust Mr Ambrosius, no matter what comes next."

What comes next. There was a darkness to those words.

"Do you really trust him?" I asked.

She nodded. "I know you think he's out of his mind. Perhaps, most of the time, he is." She smiled through her tears. "But our family has followed him this far. He'll keep you safe. That much is certain."

Before we could speak more, Dr Gibson called Grandmother to the kitchen. She squeezed my hand and walked out of the room, leaving me with a million more questions.

My mind was still on Abigail. Had last night been another hallucination, or something real? Was Abigail seeking revenge from the grave?

The Abigail I knew had never been cruel. It wasn't in her heart to be, and I hoped this meant that her spirit would not be seeking to torment me.

But if it all had been a hallucination, this meant the Annunaki was continuing to grow in strength.

Which was the worse reality – being haunted by my sister's ghost, or hallucinating ever-worse horrors, indicating my imminent demise?

SEVENTEEN

THAT NIGHT, everything changed. I don't want to remember it, but I do, and I will for the rest of my life, however long that may be.

I woke to the same screams I'd heard on our last night in Paris, but this time, they were only coming from Grandmother's room. My ribs ached as I tumbled out of bed and down the hall, my bare feet thumping on the creaky wooden floors. The screaming had stopped by the time I arrived at Grandmother's door, and no sound came from inside.

Instead, I heard laughter downstairs. I rushed down the staircase and towards a faint, glowing light in the kitchen. Grandmother's silhouette was hazy against the light of the candle she held as she paced the room, laughing.

I knew that chilling laugh. It was the same as Mama's, just before she lit the ship on fire.

The floor began swaying beneath me. Waves and waves and waves. I stepped into the room and Grandmother turned around with a wild grin on her face. I'd never seen her look so unhinged, so feral. It seemed that at any moment she might pounce on me, like a wolf circling her prey.

"Remember this?" she asked, nodding towards the candle in her hand. "Your dearest Mama? You must. It's all the same. Past and present and future."

And then she moved towards the kitchen curtains. The flame from the candlestick was dangerously close to catching on them.

Without thinking, I lunged toward her and wrangled the candle from her grasp. Grandmother didn't seem too concerned. Instead, she continued laughing, that strange, mangled grin growing ever wider on her face. "Past, present, and future. It's all the same, anyway."

I placed the candle on the shelf behind me, in a spot that would be impossible for her to reach without dealing with me first. I grasped her by the shoulders.
"Grandmother, can you hear me? Tell me what's wrong."

"Past, present, future..." She continued to repeat this.

I called out for Mr Ambrosius. When both he and the American rushed downstairs with their oil lamps, I blew out the dangerous candle behind me.

Darkness for a second, then light again, when help arrived.

Mr Ambrosius' face was unreadable as he took Grandmother by the hand and led her to the front parlour. The American, however, was rubbing his face and grimacing. He knew what was happening. And now, for the first time, I didn't want to know.

"Is Dr Gibson coming?" I asked, glancing upstairs and listening for the sounds of his footsteps.

The American shook his head. "He won't be able to help now, Emma." His voice was low, almost apologetic. My stomach dropped.

"Past, present, and future," Grandmother continued muttering as Mr Ambrosius sat her down on a chair. She was rocking back and forth, wringing her hands around a piece of her nightdress.

"She doesn't have much more time," Mr Ambrosius' voice was rough.

How was that possible? Other than the incessant muttering, Grandmother seemed to be physically fine. "What are you talking about, Grandmother?" I asked, crouching down to her eye level. "What about the past?"

She ignored my question and continued repeating the same words. Now, the manic grin was gone, replaced with nervous energy. Her eyes raced back and forth between the front door and the fireplace, which was thankfully unlit.

After what felt like an age, she stopped rocking, stopped speaking, and stared straight into my eyes.

That's when I noticed.

Her pupils had grown to cover her entire iris, all of the blue replaced with black. She wasn't Grandmother, anymore. She was one of them.

"You're next," she whispered.

I don't know how she reached into her nightgown pocket so fast, but suddenly she had a vial in her hand and was drinking from it.

Mr Ambrosius was caught by surprise, too. He tried to snatch it away, but it was already too late. The vial was empty.

She began coughing and wheezing. All of the blood

emptied from her cheeks, and then, ashen-faced, she toppled to the floor.

"Help her!" I was screaming, over and over, and then there were arms around me. The American.

Mr Ambrosius scrambled over to check Grandmother's pulse. He held her wrist, and I watched the light in his eyes die as he found nothing there. He put his face in his hands.

No. Grandmother wasn't gone. She wasn't.

"Virginia." Mr Ambrosius was leaning over Grandmother's broken form, silvery tears dripping from his face and onto her nightgown. "You were brave, you were always brave, even when you thought you weren't. We will remember your courage."

He gently took off her nightcap and placed it over her face.

I would never forget this night, the way the oil lamps flickered over the walls, over Grandmother's body.

I'd never forget the way Mr Ambrosius looked, for the first time in my presence, completely human.

~

I DIDN'T SLEEP for two days, because I knew that going to sleep meant waking up. And then I would have to remember what happened all over again. Experience had taught me that when one was grieving, sleep was nothing but a false reprieve of smoke and mirrors, which only put off the inevitable pain.

So I stayed awake. I drank more coffee than I ever had in my life, so much so that I was sick. It didn't matter.

The American remained by my side throughout it all

like a loyal puppy. Part of me wanted to make fun of him for being so attentive and brush him off as a sentimental fool. But I couldn't. I needed him beside me.

I cannot say much more about that first week, because I've forced myself to forget it. There was the burial in the garden. I told myself that Grandmother would understand. She'd adored this house when we arrived.

But I knew deep in my heart that it was wrong. She deserved only the grandest of send-offs, in London, her home. And there was nothing I could do to make that happen.

I let Mr Ambrosius, Dr Gibson, and the American take care of everything. After we laid Grandmother to rest, I went upstairs and fell asleep.

I awoke at some point the next day to the sound of Mr Ambrosius pottering around in the kitchen. Something delicious was baking in the oven. I could smell dough rising and cinnamon and butter. And freshly brewed coffee.

My nose led me downstairs. Mr Ambrosius was taking a loaf of bread out of the oven as Dr Gibson poured from a kettle.

"Finally!" Mr Ambrosius said when I sat down at the table. "We were wondering if we needed to hit you in the head with a hammer."

"Coffee always helps," Dr Gibson said, handing me a steaming cup.

My throat was too sore to speak, so I silently took the coffee and sipped, enjoying its warmth.

"Where's the - where's William?" I asked.

Mr Ambrosius nodded his head toward the front yard. "He's preparing the carriage. We're leaving in an hour."

I nearly dropped my cup. "What?"

I was emotionally and physically depleted, unfit to travel anywhere. And Grandmother was here, stuck in this place for good. I couldn't leave her, not so soon. "I don't understand. Why?"

Dr Gibson cleared his throat. "There are things you need to know."

"You've needed to know them for some time," Mr Ambrosius added. "Circumstances have changed. We need to tell you everything as soon as possible."

"Tell me here, then."

Mr Ambrosius shook his head. "You aren't safe here. The information you're about to receive might... affect you. Remember what I told you about fear? The Annunaki love it. We'll be safer having this conversation within the Stones. They'll shield you.."

I blinked. "You mean the Carnac Stones?"

Mr Ambrosius nodded. "Have some cinnamon bread." He cut a slice and pushed it over to me.

The bread was warm and flavourful. Hopefully I'd keep some food down, this time. I let out a long breath as I realised just how weak I had become over the past few days.

If these men were going to insist on carting me all around France, then fine. I didn't have the strength to argue today. And perhaps going to the Stones meant I'd get some answers.

Mr Ambrosius left the room, and I was stuck alone with the horrid Dr Gibson. I stood up to leave as well, but the man cleared his throat before I could excuse myself.

"Miss Collins," he said, rubbing his forehead. "I will

stay here for the time being. Before you leave, I just want to express my sincerest condolences. I know you've been going through the most terrible time. And I know you don't like me very much."

I opened my mouth to deny this, as any polite lady would do, but he held up his hand. "No, you don't have to say anything. I understand. We had a difficult relationship, you and I, after the wreck. I won't rake it all up now because I know it'll hurt you. But I did just want to say that I'm sorry. I pushed you too far. I was still learning how to interact with you, and I made many mistakes."

The 'you' seemed to refer to our family and our unique relationship with the Annunaki. It can't have been easy, being the only doctor responsible for helping us over the years. I had always despised this man, but perhaps I'd been too harsh on him.

I nodded and muttered something that sounded enough like forgiveness to loosen the visible tightness in his shoulders.

"Mr Ambrosius and I are terrible with social matters," he continued. "But you and Will have a special connection. I hope you continue to find comfort in his company."

I knew based on my previous conversation with Mr Ambrosius that he wasn't suggesting I pursue anything romantic with the American. Nevertheless, the idea stayed in my mind all morning, despite my wolfing down the rest of the cinnamon bread and drinking two cups of bitter coffee.

Further to my confusion, the American was to drive us to the Carnac Stones. I didn't want him to join, and yet at the same time, I needed him with us. Despite his lacking of any social graces, his warmth seemed to be one of the only things helping the hole in my heart to heal. That and the coffee, of course.

We arrived in Carnac that evening, and Mr Ambrosius suggested we retire early in order to visit his mysterious stones at dawn.

We took rooms at the village inn. I fell asleep fast, despite suffering a cot better suited for a goat than a lady. I fell into vivid dreams almost at once.

The first found me tumbling from the top of a cliff – falling, falling down a tunnel of smoke. I tried to scream, but no sound escaped my lips. All the breath in my lungs was gone.

Then, I was lying in a meadow of blue grass, looking up at an alien yellow sky. Huge, menacing birds flew above me. I sat up and looked around. Everything was moving slowly, gracefully, as if this world existed beneath an expansive sea. The thick trees swayed in the warm, cranberry-scented wind. Unfamiliar creatures danced in the distance. As I attempted to focus on these figures, a familiar sound came from behind me.

"Emma, you can be so clumsy." I knew that voice, so charming and bitter. I turned to face him.

Richard broke into a devastating, deep laugh. Suddenly, my body grew limp and heavy. I couldn't move a muscle. He wrapped my arms around him and picked me up. My weight slumped against his chest, my hands grasped at the air.

He stumbled, grunting at the growing burden. Deciding there was only one way to move me now, he dropped me to the ground, then took my icy hands and began dragging me.

Grass and pebbles scraped my back, burning red marks into my skin. Above us, the birds grew larger, angrier. The sky turned crimson. A crackling boom filled the thick atmosphere, and fiery sunlight glinted off the birds' wings.

We came to a rapid river, and Richard dropped me into it. My head fell back into the frigid water. It thrashed into my aching ears, around my red-raw eyes. I needed to say it once more, so I lifted my head for just long enough to whisper, "I love you." My final confession before drowning.

Richard smiled as he pushed me under the river. From beneath the waves, I watched his distorted shape transform into that of a girl with long, brown hair and pale, ghostly skin.

She mouthed the words so clearly. *"They killed me."*

I awoke with a jerk that cracked my neck and made the bed spin. My small room was still sheathed in darkness, only a lone streetlamp lending me any light. Sweat trickled around my hairline. Never had I suffered such a horrendous dream.

Richard had murdered me, but despite his terrible villainy, I found myself aching to be held in his arms.

Mr Ambrosius had made me question whether I'd ever felt anything real for Richard. Anything deeper than a liking for good manners and pretty things. But he was wrong. My feelings weren't just the shallow longings of a soulless girl. He knew nothing of the pain I'd faced in the past, or the guilt, or how both had forced me to stifle my emotions for all this time.

Richard was wrong, too. I had loved him. Perhaps I'd

been childish in my love – keeping my secrets and assuming he'd never feel the same for another woman, despite our distance – but it had been love, nonetheless. And perhaps it could still be again.

Maybe the hallucinations accosting me were only the reflection of an unhappy mind. They were telling me I needed to be free of my past and my guilt, to move on with my life and be with the man I'd dreamt of for years. The man who had been in my dream tonight.

I didn't need this ridiculous journey. I needed *Richard*. The mattress whined as I curled deeper into it, sobbing with loud, ugly tears that would were likely turning my face red as a turnip. It didn't matter. Richard was no longer mine, and yet I was starting to wonder if he was the only one who could save me.

~

We met outside the inn an hour before dawn the next morning. The American had lit two oil lamps at the front of his carriage to navigate the darkness and fog, which had settled into a thick curtain all around us. We rode onto a narrow dirt path that led through a forest. I could only see the silhouettes of tall, slender trees bordering our path, clawing at the still air. I shivered despite myself.

Mr Ambrosius poked the top of the American's hat with his cane. "Stop here."

"But we're still far off—"

"Just stop."

What was Mr Ambrosius thinking? We couldn't walk through this nightmarish forest, especially at night. Road or no road, this place seemed to scream danger from all sides. I said as much, but as anyone with half a mind and half a day with the Great Mr Ambrosius would expect, he didn't listen.

Our fearless leader grabbed a lantern from the front of the carriage and began walking away from the path, through the trees.

A flash of judiciousness (which had been rather lacking in recent weeks) ran through my mind. Mr Ambrosius was, after all, a madman. Anything could lurk in this forest – ravenous wolves, or worse.

But, despite rationality, or maybe because of it, I stepped out of the carriage and followed him, as did the American. The shadowy trees were even more ominous as we walked, now unsheltered. I kept my eyes on them, just to ensure one didn't uproot itself and grab me with its claw-like branches.

Soon I found I could see a little farther, and the green shrubbery ahead of us began to reveal itself. Everything was shrouded in a grey, foggy haze, slowly turning golden in the dawn's light. Leaves were gliding to the ground and birds flitted from tree to tree. Farther ahead lay a clearing.

Mr Ambrosius extinguished the lantern, set it down, and began running. "Hurry, before we miss it!"

"Miss what?" I called to him as I huffed my way along, trying to keep up. Should a medal become available for running in a crinoline, I'd win the gold.

The American kept pace with me, despite my slow progress. At least he had an ounce of gentility, unlike Mr Ambrosius.

After some excruciating minutes, Mr Ambrosius

stopped still and looked back. His eyes were wild with excitement. "We're here!"

I gasped for breath and leveraged my dress's weight as I came to a stop beside him. My indelicate panting lasted for far too long, as I heaved in deep lungfuls of icy air. "This... field... is what you dragged us here for?"

Mr Ambrosius pointed to my left, and as my dizziness subsided, I took in the scene before me.

There were rows and rows of tall, pointed stones, pale grey with patches of white, placed in orderly patterns, filling up a field that seemed to stretch for miles.

"What is it? A graveyard?" I asked.

Mr Ambrosius laughed. "Some think it is. But I'll let you in on a secret." He leaned back toward me with a discomfiting smile. "It's a passageway."

He leapt toward me and laughed, then pressed his thumb to my forehead before turning around to walk away.

"What the blazes was that for?" I asked, only to be ignored by both of them.

Mr Ambrosius made his way toward the closest stone, which was nearly as tall as he, and looked at it with admiration. Then he put his hand on a circular symbol carved into the rock's side and smiled.

I placed my hands on my hips. "This had better be worth it."

The American leaned into me and whispered, "It is. Just wait."

The buttery sun rose over the trees. Mr Ambrosius took out a tiny flute from his pocket and put it to his mouth. An awful high-pitched screech came out of the thing, so ear-splitting that the notes would break glass. I pushed my palms hard to my ears and yelled at him to stop, lest he deafen us all.

Thankfully, he did, but only because his song had changed pace. Mr Ambrosius was now coaxing out deep, vibrating tones from the instrument. The noise seemed to pulse through the ground itself, touching each stone as it went.

Then, the most peculiar thing happened. So peculiar, in fact, that I stepped back, my mouth as loose as a panting dog. Fortunately, none of my society fellows were here to witness the spectacle. Otherwise, my awful countenance – battered hair, heaving chest, ruffled gown and slack jaw – would be all over the newspapers back home.

The stone beside Mr Ambrosius had begun glowing as if lit from within. It reminded me of the messenger crystal I had found in his travelling chest. Soon the other stones began illuminating until the field was dotted with an earthbound constellation of radiant white lights.

And then something worse than a loose hair bun affronted me. A sudden, total darkness, and a falling sensation. I was dropping down, down, down, for what seemed like miles into the blackness. The air rushed up at me, forcing the breath from my lungs and gargled screams from my throat.

Thump.

It took all the strength left in me to open my eyes. I was glad that I did.

We were in the same field, with the same stones, only now everything was brilliant and otherworldly, alive with roiling rainbows of energy.

The sky above was a magnificent mixture of every

colour I'd ever seen, and colours I was certain I'd never seen before, all intermingling with the movement of the wind.

Bright white orbs of light floated just above my head, like wayward soap bubbles from Ms Wright's laundry basin.

I'd seen these orbs before. A memory surfaced of the cobbled streets of Paris and that dastardly green liquor. I thought of Grandmother then, and my stomach flipped.

I pushed the thought away and began wondering whether these white lights were angels trapped on Earth, trying to find a way back home.

Even the surrounding air seemed different. There was a wavelike movement in the atmosphere as if billions of particles were drifting past us on an invisible current.

"It's beautiful," I whispered. My voice sounded strange. It had more nuance in it, musical notes that I'd never noticed before in the spoken word. Even the vibrations of my vocal chords and the wheezing of air in and out of my lungs felt somehow special, poignant.

In amongst my jumbled thoughts, I pictured a diagram from one of Father's old books, which had illustrated the human anatomy. I could feel every organ inside of me, pumping and working like intricate clock pieces to keep my body alert. *Alive.*

Mr Ambrosius' face came into view then, blocking our heavenly surroundings as he looked down at me. His skin, which had always been pale, now had a sheen to it reminiscent of chiffon curtains in the afternoon sun. He seemed to glow from within.

"How's your head?" he asked.

These new feelings had masked any pain. The moment

Mr Ambrosius spoke, however, my head began feeling as if blocks of iron were falling on it with every thud of my pulse. "It hurts."

He chuckled. "That was quite a fall."

"Where am I?"

"The same place. The Carnac Stones. Except now you're lying on the ground."

"No," I began, shaking my head. That was a mistake. Another wave of pain washed over me and I groaned. "I went down a tunnel..."

"You *thought* you did. Come along, stand up now."

It took some doing to obey his command, even though the American gallantly stepped forward and offered me a hand. I stumbled, but once I was upright and the pain in my head had subsided, I looked around.

Beneath my feet, lines of light webbed their paths through the ground like veins in the earth. Everything around me glowed.

"Welcome," Mr Ambrosius beamed, his chin up in the air. Clearly, he was very proud of whatever feat he'd just pulled off. "You're finally seeing things as they are. Or at least, something close to it."

Was this madness? The idea that the world I'd seen with my own eyes for my entire life was only the surface, that all of this was hiding beneath. It was almost too much to bear.

Before I could say as much, a familiar shape flitted across the corner of my vision, darting between the stones. And a little girl's giggle sounded behind me.

I turned to see Mr Ambrosius, his eyes wide as he scanned the rocks, searching for the source of the noise.

"Something wicked this way comes," he muttered, his tone dark. "Something wicked this way runs..."

The shadow bolted out from behind a rock. Abigail was here, and she was playing with us. Taunting us.

The stones closest to me began oozing water from their surface as if they were sponges that had been soaked and then squeezed. I didn't need to taste the water to know it was briny. William stepped closer to me and clasped my hand in his own.

"Show yourself," Mr Ambrosius shouted, his voice reedy and high. Could he hear Abigail? See her, too? "Tell us what you want."

Another giggle. Salt air brushed the back of my neck, and I yipped and twirled around. Fifty feet in front of us stood Abigail's slight frame, and for just a second, she raised one mottled arm as if waving. Then the golden light of the rising sun hit her, and her image dissolved. For now, she was gone.

A bolt of something sharp hit my poor, abused head. Everything went black, and the buzzing of a million bees shook my eardrums. Just as I had felt my other organs working in harmony, I could now feel my brain swelling like a balloon about to pop.

"Oh, dear," Mr Ambrosius' distant voice sounded. "Is your head hurting?"

The pain was too strong now. Nothing made sense. I couldn't speak.

And then that damnable flute sounded from somewhere far away. It came closer, and a moment later, the buzzing subsided. The pressure in my skull relented. I could no longer feel my brain swelling, or my heart pumping adrenaline through my veins.

I opened my eyes and looked around. The sky was darker now. Sound and light were muffled, hazy. I could no longer see the white lights or the waves in the air.

"Is she gone?" I gasped, spinning around.

"Who?" Mr Ambrosius asked. His flute had disappeared.

"Abigail. The little girl. You saw her."

He said nothing, but before I could chastise him for being stubborn, a long-forgotten memory came flooding into my mind.

"Wait, I... I remember these stones," I said. "I've seen them before, in a book. They were in an illustration in a story, a Camelot legend Father used to read to us."

Mr Ambrosius seemed to perk up at this, but I ignored him and turned to the American. The images came rushing back as if they had never left my mind at all. "Merlin turned an entire army to stone. That's where the Carnac Stones came from."

Mr Ambrosius smirked. "Well, Merlin was quite the genius."

I looked at him. "He wasn't real. He was just a myth."

Mr Ambrosius let out a burst of laughter. "Yes! Yes, of course. Just a myth." He wiped a tear of mirth from his eye with his little finger and turned away. Without another word, he began walking forward through the stones.

I stood for a moment, baffled. It was a state of being I was growing ever more accustomed to.

The American and I followed Mr Ambrosius in silence, staying in step with one another, though he had long let go of my hand. I was still shaking a little, trying to piece together my thoughts.

I couldn't say as much for the American, but Mr Ambrosius had seen and heard Abigail just as clearly as I had. I was sure of it.

But then he'd feigned ignorance, asking to whom I was referring. This either meant that I was growing worse in my madness — imagining that another person was seeing the same things — or he was being deceptive.

The latter was both more palatable, and likelier. But what did he have to gain from bringing Abigail forth and then lying to me about our encounter?

A sinister question edged its way into my mind. Was Mr Ambrosius taking me to places where he *knew* my hallucinations would intensify?

Mr Ambrosius stopped walking then and turned to the American and me, leaning against a stone. It glowed particularly brightly where his hand met its rough, grey surface.

"Virginia was reluctant for you to know any of this, Miss Collins," he said, sighing. "She wanted you to live a normal life for as long as possible, whatever 'normal' means. After your parents died, all she wanted was to protect you.

"I told her that the best way to keep you safe was to keep you informed. She wouldn't listen. Instead, her goal was to raise you in polite society and to find you a husband and a family of your own as soon as possible. Her hope was this would keep your life stable, as it seemingly had for her when she was younger. To be fair, it was a good plan. At least, a better plan than she ever realised."

I said nothing. I felt the loss of Grandmother so strongly at that moment, I almost couldn't breathe.

"Your grandmother knew the Annunaki had been attacking your family for generations. She knew much more than she ever told you, but there is one part I've always kept from her, and the rest of your family. I always thought it would complicate matters, but things have changed, and Virginia is... well," he swallowed and averted his eyes. "I'm realising that I might not always be right."

Mr Ambrosius took a deep breath. The birds stopped chirping, the air grew still. Everything around us was waiting for his words. "You and your family – your ancestors – you all have a unique gene."

I blinked. "A gene?"

"Have you heard of Mr Charles Darwin, the naturalist? And his new book, *On the Origin of Species*?"

I remembered hearing something about it from Mr Carmichael. He mentioned something about birds who shared common traits across generations. "I know of it."

"Well, it's somewhat accurate," he said, "in the sense that humans pass on certain features from one generation to the next. These features can grow stronger or weaker, depending on what happens in the intervals between generations."

He straightened and pointed to me. "Your family has a feature that is extremely rare. Rarer than rare. In fact, you, Miss Emma Collins, are the last known human to have it. That's why I'm here. It's why we're all here." He gestured to the American. "To protect you."

I took a deep breath, trying to order my thoughts. "So... the Annunaki are trying to kill me because they don't want me to pass this feature on? They don't want me to survive to have children?"

Mr Ambrosius' eyes softened. "Smarter than I thought. Yes, that's right. They don't want humans to have this feature. They want this gene extinguished."

"Why?"

He sighed and glanced at the American, who was staring hard at one of the stones. "Because they believe it will destroy humanity for all eternity. But in truth, it's the only thing that will save you."

"Without it," he continued, "the human species has only a few thousand years left. Which may seem like a lot of time, but it's really only seconds on the universal clock."

The American looked at me then, with something like admiration in his eyes. "The gene you carry unlocks the ability to become more than your physical form. It helps you to become pure energy."

Another memory flashed before me. The day I had gone to church alone. When a strange man with black eyes – perhaps an Annunaki – had attacked me. When my entire body had burned with a bright light and I had somehow reduced him to ash.

"Are you saying I can change at will? Become energy whenever I like?"

Mr Ambrosius shook his head. "No, the gene is recessive. You don't have any ability to do anything of the sort. But your descendants, should you survive to have them, will be able to transform. To become Light, as we call it."

He was wrong. I could do it. Memories of the church in London, of the man turned to ash, played through my mind. Now that I knew what becoming Light meant, I also knew, without a doubt, I had done just that. And somehow, it had helped me destroy that man.

Morgana had told me I'd killed one of her own. That man must have been an Annunaki.

The realisation hit me like a brick. No one else had seen him, nor the pile of ashes that remained after. It had all been a vision of what I was doing to the Annunaki in my mind.

Mr Ambrosius tapped the ground with his cane. "This planet cannot support the human race," he continued as he pushed his cane into the earth. "No planet can, really. At some point, all of the Earth's intelligent species will die out. The only way for an advanced species to survive – for your species to survive – is to break out of its physical form."

I remembered my last conversation with Morgana. She had said that I had to die in order to *save* the rest of humanity. The opposite of what Mr Ambrosius was telling me.

"So, the Annunaki want humans to die out?"

Mr Ambrosius glanced at the American once again. "They have seen what a transformational gene can do, and they don't agree with it. Their belief is that it's better for a species to die out organically. They think that what they're doing is noble. Merciful, even."

I couldn't help but laugh. "They don't seem all that merciful, considering they're working so hard to kill me. If anything, they're evil."

"True, *merciful* is not the right word," Mr Ambrosius muttered. He stared up at the sky. "But neither is *evil*. The Annunaki are much more dangerous than that."

"What can be more dangerous than evil?"

He looked back down to the earth and closed his eyes. "Self-righteousness."

The American cleared his throat. "They started out as a different species, far away from here. And they evolved beyond their physical form. But they weren't happy about the results."

He looked at Mr Ambrosius. "Something went wrong during the process of becoming Light. We were helping them evolve – that's what we do, help others transform and survive. For the Annunaki, things went a little… sideways. They're trapped in their energetic form, which means they can't exist physically, at least not without a host body."

Morgana's face reappeared in my mind, filled with sadness and an overwhelming sense of loss.

"Things could go sideways with humans too, then." I thought of my potential children. What would they want? Would they choose this existence?

The American nodded. "True. But it's a rare occurrence. And still, it's better than the alternative, don't you think? The end of humanity, forever?"

I didn't know what to think. These concepts – genetics, evolving, turning into something other than human, it was all making my head feel fuzzier than Violet's winter riding muffs.

"Your grandmother wanted you to survive," Mr Ambrosius said. "That was why she took the Annunaki from your body and hosted it herself."

"*What?*"

Mr Ambrosius' pain crawled across his face. "Your Annunaki was getting stronger, Emma. There was little else we could do." He let out a long breath. "Dr Gibson and I have a process which allows us to pull the Annunaki from one host, and force them into another. When that host dies, so does the Annunaki."

Everything started spinning.

Will wrapped a hand around my shoulder. "The Annunaki can only attach themselves to humans who share the gene to become Light," he said gently. "Grandmother was the only other person left."

I couldn't speak. Grandmother had given her life to save mine. I didn't even get to say thank you.

And at the end of her life, she'd thought she was selfish. Had it been because she'd had the opportunity to save Mama? My uncle, too? And she'd decided against it?

Grandmother told me the truth even though I hadn't understood it. She'd been afraid of losing her life. And yet, she did exactly that for me.

"Virginia bought you time. We owe it to her to make the most of it." He cleared his throat, steadying his voice. "The Annunaki are always seeking you out, Emma. When they smell your blood, sense your fear, or see one of our communication beacons, they can hunt it down and find you."

My blood. That was why I was taking the pills to stop my monthlies. That was why Grandmother was always so afraid of bleeding...

A sob caught in my throat. Was that why my uncle died? The day he'd bled, and Grandmother had reacted with such fear, had only been a few months before his death. My parents never told me how he'd been killed, but I'd known it was rather unexpected. A supposed accident.

"These stones," he continued, "emit a unique energy that blinds the Annunaki. You're safe here. Hidden most effectively."

Mr Ambrosius was pacing up and down, his speech a torrent of words. "The stones also have cleansing properties. To come here is to strengthen yourself against them.

"Our plan of action now will be to get you married. You'll need to have children, many of them, to replicate the gene as many times as possible. Then Dr Gibson will perform a procedure to keep you from having more, and you'll be safe. The Annunaki only seek those able to bear children and pass along the gene."

"So I'd be leaving my own children in danger?"

The American shook his head. "We'll protect them, forever. Just as we've protected you."

"And my mother? You didn't protect her, did you?" The words came out fast and angry. Mama's eyes, black with the Annunaki's possession, flashed through my memory. Waves and flame intermingling in a stormy sea.

Mr Ambrosius stared past me, into the forest. "We tried so hard. Harder than you'll ever know. But we were too late."

Now, my heart was pounding.

I had been reduced to a bodily function. I was a breeder, not a person. And all of this had been planned, had been a part of my fate before I'd even been born.

My legs grew wobbly. The American reached out to help steady me, but although the world was spinning, I snatched my arm away. Everything in my life had been a lie, and I was furious with both him and Mr Ambrosius.

I turned on my heel and made my way out of the field as fast as I could, away from the safety of the stones and back into the darkness of the forest.

~

I didn't say a word to Mr Ambrosius or that damned American for the rest of the morning. During our carriage ride back into the village, they each tried to break through my heavy silence with attempts at conversation, but I was having none of it.

In truth, it wasn't necessarily that I was still angry with them. They had done only what they thought was right, and it had been Grandmother's choice to keep me in the dark about much of this.

My silence was due to my mind running a thousand miles a minute. Every bit of my energy was going toward unfurling the information I'd received, bit by bit, like an obstinate ball of knotted twine.

Grandmother had known about our family *curse* – the only word I could think of which appropriately illustrated our predicament – for my entire life. Mama must have known, too. And neither had told me.

Had Abigail known? She was only twelve years old when she died, but perhaps they'd told her when she'd begun taking the tincture to stop her monthlies, just before the wreck. And then when I'd turned twelve myself, Grandmother had just decided that my mind wasn't up to snuff.

These thoughts continued to rampage their way

through my head. I knew I needed to stop, and focus on what was to be done next.

I didn't want to leave Grandmother behind, but I couldn't return to that house in the countryside. It was too difficult to imagine being in the rooms where she'd suffered, and died. For now, I would have to say farewell and let her rest.

I wanted to be back home in London. I wanted a family. And it seemed, finally, that my goals aligned with those of the Great Mr Ambrosius.

EIGHTEEN

Dr Gibson met us in Carnac later that day, and we hired a driver to take us straight back to Paris. I was silent most of the time, staring out at the same fields that Grandmother and I had passed only a couple of weeks ago. Everything was different now. The skies were darker. Was it because autumn had begun, or was my own misery shading everything?

I did my best to conceal the deluge of tears running down my cheeks. Thankfully, Mr Ambrosius and Dr Gibson had both fallen asleep. But the American was as alert as always.

"You okay?"

Of course he would comment when all I wanted was to be left alone. I wiped my cheeks and forced a smile. "Just fine, thank you."

"You don't look it."

I did everything I could to keep that smile plastered on my face, but the sadness was overwhelming. "I'd appreciate being left alone."

He sighed. "But you *aren't* alone."

Was that annoyance in his tone? I'd never heard the American express as much before. His irritation allowed the floodgates to open on my own. "Why do you care? To you, I'm just another one in a long line of breeders."

The American blinked, shocked. "Is that really what you think?"

I didn't answer, but looked out of the window. The golden fields twinkled under the lowering sun.

"I - I am so sorry if I have given that impression," the American sputtered. "That's not at all how I see you."

I turned back to him. "Then what do you see?"

His mouth turned into a hard line, as if he was trapping his words within. He looked at the floor as his cheeks began to flush. "I think you're an intriguing person, Miss Collins. I think your mind runs a million miles a minute, 'cause you're smart-mouthed, fast to learn and quick to get the measure of anyone who dares cross your path. And I think folk have underestimated you all your life, because you're a damned pretty girl with fine dresses and jewels to match. But that's their mistake." He looked up then, with a shy smile. "You're real funny, too, though I don't think you realise it."

I gaped at him. I hadn't expected candour from the American, and I didn't know quite how to respond. So I opted for sarcasm. "You're saying I'm only inadvertently funny? Well. What a lovely compliment."

The American laughed. "You know that's not what I meant."

I looked away. "I'm just one of a long line of people

you've protected." I don't know why this bothered me, but it did.

"Actually, no. I'm new to this. It's Ambrosius and Dr Gibson who have all the years of experience."

I looked back at him. "You're not a thousand years old?"

He laughed again and shook his head. "No. We're not all ancient like those two." He nodded to the men sleeping opposite us.

"But you're definitely not human?"

Another shake of the head. "I'm not. But I don't think we're as different as they believe. I think..." He trailed off, as if about to say something he knew was forbidden.

"What?" I pressed.

"Nothing," he said with a sad smile. "Do you want to know about where I come from? I don't think we need to keep all these secrets anymore."

He was deliberately changing the subject, but curiosity overtook me. I adopted an innocent expression. "America?"

He grinned. "Very funny. That's where I acclimatised, when I arrived on Earth." As he spoke, he lifted his arm and wrapped it around the back of my seat. We had shifted a few inches closer together. I could feel the rise and fall of his chest, see every detail of the stitching on his shirt.

All of this distracted me from what he'd just said. It took a moment for me to regain my senses. "When you... arrived on Earth?"

He chuckled. "Yep. I'll show you what I mean. Later tonight."

The promise sent a jolt of electricity up my spine. I remembered Mr Ambrosius' warning that I was not to get too close to the American.

No, Emma. Whatever the American meant by this, it was far too inappropriate a suggestion. He would not be showing me anything later tonight, especially not without a chaperone.

~

Of course, I changed my mind. That night, after arriving in Paris and bidding goodnight to our travel companions, we met on the restaurant balcony at the Hotel Westminster. It was a small space, and we were forced to stand rather close to one another.

Since I was already throwing all social proprieties to the wind, I thought I might as well do it with a flourish.

The American had insisted upon this particular meeting spot, as whatever he had to show me involved looking up at the night sky.

"It's so bright in the city," he said, as he craned his neck and leaned over the railing. "You can't see it very well."

"What are we looking for, exactly?"

He turned to me with a smile. "My home."

"Your home... is up there?" I scrunched up my eyes and pointed to the sky.

The American took my hand and manoeuvred it to point at a faint cluster of stars, rising above a building opposite us. That spark of electricity hit me once again. What was it about this man's touch and my senses? It was all horribly indecorous.

"There. That's the Pleiades. That's where Mr Ambrosius, Dr Gibson and I are from."

My throat had seized up at his touch, but I still managed a weak reply. "Really?"

He was still smiling, but he didn't seem to be teasing me. "I know it's hard to believe. But it's true."

I didn't believe it. I couldn't believe it. My world had flipped upside down since leaving London, but there were still some things that were completely impossible.

The American did *not* fall from a cluster of stars. This man needed a good sound bump to the head to regain his senses.

But we were alone on a balcony at night. I didn't want to question a possible lunatic at this juncture. And besides, he was still holding my hand. I rather liked it. I wanted him to continue. "So you came here to protect my family?"

He nodded. "I have a confession to make, though."

We looked at each other, and my stomach flipped. Was he about to admit his love for me? Right here?

"I didn't want to come."

Oh. Why did I feel so disappointed? "Why not?"

He glanced back toward the Pleiades. "I'd heard stories about Earth. How tough it is to live like this. Like a human being." He motioned to his body with his other hand. "I always knew I'd have to go somewhere. Our society requires us to travel to help other species, and since my uncle was already here, my mother thought it would be a good idea to send me to work with him. So Earth it was."

I looked down at his hand clasping mine. His shirt sleeve was rolled up, and for the first time, I noticed a strange mark on his wrist. I lifted his arm to inspect it more closely in the dim light.

I'd never seen a tattoo this close before. It was a crimson

cross, with a white diamond in its centre. It was beautiful, in a haunting sort of way.

"It's a cross." He said.

I looked up and rolled my eyes. "Really? I had no idea."

He laughed. "It's a promise, sort of." He thought for a moment, then shook his head. "No, more of an enforcement. To serve others, and never kill."

"Never kill?"

"This mark prevents us from doing mortal damage. It's part of an oath we make when we turn of age and go out into the universe to serve."

I raised an eyebrow. "And what prompted the need to make this oath?"

"Good question," he said with a shrug. "I actually don't know."

We were silent for some time. The American looked back up at the night sky.

A thought struck as I was attempting to unravel everything he'd told me. "Are you going to leave one day?"

He was silent, his eyes on the stars. "Maybe. Probably. I wanted to, before all of this."

"All of what?"

The American faced me and smiled. "You."

And that electricity rampaged through my veins again, lighting me up from the inside. My heart thudded in my chest.

Whatever happened next, I could no longer call him the American. He was Will, and there was something deeper between us than I'd ever imagined.

Then I remembered London and having a family and

my fate. And that my plan did not – could not – involve him.

I pulled my hand from his and turned away, back toward the hotel. "W-we should really get to bed." My damned stutter had returned. I avoided Will's gaze as I rushed back inside.

~

It was strange being in Paris without Grandmother. I finally felt the full weight of her loss. She was truly gone. Here, where dress shops lined the streets and mothers and daughters walked arm-in-arm, I felt her absence more keenly than ever.

The next morning, I asked Dr Gibson to accompany me to the post office. My two other options – one being a madman, and the other a madman who was also affecting my senses – were not to my liking. The doctor would have to do.

As we walked, Dr Gibson asked with whom I was corresponding. I told him I'd sent word to Violet about my journey to the French countryside. By now, I should have received a letter from her.

What I didn't expect was for the postman to hand me an envelope with the Jameson family crest stamped decisively on its seal. My hands began shaking right in the middle of the post office.

"You look like you've seen a ghost," Dr Gibson said with a chuckle.

"It's nothing." I stuffed the envelope into my purse and began walking out of the post office.

Something in my stomach dropped, then. Nothing? Why was I saying that? It was everything I'd hoped for, wasn't it? A letter from Richard?

Back at the hotel, I excused myself to my room. My heart was sputtering and my hands were shaking furiously as I struggled to open the envelope.

Dearest, dearest Emma,

I cannot begin to explain how enthralled I am to see your handwriting. To know that you have forgiven me is a miraculous revelation. You must have known my heart was still yours, and that I still yearned for you, just as I always have.

You may have heard that I ended my relationship with Miss Klepakhov, but you may not know why. Or perhaps you already do.

It has always been you, my dearest Emma. I cannot stop thinking about you, wishing for your return, missing your sweet smile. Will you come home to me soon? Will you be mine once again?

I wait in desperate earnest,

Yours,

Richard Jameson

The letter slipped through my fingers and began a fluttery descent to the floor. He ended things with the Russian. He wanted me back. It was the greatest possible news, everything I'd wanted and more than I had dared to hope for.

So why wasn't I jumping for joy?

A knock sounded at my door. "Miss Collins? You in there?" It was Will. As usual, his timing was awful.

"I'm fine!"

Why did I say that? I was so fraught that I didn't know the words coming from my mouth. My voice was thick with emotion.

Will seemed to notice my strange response, because he asked if he could come in. I picked up the letter and opened the door, trying to arrange my face into a pleasant, neutral expression.

Will grinned at me, his eyes alight as his gaze met mine. Then he looked at the letter quivering in my shaking hands. I watched him spot the Jameson family seal, and his face turned into a strange mixture of ashen-grey and red.

"Good news?" he asked, his voice calm. Distant.

"Richard wants to, erm... rekindle our relationship."

His jaw tightened at my words. I swallowed.

"I see. And you'll go back to him?" That last word hit like a boulder falling on the floor between us.

I couldn't speak, but I didn't need to say anything for him to ascertain my answer. He must have seen it all over my face: the relief that I would likely now be married to a good suitor. The one thing I had been trained to fight for all my life, finally within my grasp.

He sighed. "Well. Wishing you all the luck," he said, in a somewhat strangled voice. Then he turned around and left.

Something within me broke. It felt like sinking, like losing a last shard of hope.

I STARTED WRITING a letter back to Richard. The sooner he received my declaration of undying love, the better. Richard was a sought-after bachelor, and I didn't want to risk him being swept off his feet by another European temptress while I travelled back from Paris. I couldn't lose him again. My sanity wouldn't survive it.

After sealing the envelope and getting into my bedclothes, I turned off the oil lamp on the bedside table and got under the blankets. I prayed for no more nightmares, only happy dreams of Richard and our wedding and perhaps — dare I say it — a baby's nursery.

It seemed only seconds had passed when I woke up again. The sunlight was streaming through my window more harshly than I was used to.

I squinted and looked up to see the window had moved. That was... impossible. It was beside me now. Last night, it had been across the room. This made no sense. And where were the curtains? I sat up and gasped.

The window hadn't moved. My cot, with me in it, had.

In fact, everything in my room had been moved. The water basin, which had been beside the doorway, was now in the far corner, sitting on top of my trunk. The curtains had been removed and folded neatly beside it. My blanket was no longer on top of me. It was now beneath my feet, at the edge of my bed.

Something — *someone* — had moved everything while I was sleeping. I felt sick to my stomach. My space had been invaded without my knowing, by someone utterly unknown.

This was madness. Someone was trying to frighten me. Will wasn't the kind of man to undertake such a prank, and Mr

Ambrosius and Dr Gibson didn't care for secretive, underhand tactics. It couldn't be anything to do with Morgana, because she'd been destroyed. Grandmother had saved me from her.

Hadn't she?

I jumped out of bed and began moving everything back to its rightful spot. None of this had happened. None of this had happened. I chanted this mantra in my head, committing to total denial as I dressed and fixed my hair.

I WENT DOWNSTAIRS to meet the others for breakfast, praying my exhausted face didn't prompt too many questions. As I descended, I began wondering if the bedroom matter had even occurred at all.

Perhaps it was a very realistic nightmare, or maybe I had forgotten that, for some unknown reason, I'd rearranged everything in my room the night previous. But it was impossible to convince myself of this.

Everyone was sitting at a table in the dining room, and I sat down to join them. "You look like a rotting fish," Mr Ambrosius said.

I thanked him with the thickest sarcasm I could muster before glancing at Will. He was staring into his porridge as if seeking a golden nugget from the western regions of his homeland. Dr Gibson stopped eating his apple and regarded me with the look of... well, a doctor.

"Did you sleep well?" he asked.

I smiled. "Just fine. Anyway, I have good news." Best to change the subject. Will coughed, but didn't look up from his bowl. "Richard has written to me. He wants me to come home."

"You mean, he intends to court you again?" Dr Gibson's eyes brightened as he turned to Mr Ambrosius. "This is wonderful news."

"Fantastic!" said Mr Ambrosius clapped his hands together with joy.

"Excellent," Will said quietly, with a smile that didn't quite reach his eyes.

I raised my chin. "I think we can all agree to go home to London. Let's leave first thing tomorrow."

~

We all had a lovely day, touring the city and sharing remarks about passers-by and interesting architecture.

Mr Ambrosius and Dr Gibson were in high spirits, which made me even more hopeful that we had vanquished the Annunaki. My life would go on, with parties and family and love, just as I'd always dreamt it.

Will was more subdued. This couldn't be because of me, could it? The idea was ridiculous, considering we'd spent little time together and his own uncle had warned me away from him.

What did he expect, anyway? That I'd turn Richard down when he was my best chance of marriage and children? That would go against our collective goal of preserving my bloodline.

Whatever his wildly inappropriate expectations had been, they didn't matter. I needed to return to London and be with Richard. There was no reason to get myself in a twist wondering what Will thought about it.

And perhaps I could also let go of my guilt over Abigail's death. Those terrible thoughts would fade now that Richard and I were together again. With him, I would allow myself to revel in romance and fine company and frivolity. As long as I returned home to him, I'd still have a chance at happiness.

So I blinked away the visions of Abigail's upturned nose and brown eyes as we walked past some children playing beneath a church awning, and I convinced myself that the little girl hugging her stuffed bear in the carriage passing beside us looked nothing like my sister

Instead, I turned my gaze to the afternoon sky, where steepled Parisian rooftops prickled upward to meet the clouds.

We stopped back in Worth and Bobergh to try on my dress. I was shocked to discover that it fit perfectly, almost like magic. The fabric accentuated my body in a way that no other dress had. I felt almost scandalous wearing it, but in the same breath, I could imagine myself wearing it to the Jameson Christmas party. I'd be on Richard's arm, beaming.

Mr Ambrosius and Dr Gibson both gave a hearty applause when I emerged from the dressing room with Worth's assistant. Will's eyes widened. I looked away from him and prayed he wouldn't notice the flush coming to my cheeks.

Think of Richard.

After expressing our heartfelt thank-you's to Worth and

his assistant, we emerged with the dress carefully packaged and continued our tour of Paris.

We passed ornate buildings where women threw laundry over second-story clotheslines with vigour. The men seemed to do none of the work. They clustered together in doorways and on patios, smoking pipes and yelling merrily into the street.

Despite all of these sites, Will's expression in the dress shop continued forcing its way through my thoughts.

I closed my eyes as tight as I could and re-read Richard's letter in my mind, over and over. He was my one hope things would get better. God, or the universe, or perhaps even Abigail, was telling me I had been forgiven for my sins.

I just needed to get home to him. But then what? We'd marry and have children. Then, another Annunaki could come to kill them. Would our lives be spent running and hiding? I'd be putting my own children in danger simply by giving them breath. Could I do that to them? To Richard?

How does one even tell a suitor she's cursed with otherworldly demon parasites?

No, I couldn't allow myself to think too much about it. I had Richard. That was enough. We would figure it all out, somehow. We just needed to marry and start the next stage of our lives together.

Morgana was gone, and if we were careful, all would be just fine.

BUT MY DREAMS that night would not allow me to hide in denial.

First, Grandmother came to me, trying to warn me of something. But I could not hear her voice. She spoke, but it was muted, as if we were both underwater.

And then Morgana was smiling as she stood atop a steep cliff overlooking the sea. I was far beneath, on the beach, and I began climbing the sandy cliff to get to her.

As I climbed, I noticed something jutting out from the cliff face around me. I recoiled as I realised they were limbs - mottled hands and arms, decaying, reaching out for me as I continued my journey upward. I screeched as they brushed my cheeks, pulled at my hair.

Even more frightening was my next dream. Will was sitting beside me on a beach, in the dark. It was midnight. The waves spread themselves in wide arcs over the pebbles, barely breaking, creating hairlike ripples across the clear water's surface. I'd never seen such a gentle sea in my life. It was as flat as glass and reflected an eerily green full moon. The air was heavy with moisture as I breathed in and smiled at Will.

Had I not been so relaxed, I might have laughed at his clothes. He was wearing a bright purple overcoat with a tail that fanned out behind him. A matching hat sat upon his head and reached as high as his torso was long. His ascot was a mustard affair that puffed out so far it almost licked the bottom of his chin. The entire outfit reminded me of something one might see at a circus.

He took my hand – even in my dream, this made me shiver – and studied the lines of my palms. "You've found your soulmate." His breath carried the whispered words across the exposed skin of my neck.

I leaned closer to him. "And who might he be?"

Will grinned, but remained silent for some time. We stared at each other, waiting, coaxing the other into saying the words we wanted to hear.

I'd never noticed the deep, green darkness of his eyes before. They seemed as ancient as the stones at Carnac. I'd underestimated this man – a traveller from across the stars, a wild and gentle wanderer. There was much more to Will than I'd known.

Will stroked a finger down my cheek, then pointed to the sky. "Look up, Emma."

Above us, thousands of fireworks exploded among the stars. Beams of light in all colours of the rainbow.

Then we were kissing. It was rough and full of a need I'd never experienced in waking life. I found myself deliriously grabbing at his waistcoat, pulling him closer to me than any man had ever been.

I awoke with a start, my forehead sweaty in the nighttime heat.

I COULDN'T MEET Will's eyes the next morning as our driver loaded our things into a carriage that would take us to Gare du Nord.

Of all those dastardly dreams, his was the one which had affected me. I couldn't stop wondering what it would feel like to kiss him, which was infuriating. I'd finally secured Richard's love, only to go and have a silly dream about an obnoxious American. This was an undesirable state of affairs, to put it mildly.

The uncertainty would all go away once I was back on good English soil. I only needed to look into Richard's brilliant blue eyes and I'd forget all about Will.

In fact, I didn't need to *forget* him at all. How could one forget when one wasn't even thinking about him to begin with?

We travelled from Paris to the port at speed, and boarded our ship without too much ado. I worked hard to keep my wits about me. I settled into my day cabin. The last time I had been in one of these rooms, Grandmother was still alive. I pushed the thought away.

Instead, I focused on maintaining my breathing, just as Dr Gibson had instructed: long breaths in, longer breaths out. The method seemed to work.

And then, everything changed.

One moment, I was sitting on the daybed. The next I was standing in the hallway. The ship was swaying, indicating we'd not only departed, but enough time had passed that we were now in open water. At least an hour must have passed.

A scratching noise coming from the walls broke through my thoughts. And then, her voice.

"You will never be free."

It was Morgana. I knew it. But she couldn't be back. If she was, then Grandmother's death would have been in vain. This had to be a genuine nightmare, a ghoulish vision brought on by my inability to tolerate travel by boat. Morgana was *not* still attached to me.

More scratching. I hobbled forward, unsteady on my

feet, leaning against the walls and trying to ignore that terrible sound.

The hall began bending and twisting, warping my vision. I blinked hard to right myself, but it was of little help. I couldn't deny it. Morgana was in my head, scratching, scratching, scratching.

Then, Will was there. He had found me crouched at the very end of the hall. I didn't know how much time had passed between the first sound from Morgana and his arrival, but I found myself shaking in his arms.

"Is it your nerves?" he was asking, and at first I didn't understand his meaning.

When I didn't answer, he lifted me to my feet and helped me up to the deck for some fresh air.

As my wits came back to me, I realised Will thought I was feeling fearful over our sea voyage. It seemed so easy to let him keep believing that. And so, I did.

The day was lovely, without a cloud in the sky. We found a couple of empty chairs and sat in silence, staring out at the sparkling water. After some time, my breath started to settle.

"So," Will began, "let's take your mind off things. I want to know something about you. Something Richard doesn't know." He smiled, and I took this to be a peace offering. "Something no one knows, except you."

"Why?"

"Well, when you go home, you'll be with him forever. He'll know everything about you. Wouldn't it be a thrill to know there's still someone out there who knows one thing he doesn't?"

"You mean, like the fact that my family is being

pursued by demonic parasites?" I said, with a raised eyebrow.

He laughed. "Not that. Something about *you, from your heart.* Something meaningful, so that if one day you're feeling lonely in your big London house with your dozen kids and distant husband, you can think of that dreadful American cad, and know he's out there, holding tight to your secret until the day he dies."

I sat there, lost for words. Will was in love with me. I couldn't deny it anymore. The bright, gentle energy of him reached out and wrapped around my shoulders. He loved me, and I would soon say goodbye to him.

We'd return to London and become nothing more than acquaintances, connected only by our practical need to avoid the Annunaki. I could see in the set of his mouth that he knew it, too. Feared it, even. He wanted to take a piece of me with him as a comfort, to help nurse his heartbreak.

And I wanted to give it to him.

For the first time since the wreck, someone had made me feel safe enough to reveal my secret. Abigail's screams rang out somewhere among the waves lashing our ship.

"You're more right than you know." My breath hitched in my chest, but I forced myself to continue. "I have a secret. One which I've never told."

My voice was so small that Will had to lean in to hear. I felt the soft wisp of his breath on my cheek and forced back a shiver.

"I did something – a terrible thing." My heart was pounding against my corset hard.

He shook his head. "You were just a little girl. I'm sure it wasn't so terrible."

"Well, it *was*," I said, but it came out as more of a shout. Will's eyes went wide. "I did something. But I can't – I'm sorry, that's all I can tell you. Nobody else even knows that much."

Will's jaw softened, and he tilted his head. "That's okay. Sorry I pushed you. I didn't think you would share something so serious. I figured you'd tell me about some silly social scandal."

I shook my head. "Mr Ambrosius and Dr Gibson – everyone, really – they think I'm a simple, frilly girl with no care for anything. I want to be that girl. I wish I was." The tears came without my permission, and I found my face buried in Will's shoulder.

The waves had grown coarser by the time I calmed myself. Will's eyes were red, as if he was trying to hold back his own tears. What a sweet, silly man. I'd miss him.

We were much too close. It was inappropriate. Richard would be furious if he knew. But I didn't want to move away.

I wanted to lean forward and kiss the skin around his eyes, make the tears resting within them disappear.

Will took my hand. His grip was powerful. Our eyes were locked on one another, each silently daring the other to move.

Just like my dream.

Was I making the right decision, going back to Richard? What would my life be like if I chose Will instead? Would we run to another continent and lose ourselves in the world? What would it be like if I found the courage to tell him what had really happened to Abigail? If he told me he loved me, anyway?

Nights huddled together in snowy cabins flashed through my mind. Days resting beside wide lakes, our feet dipping into the clear water. That dream I'd had of us on a beach, drenched in moonlight and happy.

I stared into those green eyes. They promised another lifetime, one different from anything I could imagine back home. And, most curiously of all, I found myself wanting it.

He grazed a finger down my cheek and everything within me buzzed like an electrical storm. I rested my hands on his chest. The oddest, most unbidden thought came to me: *This was home*. Not London. Not even my friends, or Richard. Just this.

Will paused. His eyes grew intense, as if he was wrestling with a difficult thought. Then he lifted one of his hands and guided my chin up, bringing my lips toward his.

Just before I closed my eyes, a movement flashed to our right. As if timing her appearance to cause me maximum distress, Abigail stood a short distance away from us, on the deck, in her tattered night dress.

I could have ignored her. I could have closed my eyes tight and let Will take me away from it all. But I also knew, somewhere deep inside, that I had to fix this problem for good. I couldn't keep hiding.

So I pulled myself away from Will. I imagined, in this half-moment, that he would probably assume I was regretting our closeness.

He likely didn't see the apparition of Abigail, staring at me with black eyes before turning around and running toward the bow of the ship.

What Will did see, however, was the woman he loved

apologising and running down the deck, seemingly trying to get as far away from him as she could.

Thanks to my thick petticoats, I tripped every few feet, despite picking up my skirt edges. I half-ran, half-stumbled across the ship, following the trail of mud that my sister had left in her wake.

She stood at the bow with her back to me. Her brown hair fell in loose tendrils down her back. It didn't move a bit, despite the strong wind that whipped around me.

"Abigail!" I shouted. The wind cut off my voice, but she seemed to know I was there regardless. She turned and looked at me with lost eyes.

I could see her more clearly than ever, and it gave me pause. Her face seemed different. It was something in her eyes and the set of her nose. God, was I forgetting what my own sister had looked like?

Before I could get close enough to see her better, before anything at all could happen, she faded into sea mist.

~

I COULDN'T FIND Will for the rest of the journey, so I spent the remaining hours lying on the cot in our day cabin, thinking about Abigail.

Seeing her again meant either of two things. One: my hallucinations had nothing to do with the Annunaki, and I was well and truly mad all on my own. Or two: the Annunaki was back, and my most recent Morgana dream had been real.

Both options were disagreeable.

I needed to speak to Mr Ambrosius and Dr Gibson.

They were the only people I could turn to for advice on this subject, now that I had pushed Will away. But I couldn't seem to find them anywhere on deck, so I went back to my room and laid on the cot, exhausted.

The waves beneath me lulled me into an unexpected sleep. Dreams drifted in and out of my cabin, but one in particular caught hold, wrestling itself into my mind and refusing to let go.

Richard and I were standing on the bow of the ship. He smiled down at me, through a thick moustache and eyes so blue they rivalled the sea. I asked him what he was doing here. Shouldn't he be in London, waiting for me?

"What do you mean? I've been here the entire time."

A cold wind lifted my skirts, and I caught sight of Abigail's form beside us. Her bare feet were grey as a storm cloud, her toenails an inky black. I looked up at her face, which looked equally pale. Her mouth gaped abnormally wide.

And then the screams of a thousand animals emitted from deep within her. I cupped my hands over my ears and huddled into Richard's chest. He wrapped his arms around me and whispered something meant to comfort, but Abigail's screams drowned his voice.

Mr Ambrosius appeared beside her then, laughing. He held his strange crystal between his thumb and forefinger. Abigail's coal eyes turned to him, and she smiled as well.

Sea water dripped from the edges of her mouth as she walked slowly towards him, her limbs jolting in awkward angles all the way. Mr Ambrosius flicked his wrist, and then she was gone, as if he had imprisoned her within the crystal.

"Such a silly girl," Mr Ambrosius laughed. "You know nothing of me, or of us."

Will appeared then, standing beside him with a queer smile. They were both working against me, weren't they? Of course. I was a stupid girl after all.

"Miss Collins," Richard began, unsheathing a sword I'd never seen before. "Step aside. I shall vanquish them both in your honour."

Had this been any other situation, I might have giggled at his ridiculous words. But there he was, approaching Will and Mr Ambrosius with his sword held high.

They dropped their smiles and looked at one another in horror. Before they could react further, my heroic Richard swung his sword hard and beheaded both men in one swoop.

The crystal fell out of Mr Ambrosius' hand and grew bright, brighter than even the sun. Richard shielded me from the blinding rays until they diminished, revealing Abigail — not the decaying ghost, but the real, living girl. *My sister*.

She wore a frilly yellow dress and smiled wide. "You saved me, Emma. Thank you." I walked toward her, but before we could embrace, she had faded into nothing but a sea breeze.

I awoke sobbing so much that I couldn't breathe through my stuffed nose for hours. During that time, I contemplated the dream's meaning. Was my intuition telling me something about Mr Ambrosius and Will? Could Richard save me from everything?

As we made our way closer to England, a thick fog descended over the sea. Soon it was impossible to see farther than a few hundred yards ahead. The ship seemed to slow, as if uncertain of its destination.

My heart began pumping faster. What if we hit an unseen rock or another ship? I peered as far over the railing as I could, gripping the slick wood whenever a wave crashed against the hull. The fog needed to lift just enough so I could see the coastline and know I was safe.

As if the heavens had heard my silent plea, a beam of sunlight burnt through the fog. It thinned the clouds until I could see grey and violet hills in the far distance.

England. My eyes filled with tears. This journey would soon be at an end. Before long, we'd be off this ship, on dry land, and headed to London. I'd see Richard soon.

~

We docked just before sunset and left the ship as we'd embarked on it in France: as a group of four.

But as soon as we reached the end of the docks, Will stopped and turned to Mr Ambrosius, Dr Gibson and me. "Since Emma seems to be fine, I'll be staying in Southampton for a few days." His voice was more formal than usual. "I'll leave you here."

A low, thudding ache began in my chest. I'd assumed that Will was coming to London with us, to continue protecting me from future Annunaki attacks. Wasn't that his duty? If he left now, would I ever even see him again?

He shook Mr Ambrosius' hand and tilted his hat to Dr Gibson and me. Then, without further ado, he turned on his heels and walked away, his suitcase in hand and back straight as a pole.

Will was gone.

I let out a long breath. I needed to carry on, to force myself not to care. He was just one man – or one Pleiaden, as he claimed – with whom I could never have had a real life.

In a matter of hours, I'd have Richard and my dear friends and my comfortable, beautiful home. Over time, I'd forget all about Will.

I was thrilled to see the fine steam engine as we arrived at the station in Southampton, but our home itself was an even better sight.

Our home. I caught myself, and made a mental correction. My home. There was no 'our' now, no Grandmother with whom I shared this place.

I perched in the parlour after arriving and stared at her spot on the chaise longue. Was this really home without Grandmother? It wasn't right, returning without her. It would probably never feel right again.

After a long conversation and an even longer cry with Ms Wright, I went to my room and sat on my bed. All was silent. Everything was just as it had been before. The wardrobe was across from me, the vanity beside it, and all my knick-knacks resting atop. The wash basin was there too, along with my powders. Everything was the same.

Yet something was still different. It was the energy, perhaps, without Grandmother here in the house.

Maybe I just needed to give it time. Within a few days, things would start feeling more normal. I'd see Richard and Violet and Florence, return to my charities and perhaps even secure a last-minute invitation to the Fredericks' annual Christmas party.

Everything would be all right again. I forced myself to smile, hoping I'd shake off the heavy grief that blanketed my mind.

It didn't work. So instead I laid on my bed, let out a long breath, and succumbed to tears.

~

Ms. Wright knocked on my door fifteen minutes later. "Violet would like to call. Are you open to visitors?"

I wiped my eyes, jumped off my bed and answered with quick enthusiasm. "Yes, of course." Violet would update me on all the gossip I'd missed while out of town. I needed to prepare to re-enter society over the following days, and she was the perfect person to help. Besides, I sorely wanted to see my friend, and to be reminded of all the wonderful things about being home. She'd help to lift me from my fog of depression.

An hour later, Violet arrived in a ball of energy and taffeta. "Oh, Emma, you're really here." She hugged me so tightly that all the air left my lungs. It seemed she'd become even more Continental than me. "I can't believe it. You've been gone for *far* too long."

We took tea in the parlour. She asked me about Grandmother, and how I was feeling. Then she told me all about London's greatest scandal of the moment: Miss Aniston and Mr Sprouse were found alone and indecent in the back of a carriage, and worse, in the middle of the night! No escort in sight.

I reacted in the same crafted way as always: a slight gasp that I covered with a dainty hand. A speck of blushing. But strangely, Violet's stories didn't enthral me as they used to. She hadn't yet saved me from my deep sadness, which was now growing more potent by the hour.

Perhaps talking about Richard would help. I moved the subject in that direction with a reserved excitement, not wanting to not appear too unkind to Miss Klepakhov. However, the moment I brought up his name, Violet's eyes darkened.

"Oh, um... yes. Richard has been well."

My stomach dropped. Violet's tone was bordering on murderous. "What's wrong?"

"Well, nothing, really. He's telling everyone all about your reunion. It's just — Emma, do you know how he ended things with the Russian?"

"Of course." I kept my voice steady. *Everything was fine.* "He realised his mistake after I left and wrote to me asking to mend our relationship. He can't court me with another girl hanging on his arm, can he?"

Violet bit her lip. "Oh, this is quite terrible." Her voice was low as she put a hand on my shoulder. "I hate to tell you this, but I don't think Mr Jameson was being honest with you. From what I've heard, it was Miss Klepakhov who ended things with *him*."

The air caught in my throat. *He hadn't left her for me? He'd lied?*

No - I wouldn't have it. Not after I'd come this far. There had to be an explanation. Rumours abounded in this city, and most were untrue. I straightened my spine and forced a smile.

"What does it matter how it ended? The fact is, it's over. Now, how is dearest Florence?"

I SENT A CALLING card to the Jameson residence as soon as Violet left. It had never been like Richard to lie to me — unless, of course, one counted the silence that had ensued when he'd met the Russian.

My stomach was doing flips as I waited for him, but they were unfortunately not the tosses and turns of giddy excitement that I'd been so looking forward to. Instead, anxiety coursed through my blood, thick and menacing.

I paced the parlour dozens of times, and Ms Wright checked in on me almost as many. With each peek through the hall door, her frown grew deeper. I suspected that she'd never liked Richard, and now that I was looking so nervous, she seemed even more wary.

The door knocker clanked. My nerves were so frazzled that I nearly jumped up to answer it myself. I patted my dress skirts, pinched my cheeks one last time and took a deep breath. In times of stress, one should try to look serene. Never show an abundance of emotion, especially to a man one hasn't yet married.

Richard walked into the parlour wearing his brown tweed jacket and a delightful yellow ascot. His eyes crinkled at the edges when he saw me, and a second later, and his trademark smile followed suit.

Combined with my nerves, the entire experience turned me faint. I covered this weakness by rushing toward him and into an indecent embrace. Better to be scandalously affectionate than show my genuine emotions.

Richard didn't seem to mind, anyway. For a moment his spine was stiff, but then his hands patted my back and he pulled me closer. His spearmint breath filled my nose.

We sat in our old spot on the chaise longue, as close together as ever. His eyes - much sharper than I'd remembered - scanned me up and down. "You look nice."

Was that the best he had? It was rather a mild compliment, considering the dramatic nature of our parting and reunion. Did he have nothing else to say, besides an unflorid comment on my pleasant appearance? I cleared my throat delicately. "And you look handsome."

He smiled and took my hand.

I looked way. "Violet told me about the — um, Miss Klepakhov. That she'd been the one to leave you?" Best to rip off the bandage.

He blinked fast. "Ah, yes. I suppose I wasn't all that clear in my letter, was I?"

"No. The opposite, in fact." I bit the inside of my lip, to keep myself calm.

"I'm sorry." His shoulders slumped as he gazed at the rug beneath us. *What was it with his deceptions and that blasted rug?* "It's just, I was so terrified you would despise me. I suppose I wanted to win you back first, and then I'd tell you everything afterwards."

He wanted to win me back. That was something, I supposed. The most important thing, really. It was the entire reason I'd come back to London. His shoulders relaxed, and he took my hand in his. "Marry me, Emma? As soon as possible? We'll have a grand wedding and a beautiful house, and dozens of children to fill it with."

My smile stayed frozen on my face. Such a pleasant sentiment – children, a life of safety and comfort. Everything I'd wanted. He was saying exactly what I'd yearned to hear all along.

I breathed in. The air smelled stale.

"Next month?"

~

My thoughts were rather muddled over the next few days. People were trickling back into London early for the start of the new season, including Florence.

She called for me as soon as she arrived. Her home was just beside Kensington Gardens, which lent it a gentle floral scent that delighted the nose. I arrived after lunch in hopes of a cup of piping hot Earl Grey tea and a slice of her cook's famous shortbread.

I was met with both, and a graceful hug from Florence. Her dark curls were pulled up into the highest bun, a couple of tendrils falling beside her cheeks. Her smile was wider than it had been in years, and there was a telltale flush to her cheeks.

This only could mean one thing. "You're engaged," I said, more as a statement than a question.

She nodded and held out her gloved left hand, atop which rested a precariously bulbous ruby. "We're announcing it tonight, but I wanted you to know first."

"He must be a duke," I said with a gasp. I couldn't take my eyes off of her ring. It was a delightful monstrosity.

She leaned in and giggled. "It's my cousin Marty. Papa didn't see the point in any other suitors. None of them had the money or breeding to match our own. 'Might as well keep it in the family,' he said."

That seemed about right for the Winstons. They were nearly royalty, after all. None of the new money were palatable, and anyone holding a title lower than that of a count was an unacceptable prospect.

It had always left poor Florence with a dance card full of wanting suitors and few genuine options. Those who fit the bill were usually looking to improve their own circumstances, and poor Florence, despite her popularity, had been close to spinsterhood.

"I'm so happy for you." My cheeks hurt from smiling. We were all going to be just *fine* — Florence and I would be married this year and I was sure, with Violet's striking looks and disposition, that she'd be soon making her own announcement.

Everything was perfect.

We sat in the parlour, and Florence set into a long explanation of her cousin's habits and looks. She'd always been attracted to him, and had secretly wished her father would suggest the match. She went on and on about his smile and the adorable way he lifted his soup spoon to his moustached lips.

I continued nodding along, but my mind was drifting elsewhere, to far-off fields of wheat glowing golden. Was I missing France? How silly. I was home and safe and happy, and about to be married.

The curtains at the parlour window began drifting back and forth in a regular rhythm, like a clock pendulum, or the pulse of a slow heartbeat. I found my eyes fixed to the window pane, the shafts of sunlight coming through it and the sparkling dust that hung limp in the air.

Back and forth the light swung. Back and forth, like the beat of a song. I was lulling myself into a gentle sleepiness.

A shadow appeared then, breaking up the light. It lasted for only a second before the light moved across the floor again. I blinked the vision away. But then it returned, and the shadow was decidedly of a little girl, peering in through the parlour window.

I looked up, straight into Abigail's black eyes. My body stiffened. The curtains continued their clockwork sway, despite the lack of a breeze, and I knew Abigail was doing this. Her shadowy shape grew closer, larger, more consuming with every moment. Salt water filled my nose. I couldn't breathe.

I threw myself out of my chair and stuttered something apologetic to Florence about needing to get home and rest.

Florence's eyebrows lifted, a warning that she didn't believe a word of it. But I wasn't concerned with social niceties now. There were far more terrible things at stake.

My hallucinations were continuing. I couldn't deny them anymore.

NINETEEN

Thankfully, I had no more hallucinations over the next few weeks.

Richard and I planned the wedding at breakneck speed. We secured the Jameson's family church and used their good name to cajole wedding vendors into last-minute agreements. My dress was nearly finished, Mrs Havendish having dropped all of her other clients to get it made in time. Everything was going according to plan.

One sunny December morning, I sat in the parlour and began rifling through our RSVPs. So far, no one had declined, which was of little surprise considering our social standings.

I hoped it wasn't also to do with the scandal surrounding our previously tumultuous relationship and the saga of Miss Klepakhov.

And then, on one RSVP, I spotted an unexpected name.

Mr M. Ambrosius and his nephew will be delighted to attend the wedding of Mr R. Jameson and Miss E. Collins.

Bile shot to my throat. How on Earth had they received an invite? I had never added them to the guest list.

And his nephew.

I tried to imagine Will sitting beside his uncle in the pews, dressed in formal wedding attire. I couldn't turn his expression into anything but a frown, no matter how hard I focussed on changing the vision in my head. To my dismay, I felt my chest ache the same way it had when I first saw Richard with Miss Klepakhov.

No. I wouldn't let Will or his blasted uncle ruin this. My time for true happiness, true *normalcy*, had come. The visions of Abigail had stopped since I took tea with Florence, and soon I'd be too busy with my new family to worry about them anyway. I would have many children, just as Mr Ambrosius instructed, and everyone would be happy.

As if some higher power wanted to remind me of my good fortune, I had a dream of Richard.

We were in a lush garden of white and pink roses. Their perfumes were so strong, I almost choked. Richard turned to me and wrapped his hand around my own. His smile brought out the golden sun from behind the clouds above, so that it glittered down on our garden.

Two little children – one girl no older than five or six, and one boy that may have been four – were sitting on the lawn in front of us and playing cards. The girl looked frightfully like Abigail, with long brown hair falling down beside her cheeks, her skirts spread wide and wildly over the grass.

Even her movements stirred up the memory of my sister — the rashness of them, the forcefulness.

She was my daughter. She was Richard's daughter. And beside her, our son.

Something tightened around my finger. Richard's engagement ring was growing smaller and smaller, until it began cutting off my circulation. I tried to pull it off of my finger, but to no avail.

Richard laughed and stroked my throbbing hand. The ring was hurting me so badly that I couldn't breathe, couldn't think straight.

"Watch Abigail play," he said.

I felt a falling sensation, and then woke up in my bed - only to see Morgana's figure standing beside me.

Was this real, or was I still dreaming? She looked the same as ever, her red satin gown reflecting the moonlight, a wide smile slithering across her pale face. She reminded me of a bloodthirsty hound, readying itself to pounce.

"Tomorrow, you have a choice," she said. Her voice was low, insistent. "Let me in, Emma. Let me end this for you, fast. Or, you can marry, and succumb to the same torture your mother and grandmother experienced. I promise you, had they been given a chance, they would have chosen a quicker death."

And then, suddenly, it was daybreak. Morgana was gone, and Mr Ambrosius was standing in her place beside my bed.

"You don't *look* very bridal," Mr Ambrosius said, peering at me judgementally.

I came to my senses and pulled up my bedsheets. "What the blazes are you doing in my bedchamber?"

"Your maid let me in." His voice was flat. "You've been staring out the window for an hour. She couldn't wake you from your stupor."

I blinked hard.

"Don't stare at me like a fish," he said. "Do you want to tell me something?"

Morgana. Her warning about the wedding, the choice I would have to make. The memory came crashing down on me like a brick.

"If you won't be honest with me, I can't help you."

I raised my eyebrows. "Are you certain you can help me, regardless?"

Mr Ambrosius furrowed his brow and stared at the floor. After some time, he let out an exasperated huff and left my room without a word.

As Ms Wright helped me with my morning ablutions, I couldn't stop thinking about my mother. She'd kept a diary at my age, one filled with the dreamy scrawling of a young girl in love. I'd discovered it months before my seventh birthday and begged her to read me some passages.

Mama acquiesced and sat me down by the fire. She read out stories of suitors and dances and flowers, which were all magic to me. There had been an odd breathiness in her recitation that I hadn't understood then. As I grew older, I realised it had been a yearning, a reminiscence for something long lost.

I wanted to relive those golden years for her. And I did, when I became the Light of London. I knew she had wanted me to find a good husband and start a family, too. Something that was now within my grasp. With all my efforts, I hoped she was looking down from heaven, smiling at me. Proud.

I coughed back a sob and apologised to Ms Wright. Such a thing was impossible. Mama could never be proud of me, not after what I'd done.

~

Florence and Violet came to the house for a celebratory breakfast that morning. It was strange having them over so early, outside of normal calling hours, but I was glad they were here all the same. The more people around me, the better I felt after my encounter with Morgana.

It helped too that everyone was full of energy and excitement. Ms Wright was directing a bevy of wedding staff around the house, shouting orders about cream puffs as she polished my shoes. I fiddled with Grandmother's necklace, its pendant dangling from my neck. I'd decided to wear it today, in memory and honour of her.

We ate in the parlour. Florence was wearing a new baby blue dress with the widest hoops I'd ever seen, and I marvelled at the way she manoeuvred them through the doorway.

Violet wore her mint gown, which brought out the flecks of green in her eyes. Both looked lovely. I found my chest warming at the thought of attending their weddings. We'd all have husbands and families soon.

Everything would be all right. And just to be on the safe side, I wouldn't name my daughter Abigail.

"I'm so proud of you." Violet squeezed my hand as she sat down. "All the heartache you've endured, and here you are, stronger than ever and about to get married."

"Oh, yes. Much stronger. And much more put together." Florence added. "Barring your antics at my house the other week, of course."

"Antics?" Violet asked.

Florence waved her gloved hand, as if batting away a bothersome housefly. "Oh, it was nothing, really."

"Do tell." Violet leant forward, her face a mix of curiosity and concern.

"Well, I'm sure it was just nerves, but poor Emma was in a frightful state when she came calling last month. Do you remember, dear?"

Of course I did. It had been the day I saw Abigail's shadow behind Florence's curtains. I thought I'd hidden my terror well that afternoon, but evidently not. I gave a curt nod and took a long sip of tea.

"What were you doing?" Violet's frown was now deepening.

Florence turned to Violet and took her hand, a florid gesture which annoyed me. "Staring blankly at my curtains for a full ten minutes. I asked you a dozen questions, didn't I, Emma? And you didn't even reply with a murmur to pretend you were listening."

Florence giggled, and Violet continued to look at me

with worry. Something within me cracked, allowing all the poison I'd been holding back to seep through to the surface.

I dug my nails into the sides of my chair. "Did you not see that horrible shadow flitting about in the sunlight?" I said this with calm patience — like a parent trying very hard to make her child memorise the Latin alphabet.

Florence sighed and turned to me. "I love you like a sister, Emma, and so I must be truthful. No, I did not see it. You put far too much energy into your wild imagination. You need to focus on things that are more important." Her smile was so wide and so false, I wanted to jam my teaspoon into her teeth.

"What *is* important, then?" I replied in barely restrained fury.

Violet squeezed my hand. "Richard, of course. Marrying him, before he gets any more ideas about Russian girls." She was trying to be supportive, but I didn't appreciate the mention of Miss Klepakhov.

"Yes. Once you're married and Richard is no doubt distracted again, you can stare at lights and shadows all you want." Florence nodded as if she had been vindicated.

"What exactly are you inferring, Florence?"

Florence, unperturbed by the tension in my tone, lifted her chin. "Well, only that it won't matter what he does after the wedding. You'll have his name, and whatever girl comes next will only be a bit of fun."

Violet couldn't meet my eyes. Once Florence had concluded her statement, neither could she. Apparently, neither had realised that I expected Richard to be faithful. Insinuating he could stray was an arrow to my heart.

There was nothing more to say. I left the room without saying a word.

~

Ms Wright was speaking with someone at the door as I left the parlour. I peeked over her shoulder to see Will, and everything began spinning.

He was in a fine suit, trying to explain his presence to poor Ms Wright. As if things weren't already difficult enough, now I had to contend with him being here. Did no one respect a bride's peace on her wedding day?

He looked past Ms Wright and grinned at me. "Miss Collins. May I speak with you?"

Ms Wright stepped aside a little too eagerly, suppressing a smile as she let him in.

To my utter shock, Will then gave me a genteel bow. Something in my heart folded. "Of course," I said, and we entered my father's study.

Alone, mind you.

Something in the back of my mind was warning me to ask Ms Wright or one of the girls to chaperone this meeting. However, I was finding myself feeling woozy and unable to think. Will closed the door behind him.

"I know you plan on marrying him today," he said, with no hesitation or polite chit-chat to warm me up to this conversation. "And I know I'm supposed to make sure you do, for the good of your species. I - I know I shouldn't be here, and I know it's a mistake, but I need to tell you–"

"You're right," I said, finally finding my voice. "It's a mistake, and you should go."

He nodded and turned to leave before pausing. He looked at me with that beautiful sparkle in his eyes. "Will he make you happy, Emma?"

I thought of Richard's lukewarm enthusiasm at my return. Of Miss Klepakhov and the conversation I'd just had with Florence.

Will took my delayed response as an invitation to step closer to me. He brushed his fingers down my cheek before pausing, waiting for me.

I pressed my lips to his.

A rush of warmth rose through my body, made me feel like I was floating and exploding all at once. It was as if lightning had touched me and frozen me in place, but even if I could move away, I wouldn't. That kiss was like nothing I had ever felt, and I knew I would feel nothing like it again.

He pressed his body against mine and that electric bolt ran down to my stomach. I wrapped my arms around his waist and pulled him closer to me. Our breathing grew faster, more urgent. Never had I wanted anything so much, nor had I ever felt so wanted in return.

Then, the worst sound in the world. A clearing of the throat. We broke our embrace and turned to find Mr Ambrosius standing in the doorway.

For the first time since I'd known him, he was seething with anger. "William. Get out."

Will stood in place. "This can't go on, Ambrosius. She deserves to be happy. We both do."

I turned to Mr Ambrosius and stepped away from Will. I knew what I needed to say, though it would kill a part of my soul. "Mr Ambrosius, I apologise for our indecency. Please, may we keep this between ourselves? It was a brief lapse in judgement. Just a silly mistake." The knot of lies nearly choked me.

Will moved toward me, but I would not meet his eyes. A silence, then Mr Ambrosius sighed. "Of course. Let's get on with the wedding."

I didn't look at Will as I left the room.

I FOUND myself in the back garden, heaving in deep breaths of the December morning air. What had I just done? Such a passionate kiss could not be forgotten. I'd never felt anything like it.

But Richard and I *needed* to marry. I'd dreamt of this day for years. And now, our union was also apparently for the good of humanity. I needed to have human children, and carry on the bloodline.

For the first time, I forced myself to look at the harsh reality of it all. Mr Ambrosius had boiled down my reason for existence to that of a breeding horse. And worse than that, by giving my own children breath, I was cursing them. Committing them to a lifetime of running away from a relentless and horrifying otherworldly race.

And then there was Richard. He knew about none of this. Throwing this life into his lap with no warning or chance to abstain was just as immoral as doing so to my children.

And what of my own life?

I was not confident that Mr Ambrosius and his fellow Pleiadians could protect me. They hadn't saved my poor grandmother and Mama from succumbing to madness. But if I truly believed their assertion that passing on my genes would save humanity, then who was I to value my own happiness over that of my entire species?

Staring at the begonia bushes, which had long lost their flowers, I realised everything boiled down to whether or not I trusted this ludicrous, maddening and most eccentric man, who'd so far failed to save my family at every turn despite leading us all over land and sea.

As if he'd been reading my mind, Mr Ambrosius' telltale musical humming joined me on the patio.

"What did I tell you about Will?" he asked.

I looked up, expecting to see a face of pure fury. Instead, there was a profound sadness, maybe even a glimmer of guilt.

"Please, can we never speak of this again?"

He nodded. "As far as I'm concerned, it never happened. Anyway, more worrying to me is that thing around your neck."

I touched Grandmother's necklace. "This? It's just Grand-"

"It's a messenger crystal, and you don't know how to use it." Mr Ambrosius reached toward my neck, as if to rip it away from me.

I backed up and pressed my hand to the gemstone. "What on Earth are you talking about? This is Grandmother's favourite necklace. Grandfather gave it to her on their honeymoon."

Mr Ambrosius dropped his hand and sighed. "Your great-grandmother gave that necklace to Virginia, as her own mother did before her. It has been passed down for generations, but should only be worn when the new owner can properly operate it."

"Operate it?" None of this made sense. It was a necklace. How would one operate it?

He reached forward again. "I'll show you."

This time, I let him touch the gem resting on my collarbone. A second later, the thing was glowing as bright as the sun. There was a faint buzzing tickling my skin. He tapped again, and the buzzing and light were gone.

I fought a gasp and backed away once again. "Why did she have this?"

He smiled. "To contact me in case of an emergency. But if you wear this necklace without knowing what it does and how to use it, you might contact someone else." He paused and raised an eyebrow. "Of the Annunaki sort."

I grabbed the necklace's clasp and threw it at Mr Ambrosius' chest. "Oh dear God, it was *this*? This called Morgana to me?"

Mr Ambrosius' mouth dropped open as he caught the necklace. "Morgana?" he whispered. The birds stopped chirping, and everything in the garden around us turned deadly silent. "Where did you hear that name?"

"It was the Annunaki who was trying to possess me. She told me herself, in a vision," I said. My heart pounded as his expression changed from shock to sheer terror.

He swallowed so hard I could hear it from where I stood. "The Annunaki identified herself as Morgana? Are you sure?"

He seemed to desperately want me to tell him that no, I wasn't sure.

I nodded.

Mr Ambrosius buried his face in his palms and groaned something in a language I couldn't discern. Suddenly, things that had seemed quite ordinary – a necklace, a name – had a weight which I couldn't comprehend.

I needed to find my voice again, fast. "Who is she?"

He looked up. For the first time since I'd met him, Mr Ambrosius looked as ancient as a Greek statue. "Morgana is more powerful and more terrible than you can imagine. The leader of the Annunaki. I thought she was long gone, but if she's after you, then –"

"She's dead." My voice was flat, unwavering. But something toxic was burning in my veins. "You told me that the Annunaki died along with Grandmother."

Mr Ambrosius looked lost. He didn't need to tell me more.

I'd worn that damned necklace to that ball. I'd called Morgana straight to us. And she couldn't be killed with mere poison.

Grandmother had sacrificed herself for nothing.

TWENTY

ONE MIGHT PRESUME, that had a lady just learned she'd inadvertently killed her own grandmother by calling an evil entity, and that this entity was so powerful it could still be alive and lurking amongst her and her loved ones, that the lady in question might not be in a state to attend her own wedding.

This, however, is assuming the lady isn't an English debutante who had been primed her entire life for this crucial event.

My mind went blank after conversing with Mr Ambrosius in the garden. It was all too much – Will's kiss, the necklace, Grandmother, Morgana.

Mr Ambrosius rushed off to find Will and Dr Gibson, and I decided I needed to do something. So do something I did.

I went to my bedchamber and called Ms Wright to help me with my wedding dress. Violet and Florence arrived with her, both wearing their bridesmaids gowns and apologetic for our earlier conversation. I had worse things to worry about than their views on Richard, so I told them I forgave them and asked them to help find me a new necklace to wear.

My head was pounding. This was it. I was going to marry Richard. He'd be my husband. I'd work the rest out from there.

Ms Wright, Violet, Florence and I all rode in a royal barouche to the church. It was a lavish, grand affair, covered with preposterously lush Christmas roses that trailed white petals in our wake.

All of London seemed to be out for the event. It was something of a parade as we rode through town, waving to everyone. The sun glittered through the clouds, breaking up the morning fog to join us in our celebration. My body buzzed with all the energy around me.

We soon arrived outside the church, where a dozen footmen stood in a neat line. Two approached our barouche and helped the other ladies out. My cheeks hurt from smiling at all the people crowding around us. Children were squealing about my pretty dress, and adults were talking animatedly, pointing to the carriage and my veil and the bouquet in my hand.

I had never been so loved as I was at this moment. And I felt no triumph in it.

I stepped forward to take the footman's hand. Only when it wrapped around mine did I notice the glove — an atrocious, acidic green colour. I looked up through my veil to find Mr Ambrosius was its owner. My breath hitched and I glanced at the ladies, who were already at the church's entrance on the arms of their corresponding groomsmen.

"Why are you here?" I hissed.

Mr Ambrosius smiled serenely and nodded me forward. I had no choice but to walk with him. Asking another footman to escort me would only lead to whispered confusion about why Mr Ambrosius hadn't been up to snuff. "You have about five minutes before you'll make the most important decision of your life, Miss Collins. Are you up to the challenge?"

"What in God's name are you talking about?" I muttered, so that no one around us would hear. "For once, will you please speak plainly?"

"She's inside, waiting for you. It's time."

My bones turned to ice. "Who?"

Mr Ambrosius gave me a smile which didn't reach his eyes, dropped my arm, and walked away. I was at the door to the church now, amongst the flurry of bells, organ music, people rushing to prepare for the ceremony. Flower petals were falling from Lord-knew-where.

I needed a moment to gather my thoughts. There was only one person Mr Ambrosius could be referring to, but I wanted more than anything to be wrong. Morgana was inside the church, waiting to kill me.

By the time Richard's father arrived to take my arm, I was firm in my decision. There was no running away now. Wherever I went, Morgana would find me anyway. I was tired of hiding. This was my wedding day, and I needed to stand my ground.

We entered the church, the interior decorated in pink and white flowers. The pews were teeming with people. I couldn't believe so many could fit. They were all bending this way and that to get a better view of me.

I forced a smile and looked straight ahead, to the end of the aisle. There, Richard was waiting, his back turned to me, ready for my arrival.

It took everything in me not to search for Morgana. I couldn't see any bright red gowns in the crowd, so that was a positive sign. I did, however, notice the tall, blonde man standing just to the left of the aisle. Will was here. I felt his eyes on me as I walked toward the altar, and I wished that he'd decided not to come.

I couldn't think about him now. I could never think about him again. And neither would I think about the deep, wrenching ache that such a prospect brought forth.

Richard. Focus on Richard.

I arrived at the pulpit and the organ stopped playing. Richard and I turned to one another. His eyes sparkled blue as always, but there wasn't a tear in sight. I'd always imagined my groom's eyes would be just a little damp when he saw me. Richard merely smiled, calm and collected as ever.

"Shall we begin?" The rector asked, his bible opened wide.

The congregation breathed in at once, and I turned to smile at their dramatic response. But their eyes weren't on me. I followed their gaze and looked to my left, at the church's giant stained glass window.

Standing behind it was the form of a child, cloaked in shadow. They pressed their palm to the glass, little fingers outstretched. The ground groaned and rumbled beneath our feet. The chandeliers above us swayed perilously back and forth as the flowers jittered in their vases. A woman cried out, saying something about the windows.

Before I could make out her words, there was a terrible shattering sound. Richard dived in front of me, shielding us both from the flying shards of glass that had, only moments before, been a delightfully colourful depiction of the Virgin Mary peering down at a newborn baby Jesus.

I looked over Richard's shoulder to see Abigail, standing in the gaping hole where the window had been. Beside her stood Morgana. There was raw, naked hunger in her eyes. She was smiling.

Abigail began limping forward, across a carpet of destroyed stained glass. Limping toward me.

More cries about a strange girl and a woman. Someone yelled Abigail's name. The girl stopped and looked for the person who'd recognised her. A queer smile withered across her face. She turned back to me.

Richard pushed me further behind him as he unsheathed his sword, which had only been meant for show during the ceremony. His hands were shaking.

"What are you?" he called to Abigail.

What. Not *who*.

Abigail's eyes widened. She reached out her hands and stared at me. "Mama. Don't do it."

The room began moving, but this time, it was only in my own head.

Richard turned to look at me. "Mama? What's going on?"

"Don't do it," she cried, her voice feeble and rasping.

I couldn't escape her this time. There was nowhere to go. "I-I don't understand," I said. We stared at each other.

As one might imagine, the rest of the congregation was in uproar. Though I wasn't looking their way, I could hear the ladies' screams, the sound of fainting bodies collapsing, of babies howling, of the church doors opening and closing as people scrambled to escape.

Men were brandishing swords, shouting to children to cover their eyes – for no one should see this ghostly apparition, lest they suffer lifelong nightmares. I risked a glance to seek out Violet and Florence. They had found safety behind two of Richard's handsome Navy companions, and were crying into their handkerchiefs most dramatically.

"Don't do it, Mama."

She stepped forward again. Dirt fell from her tattered clothes and loose hair. Morgana walked close beside her, grinning.

Had Abigail accosted me like this a year ago - before Richard broke my heart, before Will and Mr Ambrosius and our odd travels, before losing Grandmother - I would have pulled Richard out of the church and as far away from my sister as possible. Sweep my past under a rug, neat and tidy, where it belonged. Return to my social engagements as if nothing had happened.

Now, I knew I needed to face her, once and for all.

"Please. Please, Mama."

Mama. Why did she keep saying that?

I looked at Abigail again. Now that I wasn't running away, I could truly focus on her face.

Oh, my good Lord.

This wasn't Abigail. She looked hauntingly like her, but now I could see the tiniest differences in her features. The exact shade of her eyes. A deep blue. The precise set of her mouth, the curve of her nose. It wasn't her. It had never been her.

She looked like me. And like Richard.

Now, finally, I understood.

This was my future daughter.

And now I knew what Mr Ambrosius had meant outside the church. *She* had been waiting for me. And now I had a choice. I could marry Richard and muddle my way through all of this. I could have children – have *her* – and the family I'd wanted.

But this poor girl, who looked so much like Abigail, would suffer the consequences of our curse. This fate was apparently so terrible that she was appearing to me, an apparition from the future, to beg me not to allow her to exist.

For the first time in my life, I felt genuine pain. I felt what it meant to be a mother, to love and lose more deeply than I could fathom.

I clutched Richard's arm.

He turned to me, frowning in confusion. It made him look like a little boy, one who was terrified of monsters under his bed. He didn't deserve this. He had made mistakes, of course, but it wasn't fair to drag him into an existence he wasn't prepared to face. He deserved a normal life, with a normal wife and normal children. I could never give him that.

"I'm so sorry, for everything." My voice shook more than the church had. "I can't marry you."

Richard looked even more confused. "What? Why? Just what the devil is—"

A familiar laugh interrupted his words. Morgana

stepped forward. "Smart girl, Emma. You understand, now, what your very nature will do to everyone around you." She motioned to the scene before me, my friends and loved ones cowering in horror, the church a mess of shattered glass.

My future daughter, her body in tatters and covered in dirt, begging not to exist.

"You will destroy humanity if you continue to live," Morgana continued. "Let me in, now, and I will end this quickly."

I knew what this meant. Total possession, then madness, then death.

"She's lying," Mr Ambrosius called from the back of the church. He was standing in the middle of the aisle, swishing his cane from side to side. "You will not destroy humanity, Miss Collins. Quite the opposite."

Morgana's face went as red as her gown. She turned toward Mr Ambrosius. "Of course you're here," she hissed. "Making sure you keep your line of miserable mutants going. You did a lovely job engineering this wedding by the way. Convincing this poor boy's lover to leave him. Manipulating him into going back to Emma." She turned to Richard, and her eyes softened. "You've been deceived, Mr Jameson. This girl isn't who you think she is."

Richard stared, dumbfounded.

I felt a scream threatening to burst from my throat. *Mr Ambrosius manipulated Richard? Our reunion was his doing?*

"And what are *you* doing here, Morgana?" Mr Ambrosius asked. His voice was calmer than it should have been, considering the circumstances. "You've been sending your minions to do your bidding for centuries. Why are you so interested in this particular, rather tedious young lady?"

Tedious? I was about ready to bite his head off, but Richard was still wrapping his shaking arm tightly around my waist.

Morgana's jaw moved beneath her white skin. Her eyes flickered across the congregation.

During this brief pause, something that should have been quite obvious finally dawned on me. Morgana was an Annunaki, a creature incapable of taking physical form.

I had always thought that she, along with the ash-man and possibly Abigail, were visions in my head.

Yet, she was standing in front of us, as solid as anyone else in the church. And everyone could see her.

Mr Ambrosius cut off my realisation with a hefty clearing of his throat. "My theory," he began, ambling down the aisle, "is that there is much more to Emma than meets the eye. And that you learned of this before I did."

A small hand touched my arm. I looked down to see my daughter, forgotten in all the drama, peering up at me with blue eyes. Richard's eyes. "Please, Mama," she whispered. "Come with me."

Come with her. I knew that this meant death. Not just for me, but for our family line – and maybe all of humanity, forever.

But this was my daughter. Everything I'd ever known, ever wanted, had just changed. Nothing else mattered but her.

Morgana was shouting, everyone else cowering, and Richard was holding me tight. All of it was muffled as I looked into my daughter's eyes. She could never be. I had to end this now, for her sake.

I kissed Richard's cheek. Before he could react, I wrenched myself away from him and took my daughter's hand.

Then there was nothing.

THIS WAS DEATH. It wasn't unconsciousness, because even then, one has a sense of breathing, of organs working somewhere far off in the distance. It wasn't darkness, nor light, nor anything that language could describe. It was a total lack of the universe.

But then, past death, there was an image. I saw Abigail. The *real* Abigail. She wore her favourite blue dress, the one that allowed for easier tree-climbing. Her hair was in lush, loose brown ringlets, decorated with a bright blue bow. Her cheeks were flushed as pink as springtime carnations, and her brilliant smile stretched wide across her cheeks.

"You're here!" Her voice was higher than I remembered. Perhaps, as her younger sister, I'd always seen her as more grown-up. But this little girl was so innocent.

And I'd killed her.

"Abigail, I – I'm so sorry."

She shook her head. "It wasn't you."

Behind her, a grey cloud grew, expanding into a violet and silver sky.

We were floating now, above the same waves that took our parents' lives. Took *her* life.

Below us was the wreckage of a ship, burning. Two

little girls were in the water, struggling to stay afloat. *No,* I didn't want to see this part. I turned away, but Abigail guided me to look at them.

The smaller girl — little Emma, all gold hair and petticoats — reached her arms up over the waves.

But then, her sister grabbed her, pulled her down, under the water. Why was Abigail doing that? I didn't remember this part, not like this.

The Abigail who was beside me took my hand and drew me closer to the scene. Her counterpart was cackling, a sound I did remember. I'd always thought it was the sound of the water choking her. Now, I could see that it hadn't been.

"It was them."

"Who?" I asked.

Abigail motioned back to the girls in the water. They were still scrabbling, and the other Abigail was clearly winning the battle.

My former self was beneath the water now, and the memory of it filled my mind. My lungs heaving, burning like someone had splashed boiling soup into them. Flailing, trying to get air. Hitting something hard with my left hand, something like a skull. Abigail's grip on my body loosening.

Watching her sink down, down beneath me, black eyes wide and confused.

Black eyes.

But Abigail's eyes had been brown.

I looked back at the Abigail beside me. She smiled through thick tears. "An Annunaki possessed me, Emma."

I turned to little Emma, who could now lift her head over the waves, taking in the best and most bitter breath of her young life. She glowed from the inside, and then the scene darkened.

But there was soon light again. Now, standing before me was Grandmother in her finest evening gown. Strands of pearls shimmered from her ears, and she smiled. "Emma, my dear. You must go back. This isn't your time."

Before I could respond, she pressed her thumb to my forehead.

This is the part of my story that becomes convoluted, because time and space are actually an inconvenient mashup of non-existence. Yes, I realise this sounds like something Mr Ambrosius might say, but now that I've experienced it myself, it's the only way to describe it.

I saw everything at once, as if it were all happening in one moment: my birth, when I'd almost died and Mr Ambrosius had intervened, pressing his thumb to my forehead. Mama dancing around Glastonbury Tor on our picnic, singing a strange song about turning into Light. Mama sparking the fire that burned down our ship, screaming that I needed to become Light. Mr Ambrosius, in the parlour that first afternoon we'd met, toasting to becoming Light.

And I saw the future: a baby in my arms, pyramids, people dancing beneath strange skies filled with greens and purples. Galaxies of stars I'd never seen before. And a void, blacker and emptier than anything I'd ever perceived.

These events were all connected, and each puzzle piece was a part of me. They were signs which pointed toward one crucial truth.

I knew, then, what I held within me.

The human side of me was scrambling to remember all

of this. The Light part of me was as still and calm as a lake at dawn, because it always had been and always would be.

Anyway, there was only one fact I needed to take from this timeless place of pure existence. I wasn't simply a breeder.

I was Light.

~

CANDLELIGHT BROKE through the nothingness and everythingness. It burnt into my field of vision, gently and with no need for force. I followed the flames with my eyes, flickering back and forth, back and forth, until the things around them began taking shape.

My wash basin, resting atop my vanity. The chair I sat in on my wedding morning as Ms Wright fixed my hair. My wedding dress, hanging haphazardly from the wardrobe. Someone had cared little about protecting it from harm. If left there for too long, it would crinkle.

Where was Will?

He had been at my wedding. Had I been married? The fear of it lurched me into clearer consciousness. No, no, I hadn't. Thank God. I wasn't married to Richard. My daughter had saved me. I had saved myself.

I didn't kill Abigail.

Long-awaited relief coursed through every inch of me. *I didn't kill her.* At least, not the real Abigail. She was already gone. And whatever had died at my hands that day had been trying to kill me. It had been self-defence.

I opened my eyes.

Ms Wright was hunching over in a chair beside me, her

eyes buried in her handkerchief. A tall shadow was pacing about behind her, making impatient grumbling noises and checking his pocket watch.

"Mr Ambrosius." Strange that these were my first words.

Ms Wright's head shot up so fast, I was half-worried it would fall off. Her body, thankfully, followed suit and prevented such a terrible fate befalling her. "Emma, oh, dear Lord, you're alive."

"Of course she's alive." Mr Ambrosius let out a long sigh from behind her, as if he were at the end of his tether. "She was never dead. Or, not completely, I should say. Perhaps ninety percent, give or take a few decimals—"

Ms Wright simply stared at him for a moment before patting my cheek and asking how I felt. I asked for water. She poured me a cup and began talking fast. "You collapsed at the altar, and the doctor who examined you couldn't hear your heartbeat. He told me you had passed away."

"And I told you she was just fine and dandy." Mr Ambrosius turned to me with a roll of his eyes. "Really, don't you people ever listen to a word I say?"

Ms Wright rounded on him. "The entire church was in a frenzy and she wasn't even breathing! It was clear the earthquake had jolted her nerves beyond belief."

"Earthquake?" I asked.

Mr Ambrosius smiled. "Yes, Miss Collins. Your wedding was interrupted by a rather violent and – dare I say – *impossible* earthquake. The entire city is talking about it."

"But it was Morgana. She was there. Didn't they see—"

"Morgana?" Ms Wright's spine straightened. Her eyes shot back and forth, as if she was trying to remember something she'd long forgotten.

"There was nobody there by that name." Mr Ambrosius broke in. He gave me an odd wink.

"The earthquake was terrible," Ms Wright began. "It shattered the lovely stained glass windows - which were centuries old, might I add. And you fainted." She let out a long sigh. "Thank heavens that was all it was. A terrible fainting spell. And I can't blame you. The wedding was in tatters after that. Oh, we must tell everyone that you're alive and well."

An odd thought came to me: Did I *want* people to know I was alive? Richard? Violet? "Is there anyone else at home?" I asked.

Dr Gibson cleared his throat as he stood from another chair in the corner. I hadn't realised he was here, but strangely, the sight of him was a comfort. Now I understood why Grandmother had always called on him. He was the only doctor who truly knew our family.

Ms Wright shook her head. "Only myself, these two. Oh, and that lovely man, Mr Ambrosius' nephew, is in the other room. Why?"

Will. He was nearby. I ignored my quickening heartbeat. "Don't tell anyone about me being awake," I said. "I need some time to rest." It was a silly excuse, but I couldn't think of anything else at the moment.

Ms Wright was so fraught with emotion, she didn't seem to notice how odd the request was. She nodded and hurried out to fetch me some food.

I turned to Mr Ambrosius. "My daughter – I mean,

future daughter – was there. And Morgana, too. You warned me before I went inside, and everyone saw them. Why doesn't Ms Wright remember?"

He smiled so widely, it seemed to stretch from one side of the room to the other. "Funny thing, the human brain. It decides what it sees and what it remembers. If something so horrific, so outside of its own crafted perception of reality occurs, it will paper over the event. Create its own universe, you might say. Such a wonderful trait, and even more potent when a hundred other minds do the same thing. Humans conspire together – subconsciously, of course – to change their memories to something more... palatable."

I took a gulp of air, trying to stay calm. "When I was asleep, or dead, or whatever I was... I saw things." I was afraid to tell them too much, and even more afraid to ask the thing I needed confirmation of most of all.

Mr Ambrosius nodded. "I'm sure you did."

"I thought..." I paused, but it was a question I needed to get out of my head. "Did I become Light? Or was I just hallucinating? I mean, if everyone saw me collapse and nobody said a word about me disappearing, or becoming Light–"

"Stop rambling, please," he sighed. "Yes, you did. For about five milliseconds, you were... well, Light. Like one of us. Nobody in the church saw it but Will and I."

We were all silent for some time.

"What does this mean?" I asked.

He let out a long breath. "It means, Miss Collins, that you are in even graver peril than we thought."

"Because of Morgana? Is she still attached to me?" My heart started pounding.

Mr Ambrosius shook his head. "You shook her off when you became Light. I'm willing to bet that she's rather angry right now."

"So she's still alive."

"Of course. But thankfully, your little foray into Light will have put her off your scent. She'll have trouble finding you again for some time, at least."

Just *some* time.

Then, I remembered. "I thought you said that the Annunaki couldn't take physical form?"

Mr Ambrosius blinked. "What?"

It seemed I'd caught him off guard. "The entire church saw Morgana. She wasn't a hallucination. How did she do it?"

A look passed between Mr Ambrosius and Dr Gibson.

Another realisation hit me. "And if she can take physical form, why go through all the mess of possession? Why not just take a knife to my throat?"

Silent tension ran through the room. I'd struck a nerve, and suddenly, I wanted desperately to change the topic.

"It's too long of a story to get into now," Dr Gibson said through tight lips. "You've been through a great ordeal, and there is still much to consider regarding your future."

As much as I hated to admit it, Dr Gibson was right. I was exhausted. I'd ask Will, next time we were alone together.

I let out a long breath. "So what do we do now?"

Mr Ambrosius knitted his brow in confusion. "What do you mean? The same thing as always. Get you married. Children."

"But... I can become Light. Doesn't that change things?"

"Yes." He looked at me like I was an imbecile. "As I said, you're in much greater danger now. The Annunaki know the gene is already presenting itself. They're running out of time to stop humanity from evolving, which means they're going to push harder against us. We must work all the more quickly to continue your line."

I thought of my daughter again. I'd already made my promise: no children, no more curses. How was I going to explain this to Mr Ambrosius and his Pleiadian colleagues?

Perhaps I wouldn't. Mr Ambrosius would never understand or agree with my decision. What would he do, I wondered, if I told him I refused to reproduce?

My mind was whirring at a million miles a minute. "Where's Will?"

"He's in the other room. Why?"

I stood up, slowly at first, because the room was spinning. But my legs soon felt sturdy beneath me, and I began walking to the door.

"Careful," Mr Ambrosius warned. "Things aren't –"

I touched the door handle and shrieked. A spark of electricity shot out of my hand and burned my skin.

"– like they used to be," he finished, chuckling.

Will must have heard my outburst, because the door flew open, almost hitting me in the face.

"Are you all right?" His green eyes were wide.

"What the blazes was that?" I hissed, cradling my poor hand.

Will looked at Mr Ambrosius. "Did she touch the doorknob?"

The madman had now collapsed into giggles and could only muster a nod. Will shook his head and turned to me.

"He should have warned you."

"I tried!"

I squinted. "Warned me about what?"

Will smiled at me, and suddenly I didn't mind the pain in my hand. "Your body goes into a heightened electrical state after it turns Light. You're going to want to avoid metal for a few days."

I blinked.

"Don't fit all that information into her head," Mr Ambrosius said with a smirk. "She can only handle so much at once."

I shot him a glare, then turned to Will.

"Richard thinks I'm dead, and all of my friends do, too. I think – no, I *know* – that we need to keep it that way. I need to leave London. Can you come with me?"

~

My gravestone sat beneath an especially weepy weeping willow. Its branches hunched over, as if it were trying to cover the whole earth in its sadness.

Emma Elizabeth Collins,
Beloved Light of London.
February 1840 - December 1859

It was unsettling to see my name carved into stone in such a permanent fashion. There was no going back now. I bent down and touched the stone, felt its rough wetness beneath my fingers. It had rained at my funeral, but despite the nasty weather, nearly two hundred people came to watch my empty casket being lowered into the muddy earth. Emma Collins had truly been the Light of London, after all.

Beside my empty grave were the stone memorials of my parents and Abigail. My uncle's grave was here, too, and the graves of so many other family members whom I'd never met. Each of their names was more legend than real to me. Still, we were more connected than I could have ever imagined.

During my funeral, I stood right at the back of the crowd, my face shrouded by a black veil. Ms Wright was the only person outside of my trio of Pleiadian misfits who knew about my plan. As disturbed as she was by the overall scheme, she was most distraught that I'd be attending my own false funeral.

She'd used all the negative adjectives under the sun, but stuck with 'morbid', rounding the 'or' with a strong, salty pitch.

But I wanted to say goodbye to Emma as well. It felt like the right way to let go of the life that could have been mine.

I suppose that sounds a tad melodramatic, considering I had put an end to Emma Collins myself. The truth was, this life had been of Grandmother and Mama's design. I had simply tried my best to fit in, to please everyone, to enjoy society life and to prove that – despite Mama's apparent madness – we Collins ladies were a respectable bunch.

Now that Grandmother was gone, and I knew the truth

about Mama, there was no need to prove anything. And, though I'd miss my friends, the idea of living here without Grandmother was too painful.

Richard had sat in the front row of my funeral service, next to Ms Wright, who was surprisingly good at feigning tears.

After my casket found its home and the last prayers of the service were uttered, I caught my last glimpse of my former fiancee. He led a procession of people in black down to a waiting carriage, head bowed low and hands deep in his coat pockets.

Violet and Florence followed behind him, the latter in floods of rather over-the-top tears, the former quiet and ashen-faced. They would all be just fine. I knew it. They had the memory of me to look back on whenever they liked. A girl who was confident and dazzling and sure of her place in the world, if a little off-kilter.

I wasn't that girl anymore, and I didn't want them to see what I'd become.

~

Two days later, I stepped into a second-class train carriage and did my best not to crinkle my nose. It was bad enough that my new wool dress — a horrid grey and brown number — was itching against my skin. How did anyone live like this?

For the thousandth time today, I reminded myself that this had been my decision. I didn't want to return to London society, not after all that I'd experienced. I was no longer Emma Collins in name or in spirit, so it was best to leave the city and start a new life elsewhere, in a place where nobody would recognise me.

Hence the train.

I leaned back to mutter to Will, who was following just behind me. "Does second class always smell this way?"

"What way?"

"Like... fish?"

He fought a grin. "Never noticed it," he replied loudly. "Of course, we don't all have your refined aristocratic nose."

I slapped his arm and shushed him. We were still in London and though my clothes had changed, my face had not. Someone could recognise me if they looked hard enough.

We sat in the back row of the carriage. The seats were narrow, which meant that Will had to sit close to me. I didn't mind — not that I'd be telling him as much.

The train lurched forward, and then began shaking, as the steam engine hooted its goodbyes to the station. We moved fast past the smokestacks and houses, out into the country, toward fresh green pastures and sheep and grey sky. Small flakes of snow sputtered around in a dismal attempt to blanket the surrounding land.

Will jabbed the side of my arm. "What'll your new name be?"

I lifted my chin. "Not until you give me your family name." I could see his face in the reflection as I looked out the window. He was smirking.

"Promise you'll keep calling me Will? I don't want you to use my surname under any condition."

I blinked in confusion. "All right. I promise. Do you not like your surname?"

"It's not that I don't like it. I just don't want you confusing me with someone else."

Now I was even more perplexed.

"Our family customs are different from yours," he continued. "At home, women don't change surnames when they, as you call it, *marry*."

I groaned when I realised and turned to face him. "Your surname is Ambrosius, isn't it?" No wonder he didn't want me knowing. I'd never have let him live it down.

He nodded and laughed. "Don't worry, you can keep your own name when we marry."

I knew this was a joke, but still, my stomach fluttered at his words. My cheeks were heating up so much that I needed to turn away again. The train was speeding up, and the countryside rolled past us.

"So, what'll your name be?"

Grandmother had told me once, years ago, that she had loved her maiden name. It had meant something to her, and now that I knew the weight of our familial past, I understood why. I wanted to keep it going, for her.

So I smiled at Will's reflection.

"Emma Nolan."

EMMA'S STORY CONTINUES...

Preorder the next chapter of the Becoming Light series here: www.alienunicornpress.com

Want to know what *really* happened between Richard and Miss Klepakhov? Sign up to my mailing list for a free downloadable short story: www.sarahlongwrites.com

ACKNOWLEDGMENTS

First, I want to thank my husband Daniel, for being my biggest cheerleader from the start. He never stopped believing in me, and without him I can definitely say that this book would have stayed buried in my computer.

My son Sebastian is another huge inspiration. He drives me to achieve the dreams I've let linger for far too long, and my hope is that this book will show him that he can achieve his own goals, too.

I probably wouldn't have started this story had it not been for my mom, who, after hearing me complain about poor job opportunities post-graduation (in a recession, with an English degree), told me to "just write a book."

And of course my dad, who was always supportive and spent many of our father-daughter breakfast outings patiently listening to me ramble about the publishing industry.

My friends and family have read so many rounds of edits, and for that I am eternally grateful. I can't begin to describe how much they've helped. Their feedback shaped the story in ways I could have never done alone.

A special thank-you to my editors, Victoria A Mixon and Gabby de Matteis. Your detailed notes and ideas were instrumental to not only the story, but the spirit of the Becoming Light series.

There are so many people who have put time and heart into this series. This was truly a team effort, and I am extremely grateful for such a supportive community.

ABOUT THE AUTHOR

Sarah Long was born and raised in a hippie surfer town in California before running away to New Orleans to read literature with the local vampires. After a hurricane and a degree, she found herself wandering around Los Angeles, dreaming of becoming a novelist in a script writer world. The heat was a tad too much, so she moved across the pond to pursue an MA in English Language and Linguistics, focusing on practical applications of linguistic theories on fiction. She's currently writing from her small West London balcony with her dog, husband, and toddler cheering her on.

Printed in Great Britain
by Amazon

17696557R00164